Rucklingsdorf
- An American Surrounded by Germans

Available in English as a paperback or eBook.

Also available in German as a paperback or eBook under the following title:

Rucklingsdorf
- Ein Amerikaner von Deutschen umzingelt

Other Books by Jonathan Claay:

THIS is America?!!
- A European Expat in the USA

Available in English as a paperback or eBook.

RUCKLINGSDORF
– An American Surrounded by Germans

By Jonathan Claay

© Copyright 2019 - All contents of this book, including the cover design, are copyrighted by the author.

Available in English as a paperback or eBook.

Also available in German (as a paperback or eBook) under the following title:
Rucklingsdorf - Ein Amerikaner von Deutschen umzingelt

"All stories, characters, locations (except for the cities of Düsseldorf and Munich as specifically mentioned in the text) and events in this book are fictitious. The opinions expressed by any characters should not be confused with the author's or anybody else's opinions unless stated otherwise. Any resemblance to actual persons, living or dead (except for the poet Heinrich Heine as attributed), to any specific, actual events or to any locations (except for the cities of Düsseldorf and Munich as specifically mentioned in the text) is purely coincidental."

The exclusive place of jurisdiction for all disputes regarding any part of this text shall be pursuant to §104a of the German Civil Code.

Impressum
© 2019 Jonathan Claay
Herstellung und Verlag:
BoD – Books on Demand, Norderstedt

ISBN: 9783741298172

Book Reviews

"Buy this book. And *read* it!"

  - Jonathan Claay, American Expatriate Living in
    Germany

"Insightful.
 Entertaining.
 Delicious!"

  - An Avid Reader

"You'll laugh, you'll cry, you'll wonder why."

  - Jonathan Claay, Literary Composer

"I'm Jonathan Clay, and I approve of this book."

  - Jonathan Claay, Author of *Rucklingsdorf - An
    American Surrounded by Germans*

Acknowledgement

With love to my lady friend, whose company was always the best part of all of those many travels – thank you for the sunshine.

Table of Contents

Introduction

A Club Meeting

Answering the Door

Small Town Life

At the Book Store

A Little Surprise

The Germans' German

On Vacation

A Social Visit

At the Supermarket

The Coffee Klatch

A Train Ride

Carnival

Euro Trash

The Waiting Room

At the Street Market

(Former) East Germany

Cats, etc.

The New Friend

Between Democracy and Nazism

The Playground Incident

Germans on the Job

The Doorman

Guests from Abroad

The Dark Side

The Little Dog

Conclusion

Introduction

After years of living and working in Germany and traveling around to many of its cities and small towns, I decided to head north – but I found that the nearer I got to the edge of the country, the closer and closer I came to its very center, to that one very point which is directly in the middle – the middle of the culture, of the people, of the German soul – and as I continued further, I got so close that I entered that center and came out the back end, so to say, in a place that was no longer on the map, exactly; a place that progress, globalization and evolution has in many ways forgotten… and that place is the town of Rucklingsdorf.

Tap into the brain of a Rucklingsdorfer (as I have often had the urge to do myself) and, after the bats and spiders fly and scurry out, you will find a primordial ooze, and far, far beneath that – you will see the German in his rawest form.

The people of Rucklingsdorf have some ways and behaviors that are uniquely their own (in spite of also sharing them with hundreds of other little cow towns across the region), but these are variations on a theme, mere local habits inlayed mosaically upon ancient Germanic tendencies, tendencies which are found in nearly every German and nearly every sign of Germanness, whether in a highrise office in Frankfurt, a town in the American Midwest that had been settled generations before by ancestors of modern Germans – or a Rucklingsdorfer standing over the sprouts in his corn field, silent and scowling.

This book is about Rucklingsdorf – a small cow town which is located on the border and, mysteriously enough, also in the middle of Germany – but it is also an instruction manual about Germans – how they operate, how to maintain them, and ways in which they can often malfunction. Not everything that is stated applies to all Germans at all times, but if you deal with the people of this culture, you will notice definite trends.

This book shows what it *feels* like for an outsider to be in Germany, to live amongst the Germans – what it's like to really interchange with them on a regular basis.

Do you deal with Germans in your private or professional life?

Then read this book!

Are you planning to travel or relocate to Germany?

Then *read this book*!

Are you German yourself?

Then, for your sake as well as everybody else's, please… *READ THIS BOOK*!!

A Club Meeting

It was a big day for Hans Stempelkauer, for today was the day of the evening of the first annual meeting of the "What a Town" Neighborhood Association, which itself branched out as a committee of the Rucklingsdorf Works Council.

In celebration of this glorious morning, Hans Stempelkauer groaned as he sat up and hunched on the side of the bed, scratching his sagging belly.

His wife was already out distributing leaflets for the Works Council's "Under the Apple Tree" dance, which was not as big a hit last year as had been expected, and against council from various sources (as well as not a few lightly veiled pleas) to let it just quietly fade away into the archives of town history, she decided to let herself be inspired (largely by fear) to give the occasion an extra "Stups", as she said, and do her devoutest duty to try and rally up interest, support and attendees for this year's event.

Hans was one of the voices on the nay side, but his voice was quickly blown over by the whirlwind of his wife's zeal – a result that he (and everyone else) basically expected from the beginning.

Today carried other concerns for him besides his wife's planning of the dance.

Tonight, he was going to be called upon to open and lead the meeting of the "What a Town" Neighborhood Association, a responsibility that he had never had to bear before.

He had always sat in the front with Jürgen while Karl handled the ins and outs of such affairs of various association meetings and local political events. Karl, as Chairman of the association (since he was already Chairman of the Works Council), was comfortable in this position, being accustomed to gaining the attention of the local crowd, be it at the pub or when working together with a couple of the other boys at repairing a tractor. There was always the right mixture of a light joke at the right time (sometimes a bit bawdy, depending upon the company), along with a dosage of wise statements that seemed to come from years of experience and generations of good, solid, rural upbringing.

Hans was, well, better as back-up than as the front-runner. He was more the type to let himself get caught up in the stream of current behind the man in front and make a good show of being somewhere at the head of the pack. He was not the head, though; he was more of a "neck and shoulders" type. When Karl needed someone to laugh at one of his less well-honed jokes, he just had to look over at Hans and could be sure of a throaty chuckle to set the mood.

Karl was called away from his duties due to a matter that concerned his son, who was living in the city and who had apparently gotten himself involved in a matter about which Karl did not find it best to go into detail.

As the Assistant Chairman of the association, Hans was suddenly thrust into the glaring spotlight of the village eye, and everyone knows that this eye can be as endearing as an early spring meadow or as fickle as the wind in the run-up to a late November storm.

It's a lot of stress in a little village like Rucklingsdorf to stand in front of these people, one's own people, because they are, in fact, ALL of one's people. When the whole world's events occur within the limits of Horst Peter's cow pasture to the east and the Schweinsteins' property to the west, the opinion of this few is the opinion of one's entire world.

For Hans to stand before the association tonight meant that he was putting himself in the position to be the subject of discussion, conjecture and judgment of the entire neighborhood citizenry, one by one and pair by pair.

It would start the next day with a "So, how did the meeting go last night?", or, for those who wanted to get an early start on the gossip for the next day or two, "How did Hans do last night?", in a voice a few degrees deeper than normal and with a tone of expectation as to what the answer was going to be before one was even offered.

To start with, each of the other members in the small audience would talk with each other, soon after having left the pub where the meeting was held. Then, their wives would ask their husbands "how things went", a phrase which, when everyone involved is well aware of the conditions at hand, is far more laden with meaning than such a statement otherwise would be. The wives, of course, would then talk with each other (although nothing would appear in print on anyone's social media sites; that's too scientific and definitive for a matter as amorphous and indefinable as smalltown neighborhood gossip).

Then, at some point, Karl would be back from the city, would have gotten the various coded and decoded messages and insinuations about the evening in his absence, and would approach Hans, one way or another, with a "So, Hans, I heard...", and Hans' performance tonight would be the force which was destined to shape whatever it would be that Karl will have heard.

Hans knew all this, and he was filled with a sense of unease and foreboding. He didn't say anything about it, of course, because that was not his way. He just went about his day, handling the latest matters of work and family life that arose for the moment, but with the ever grinding wheel in the back of his head, "Tonight – the meeting".

The sun started to set and cast yet another miraculous swath of pink and cottony orange across the sky above the fields, and Hans opened the door to "The Golden Mule" where the meeting was to be held.

As the door opened, Hans saw that Jürgen and the boys were already seated at the bar, waiting, and Hans suddenly remembered a scene from a mafia movie when an ill-fated member of the group had entered a room much like he had just entered this one, and in the movie, there were already a few people waiting for the guy, just like Jürgen and the boys were already waiting, and...

"There's Hans", Jürgen murmured to his neighbor at the bar, as he raised his beer just perceptibly in greeting to the Assistant Chairman entering at the door.

As he got nearer to them, Hans sat down halfway on a stool and joined the chat for a few minutes, but after a while, Jürgen said, "Well...", which to Hans was like a blare of trumpets to initiate the event.

They all collected their things (that is, their hats and beers) and marched into the back room that is used for such events as these (of which there are surprisingly many in these little German farm towns, for some reason).

Hans was uncomfortable to notice that a train of other people from the bar started to collect behind them and follow them into the room. He had never noticed how many people went to the meetings of the Works Council in the past, but he was suddenly aware of what seemed like a mass or a mob behind him (it was Paul Paulson and his wife, the two Spuck brothers and a few of the other regulars).

Everyone settled into their usual seats (the same ones they had sat in during the previous Work Council meeting, which were more or less the same seats they had occupied in the meeting before that, with minor variations).

Hans started to plant himself in his familiar place to the side of the center of the table in the front, when Jürgen unexpectedly slipped his own weight into that chair, forcing Hans to remember that his place was one step to the left this time, in the spotlight (there was no actual spotlight in the room, which was actually rather too dim, due to nobody having gotten around quite yet to having repaired one of the lamps that had broken – but Hans was not aware or conscious of such subtleties as lighting and ambience. For him, he might as well have been about to begin his speech with "Dear members of the United Nations").

He let the chatter continue a little while longer than it should have, until it started to die out on its own accord a little, and then he realized that he had no other option but to dive right in, with or without his swimming trunks on.

Jürgen handed him the little gavel that they had been using for a while to open the meetings. It was just a rounded out block on a stick that one of them had whittled, but it served the purpose.

"Oh", Hans said, almost forgetting it, and he fumbled it a bit during the hand off, making it clack and clatter on the table like a bag of marbles dropped in church in the middle of a sermon. One of the Spuck brothers chuckled low to the other one, and this low tone of laughter caught on and made the rounds of the entire audience.

Hans recovered majestically and gave the mallet a tentative little "Tap, Tap, Tap" on the tabletop, and the laughter subsided into reverent and obedient silence. They were not used to this leader, who had so suddenly climbed to the mountaintop from amongst them, but there he was, gavel in hand, tapping on the table just like Karl usually did (well, not as adroitly and succinctly as Karl usually did it, but tapping anyway), and their inbred sense of accepting their place in the hierarchy and following their leader began to work its magic in Hans' favor.

Hans looked out at the mass of faces before him, all of which belonged to people he knew long and well (as far as he understood those concepts in this regard), but now they were not only Paul Paulson and his wife, the Spuck brothers, Holger Jansen and Jens Hansen and the others; they were faces with eyes that suddenly were looking at him with their full attention, observing him, waiting for his words, his guidance, his leadership; and they were already clearly submitted (thanks to the little gavel and the seating arrangements) to his newly-bequested authority.

And this, in a town when eye contact is saved for moments of argument and discord or safe discussions about the weather and is not otherwise distributed lightly during day-to-day life, and particularly not in matters of relative intimacy.

He swallowed as he stared back at them, all of them as a faceless mass, and for a moment, Hans Stempelkauer almost let the ball drop.

Then, thankfully, the very characteristic that had settled the others into their positions of blind submission and obedience inspired Hans to a likewise respect and appreciation of hierarchy, of the necessity for order and regimented categorization that the moment inherently required.

Whoever the leader was, that person was to be obeyed and followed, and if that leader happened to be Hans himself, well, he was nobody to oppose the natural Germanic order of things. If he was to be the leader of this hierarchy, then that was what this hierarchy demanded of him, and he was to obey. He suddenly had a vague sense of himself in some kind of uniform with a shiny sash and some unknown medals, even though he was just wearing his yellow flannel shirt that he had pulled back out of the hamper that morning.

A warm wind seemed to rise from below him, and he was touched and transfigured by the gravity of his sense of duty.

He raised his hands aloft and spread his arms in greeting, wider apart than anybody in this town perhaps had ever done before, be it a wedding, a funeral, or the purchase of a new horse.

He had nothing in his mind particularly to say as a starting point, but he knew he had to say something, so he didn't let that stop him. He opened his mouth and became extemporaneous.

"JAAaaaaa…".

A great proportion of association meetings in Germany open exactly in this way, season after season, year after year. It results from a general lack of orderly thinking – not being able to grasp the overall structure of a matter and the relationship of its parts to one another, and therefore not being able to know which part is at the front, which is at the end, and how everything needs to be aligned, cohesively, all the way through.

As to summarizing the general points with an all-encompassing introduction: forget about it.

Germans generally conceive of minutiae, of individual details cut off and isolated from one another. They are able to hyper-focus upon one particular of a matter with laser precision, to a point that can shake fear into other humans… but ask them to open a meeting of a local town association? "JAAaaaaa…".

There are exceptions. After all, there must be, considering that Germans manage to produce so much high-precision machinery as to flood the world with its meticulous, state-of-the-art accuracy. Naturally, at conventions at which the forefront of medical technology is presented to a specialized public, audiences from far and wide will normally be greeted with a momentarily heartfelt "Meine Damen und Herren" ("Ladies and Gentlemen"), but if those same captains or Kaisers of industry find themselves in somewhat less formal gatherings and venues on another date, they might very well resort to the ancient, traditional Germanic opening of "JAAaaaaa…".

Hans Stempelkauer was no captain of industry. He was a man of his people, and a good portion of them sat before him on this very night, enthralled by his leadership.

"JAAaaaaa…, meine Damen und Herren", he said, following the preconceived pattern, even though there was only one female present, "I would like to WELCOME you here, toNIGHT," speaking each segment of words separately as he managed to dredge them up from his rather infertile imagination, "to the FIRST annual meeting, of the "WHAT A TOWN" Neighborhood Association…"

There was a long pause, because Hans Stempelkauer had at this point essentially reached his climax and was feeling about ready for his closing.

Sensing this, the members in the audience performed that unique ritual that I have only seen in Germany and which can thoroughly fluster a public speaker and make him take a quick step in the direction of the nearest open door if he is not aware of or expecting it: they all started to knock in unison with the knuckles of their middle fingers on the table top, creating the sound of a flock of woodpeckers to voice their approval and agreement.

It strikes me that human beings, who as a species have collectively developed the ability to express themselves in song with the grace of Maria Callas and the soulfulness of Sarah Vaughan, are selling themselves short by resorting to the smashing of their hands against hard, wooden surfaces in order to voice their approval. Then again, does slapping one's articulate fingers and poseable thumbs together in applause make much more sense, when you come to think about it?

Be that as it may, Hans was encouraged by this show of support and good will, and he carried onwards, wherever it might lead him.

In lieu of anything else to mention (since the matters of the "What a Town" Neighborhood Association were not very grave, after all, and the town itself did not offer a particularly wide milieu that would warrant such an occasion), Hans followed the current that was in his Germanic nature, for generation upon generation.

He spoke of data and history.

"Uhhh… the 'WHAT A TOWN' NEIGHBORHOOD ASSOCIATION was founded by KARL NUSSHOLZ, three years ago. It began in his GARAGE. Jürgen and I were there. Right, Jürgen?", he said, turning to his friend who was seated next to him and, to Hans' surprise, located somewhat below him at the moment.

Jürgen smiled at the recollection, and Hans' confidence and spirits soared.

'This is going well', Hans thought, so he kept saying things.

"It is THEREFORE, my great HONOR, as the DEPUTY CHAIRMAN, of the 'WHAT A TOWN' NEIGHBORHOOD ASSOCIATION, to WELCOME you, to this IMPORTANT event."

Again, the woodpeckers, knocking on the table in agreement. They all exchanged a quiet look of satisfaction with the orderliness of the proceedings, and Hans was soaring high with them.

"Karl's garage was built in 1947, when –"

"– Perhaps we should talk about what we mentioned last Saturday, Hans", Jürgen interrupted, fondling the little gavel in front of him unconsciously.

"Uh, YES", Hans responded, thrusting his entire body skywards with the interjection. "Thank you, Deputy Assistant Chairman." He looked at Jürgen with an expression of relief and gratitude, although his eyes fell briefly upon Jürgen's fingers caressing the gavel before Hans turned his attention back to his audience.

"We are gathered here today", he resumed, in his more casual and less officious manner, "to talk about the 'What A Town' plaque that stands at the entrance to our beloved Rucklingsdorf. As you may know, the plaque was granted to us by the county back in 1952. We are all very PROUD of that plaque" – a round of self-satisfied table knocking broke out, accompanied by several upwardly raised glances of mutual appreciation dispersed around the dark little room – "ja, ja… and Karl had the idea that it was about time for us to maybe freshen the plaque up a little."

He was tentative here, for he had reached a point at which action and consensus would be needed.

German farm town inhabitants are sociable amongst each other, at least superficially, as long as they have known one another long enough and find that no risk awaits them in the relationship. Exchanging and evaluating ideas together and deciding upon what parts of each suggestion to retain and which to dispose of, and integrating those suggestions into a cohesive, effective, actionable whole – these are not strengths to be found among the members of such a sociological grouping.

"Do you mean cleaning the sign up a bit?", Holger Jansen offered.

"Maybe with a little paint", Jens Hansen added. "It does look a bit faded at this point."

"NO... no", Hans bubbled, before collecting himself again. "I mean... well, it was KARL'S idea... right Jürgen?"

Jürgen nodded his assent and support of Hans' innocence in the proposal, and Hans proceeded tentatively.

"Anyway, it was Karl's idea that maybe we could win the award from the county again this year?"

There was silence among the population in the back room of The Golden Mule. Winning the "What A Town" plaque again? AGAIN? That would take a lot of... nobody was sure what it would take a lot of, exactly, but it certainly seemed like it would be hard to come by, whatever it might be.

The people began to become visibly uncomfortable. One of the Spuck brothers leaned forward on the table, balling himself like a fetus and hiding his otherwise lengthy torso behind his elbows. Then, he saw his brother slump back in his own chair and sink a bit, and the first brother then did likewise.

"Does Karl really think that's necessary, Hans?", Paul Paulson asked, in kind of a whine.

Hans felt his seat on the throne getting a little shaky at somebody else's mentioning of Karl in this way, so he added, "Yes, and so do I, Paul. Why, they did it back then, I don't see why we can't do it again." He didn't really believe in what was saying, but he said it anyway.

"We're probably going to need a lot of shovels", someone said.

"Yes, and flowers and plants," came another. "Those can get expensive, if they're going to be all over the town like that".

"We'll be up against those folks in Trottelskirschen", someone added, with a quiet tone of ominous warning while looking around the room – and everyone thought simultaneously of the beautiful traffic circle with the blossoming purple irises and yellow tulips right at the entrance to Trottelskirschen, which was about four towns removed from where they were on the earth, there in Rucklingsdorf. Nobody knew of anybody having any relatives in Trottelskirschen, and so there was a feeling of something foreign and somehow dangerous about the place – in spite of the pretty tulips and irises and the well-manicured façades of the prim little houses.

"I don't know if it's such a good idea to change everything anyway", said Jens Hansen. "Everything's going along pretty good the way it is. Why shake everything up?"

"Ja," Holger Jansen added. That would take a lot of time, too. I don't think anybody will be able to get free to do it all."

They started to think about that traffic circle at the entrance to Trottelskirschen again, and they all sank a little deeper into their chairs.

There's a sense of doom among the Germans. It's not always present, and they can be quite light and chipper on the surface in day-to-day life. But present them with a circumstance in which there has to be change, which means taking a… taking a… risk, and everything becomes different.

It *could* come out all wrong.

Maybe things will be worse.

What if we can't do it, and everything just collapses one after the other?

What if we regret it?

THEN we'll be pretty sorry that we ever took up the notion in the first place.

After all, things are pretty good as they are.

OK, there are potholes in the roads and a few houses have a progressively large amount of car parts and building scraps in their front yard… but is that so bad? Is it bad enough to warrant… doing that thing you said, taking that… what was it called? Oh yes… R-I-S-K.

Among the habit-oriented citizenry of Rucklingsdorf as assembled this evening for the First Annual Meeting of the "What a Town" Neighborhood Association (and it was a group that was rather representative of the whole), there developed the sense of looking into the abyss, of the Rucklingsdorf Apocalypse as they could imagine it. They thought of the teenagers of the town they had seen sitting at the bus stop and listening to tinny music from their cell phones and smoking, they thought of their friends who had problems at work, one of them remembered reading something about the national gross domestic product the other day, and, though it didn't have any DIRECT connection with planting flowers in their little town, it was something bad, and this competition for a new "What a Town" plaque could also turn out badly, so it was basically the same thing, and just as catastrophic.

Hans Stempelkauer looked likewise into the abyss, but as the Assistant Chairman of the Committee, he knew that it was up to him to lead his people to the light.

"Well", he offered, "there's that tree nursery just off of the highway. Has a bunch of plants too, if I remember right. Maybe he would be interested in helping us out somehow."

This is where the Germans can get particularly anxious. Here was a solution, a chance, but if they took it, they might fail... and then where would they be? Isn't it better to just stay low, keep your head down and eat your soup? It was worse now that Hans had made the suggestion, because there was no longer any good reason for sitting passively in bleak despair, and a few of them hated him a little for it.

Just to avoid admitting to himself that he felt so helpless, Holger Jansen interjected, "Now, that's not such a bad idea". He stated it more to the group than to the Assistant Chairman, almost as if he were asking permission from them for him to believe in this wild idea by such a fearless leader.

The general body posture of the audience members slowly improved with this tentative foray into optimism, and the Rucklingsdorf Apocalypse broke apart to make way for what looked like it might turn out to be the brightest, most beautiful spring the town had ever seen – including that Spring of 1952, when everyone's parents and grandparents saw the picture of the mayor of Rucklingsdorf in the paper as he was being presented with the "What a Town" plaque… the FIRST "What a Town" plaque… perhaps the first of many…

There was pleasant chatter among the audience members, and a lot of heads nodding in agreement.

Jürgen looked up smiling at Hans, and Hans look out at his audience and townsfolk, as he beheld the result of the fine work in this, his first foray as Chairman… uh, Assistant Chairman… as leader of the people who needed him.

He pulled it off. He was a hit, and he knew it. He was going to be holding his head a little higher around town from now on, and he might even be telling some of the jokes to the boys himself after Karl got back.

Then, he did it.

He had a good thing going, Hans Stempelkauer. He was pushed onto the stage and found that he was a natural orator, and all because he just said what came to his mind. How could that strategy ever fail him now?

So he added, "Yes, maybe if someone asked him to donate a few plants."

"We could offer to put his name on the plaque!", said Holger Jansen, almost in a fit of glee.

"Great idea!", Hans erupted. "Holger, why don't you be the treasurer of the association and ask that man at the tree nursery if he might wouldn't be interested?"

The knocking on the table was louder than ever, and although there would be no official inauguration of Holger Jansen as first Treasurer of the "What a Town" Neighborhood Association, this was as irrevocable a confirmation as any pact among any group of people has ever been.

Hans went on.

"Yes, Holger, I think you would be good at it. You've always been good at attracting people."

There was silence.

There was more silence.

One beat after everyone else had realized the Assistant Chairman's faux pas, Hans himself recognized the implications of what he had just said.

If there were someone present at this meeting who was not a member of this village (there wouldn't be, for nobody else would want to come, and they wouldn't really be welcome, if they did), that intruder would not know why there had been such a sudden sea change in the current that had, until so recently, been upholding the Assistant Chairman in his newly found position of leadership.

Long, long ago, when everyone present had still been teenagers in school... there was a girl.

She was a pretty girl, and all of the boys thought so, but Paul Paulson was the one who... well, Paul Paulson was the one. It went rather well for a while, to the point that Paul Paulson didn't think it too presumptuous to start bragging about the matter a bit.

Word got around, and they were a couple.

Then, somehow... maybe it was the moon shimmering over the lake that night when Holger Jansen had rowed in from fishing and saw that girl – Paul Paulson's girl – standing alone on the shore while Paul Paulson was out visiting his cousins. Maybe it was the hot breeze that came along and rustled up her skirt a little higher than it ought to have been rustled up.

Whatever it was, it happened, and everything changed afterwards.

The change lasted for a long time, even long after the girl lost interest in Holger Jansen and went off with a boy from another village. They say that girl and that other boy moved to the city somewhere after school was done, and then, who knows.

Well, the friendship between Paul Paulson and Holger Jansen was mended as well as it could be over time, like a fence with a piece busted through and then replaced, so that the cows can't get out but you can still see the different grain of the wood through the paint if you look closely enough.

Paul Paulson went on to date another girl, and that girl he married, and that married woman was sitting right there next to him when the Assistant Chairman of the "What a Town" Neighborhood Association decided to take it upon himself and call everyone's attention back to the fact that, of everyone present, Holger Jansen had a way with attracting others, particularly others who were, for one reason or another, desirable.

Nothing further was said about the matter then and there, but everyone knew that it would be said soon, and for a long time thereafter – including Hans, the Assistant Chairman.

Holger Jansen was instantly flooded with guilt and shame – for having taken the girl from his friend, for having lost the girl in front of the whole town like that, and for a blot being placed upon his reputation on this, his first day as Treasurer of the Association.

Paul Paulson didn't dare look at his wife, who, as everyone already knew but were now publicly reminded, was second choice after that other girl. Everyone tried to look away and pretend they didn't notice as she tried to pull her head into her shoulders while her face started to turn a shade of dark pink, and having nowhere else in the room for their collective glance to fall, they let the full weight of it fall upon Hans Stempelkauer, their once and short-lived leader.

Hans was now aware of his fall, and he knew instantly that the plummet would not end tonight, or even tomorrow. He would not reach the bottom of his fall from grace for a long, long time.

He couldn't, not in a little town like this one.

It was Jürgen who finally said, "Well, we'll see what happens with the plants," and with this, every single chair in the room slid instantly back, as if connected with each other. The space was tight for so many people, though, and the chairs were all pushed back up against the wall. As a result, there was no place for anybody to get out, and each chair blocked his neighbor's escape. The idea of some people pushing their chairs in and letting the other person go first simply did not occur to anyone; it was not in their nature. Instead, there was a lot of climbing over and a gangly stretching of legs.

After the crowd left, Hans stood there at the head of the room, in the cool of his faded spotlight, wondering just how it all happened and trying to make sense of it all.

Jürgen looked up at him for a little while. Then he said "Well", stood up, put the little gavel into his pocket, and left.

Later that night, after a long walk in the darkness, Hans opened his front door and closed it softly behind him. He didn't say anything to his wife, and she could tell from the way he left the room that she shouldn't ask him anything just yet.

That night, he lifted up the sheet and slipped himself into the bed where his wife already was.

She watched him, waiting.

After a period of heavy silence, and in a moment of self exposure (which, after years of further evolution, would otherwise have approached intimacy), he said. "I never should have entered 'The Golden Mule' tonight".

He was marked for life in this little German farm town.

"Hans Stempelkauer's Meeting", they called it.

Answering the Door

Usually, when someone's doorbell rings unexpectedly, it makes the person instantly happy. Their heart beats a little faster, and they anticipate the pleasure of opening their front door and beholding the pleasant surprise of finding out who it might be who has come to see them. It's like a present at a surprise party. Of all the people that there are in the nearby area, and considering how many people are accessible near and far thanks to cars and highways, from all of those opportunities, somebody has decided, "No, this one is the right one. I shall ring the bell of THIS person. THAT'S who I want to see."

Not in Rucklingsdorf.

When the bell rings unexpectedly here, it is usually someone who wants to get something from the you, one way or another. Socializing, when it occurs, usually takes place after the visitor and guest have established a specific date and time for the event, like for a medical procedure.

Moreover, he rarely comes outside of five minutes before or after that appointed time – which is incredible, considering that our watches and clocks cannot be PERFECTLY synchronized with everybody else's watches and clocks – unless the Germans are all connected by radio wave to some sort of network (which would explain a lot of other things, too, by the way).

Therefore, when the bell rings unexpectedly, it's a rather safe bet that it is not going to be a purely social encounter, with someone just stopping by to say hi, ask you how it's going and generally feel good while sharing some time; usually, it will be business, and a business of unilateral interest, at that.

After so many years of answering the door in Rucklingsdorf, when the doorbell rings now and I am not expecting a package, my reaction is, "Oh, crap. How is THIS person going to be rude and inconsiderate and soil my contentedness?".

It almost always turns out that way.

Even when the mail truck is outside, I can never be sure from one end of the experience to the other that the interchange will not end up pissing me off thoroughly, through that tendency that Germans have of stepping beyond the boundaries of civilized mutual consideration to one degree or another.

The people of Rucklingsdorf have a subtle way of casually and unnecessarily stating the inconsiderate, of disregarding how what they do or say affects the other human being standing across from them, and sometimes they go straight for the jugular.

Sometimes they clearly do so with a demonic pleasure, like a cat murdering a bird just because he can, and sometimes they really just don't get it.

There's something missing in them that otherwise serves as a certain lubricant in immediate social situations. In Rucklingsdorf, there is a dryness – not like that fresh feeling after you have toweled off coming out of the shower – it's more like those pictures of arid land with withered trees where the pale dirt cracks into separate cakes of infertile soil, and nothing grows.

Here are some of the ways it can go when answering the doorbell in Rucklingsdorf...

―――――――――――

BING-boooong.

It's Haike, from next door.

"Moin," she chirps from the front porch, as if in a state of contended joy and glad to see me.

"Moin, Haike", I say from the other side of the threshold. We use the word of greeting that is typical in this northern part of Germany. "Would you like to come in?"

Then, her state of peace is shattered, and the dance of awkward refusal begins.

"NO, no... I just wanted to borrow a hammer. We can't find ours."

"Sure, I'll go get it. Come on in", as I reach naturally to open the screen door to make way for her, glad to be hospitable and to welcome someone into my home.

"No, thanks. I'll just wait out here."

I pause in reaching for the handle and I look at her through the screen. It's like being in one of those confessional booths in a church and looking through that little grating at a priest, but this time the priest is guilty; there's a sense of shame involved in it, somehow.

"You want to wait outside while I go in and get the hammer?", I say, calling attention to the peculiarity of the situation. She expects me to close the door and leave her waiting outside, like a chicken in the front of a barnyard, while I walk through my warm, clean, secure home to spend who-knows-how-long looking for a hammer that I might or might not be able to find, after all.

"Ja, that's OK. I'll just wait here." The chirping in her voice is still there somewhat, but it has turned into more of a trill. She's nervous.

I take a moment to reflect upon the fact that people in different countries have their own ways of doing things. Then, I weigh that with the fact that this human being wants me to lend her something of mine but doesn't even dare to step foot in my own home to get it.

I have made my decision, and I throw down the gauntlet.

"That's ridiculous", I say. "Come in anyway."

Her sharp, darting eyes show that I have just broken a German covenant that, for all I know, might go back as far as the Holy Roman Empire and Karl the Great.

As I am opening the screen door, she starts shifting back and forth on her legs, like a giant, lanky whooping crane. She seems to be making the effort to maneuver the turn around the screen door and enter while simultaneously holding herself back, far back, and it wouldn't surprise me entirely if she just suddenly bolted and ran in a straight line in the opposite direction, to then just stand in the street and look away.

She makes herself enter, clearly against her will to some degree. She stands rigidly, as close to the threshold as possible, as outside as she could be while still officially being inside. The very moment after she has passed the border of the threshold, her eyes start darting wildly, searching desperately for something and, AH, she has found it – with one foot firmly planted at her scouting point in the doorway, she stretches her other leg a-a-a-lll the way to the side where there is a little doormat for people to put boots on when it's raining out. After a rather graceless and wide-spread pause, in which she assesses that she has attained sufficiently stable footing on the mat, she then hauls her other leg to join the rest of her and she stands, like a soldier, on the door mat, determinedly within the rubber border and surprisingly equidistant from all edges simultaneously.

I now call it the Prussian doormat. It's where the Prussians stand at attention and await further command.

To make conversation, I ask her how her husband is, and she lets out a quick, sharp "He's fine", a little overly loud for indoors. Her eyes are still darting around everywhere; progressively so, in fact. "He's fine", she repeats, although I did not ask again.

"I hope I'm not disturbing you", she adds, in a disturbingly high pitch, almost yelling. She is still standing at attention on the Prussian carpet, in obedience to I know not whom.

"No, *I'm* not disturbed", I say, leaving open the possibility that somebody else in the entrance hall might be.

I imagine the act of trying to continue a conversation at this point, and I see that any hope of a normal host-guest relationship is not in the cards.

I look at Haike, and I conclude that this has been a lot of effort for a German to make in one afternoon. I decide to claim a kind of victory and I go and look for the hammer.

It takes a while to go get it and bring it in, and my neighbor is still standing there, seemingly more comfortable in her transparent guard booth but still well within her self-imposed boundaries.

I hand her the hammer, she takes it and thanks me, and I reach for the screen door. Her body leans into the doorway before the screen door has been opened yet, eager to go.

"Bye, Haike."

"Bye", she says, waving the hammer at me over her head behind her.

BING-boooong.

I open the door to a man who is dressed casually but still somehow looks proper and orderly.

"Hello", I say.

"Hello", he says. I hear him say it, but I don't see his mouth move at any time. "There's going to be a parade for the Fire Department this weekend, and you'll need to keep your car off the street between 7:45 a.m. Saturday and 9:45 p.m. Sunday."

Again, it's not a polite request. It is an ordinance.

I also notice that the mentioned time-frame is precise down to the nearest minute.

Besides that, the man's voice is void of any intonation whatsoever. If we were to record what he said and look at the modulation of the sound waves in some printout, he would be flat-lining.

"It's nice that there's going to be a parade", I say.

Then he makes a comment that is entirely inaudible through the narrow slit of his thin mouth. It was evidently some comment about the parade that he found humorous, though, because he laughs a bit. When I say laugh, I do not mean a jovial throwing back of the head and a rhythmic heaving of the shoulders, and there was no sound that would echo across the wheat fields for miles, endearing everyone who heard it. The man's laugh sounds more like when you are trying to flatten a plastic bag and the last little puff of air wheezes out, barely perceptibly, before everything is deflated.

After he leaves, I stand in front of the mirror and try speaking like this to see how it even works. I even practice the laugh.

It's not easy, but after a while, I get a hold of how to do it. I look in the mirror and, like a ventriloquist using himself as his own dummy, I mumble to myself, "I think I am ready for the parade."

BING-boooong.

The door opens to a friendly face I have never seen before.

The woman is about 45 and has a version of the only hair style that German women of this age can conceive of, for some reason. It is short, with each individual strand basically just chopped off, as though instead of going to the hairdresser's, she went to the butcher around the corner, bringing her own meat cleaver (since she cannot trust that anyone else's meat cleaver will be honed to precision quite to her satisfaction), and when she sees the butcher, she bends to lay her hair on the butcher's block and shouts in a tone of domineering military command, "Chop it off. Just CHOP IT OFF!!".

Sometimes German women of this age manage to reorganize the ends of the hair strands in one way or another, curving them a little all in the same direction perhaps, but the underlying design is basically always the same.

The hairstyle makes her look like a 45-year-old boy. She is also bone thin, as though somebody at home has forced her to live on dry crackers and disappointment ever since the final days of youth passed her by. If her sweater were left on a hanger overnight, it would not look less filled out that it does on her skeletal and shapeless form, which is devoid of any and all femininity. Her body type reminds me of those pictures of prisoners in concentration camps from so many years ago, a similarity which makes her gleeful smile seem peculiarly out of place.

"Hello", she says musically, as though earnestly glad to have the pleasure of seeing me in life, finally. "I'm collecting money for the XXX (it could be anything. There is an endless stream of charities in Germany, and so there is an endless stream of doorbell ringing. I think it has to do with some kind of individual and collective soul purging for the past).

Why this can't all be organized federally and paid for through our taxes as needed is a fact which eludes me. If people are in trouble, then let's make sure that our tax dollars go there in a supervised fashion. Between that lady's jeans pocket and the needy hand in question, there are so many steps at which the donations can be siphoned off into some administrator's private fund. As a person who is interested in the wellbeing of others without myself being made into a patsy in the process, I need transparency.

She shows me her list of signatures with the name of the charity printed at the top, and she seems to just expect that I will be donating, without any question. She doesn't make a request as much as she states the cold, hard reality that she is, in fact, collecting money for XXX and that this is clearly the right time to hand over a few bills to her, so that she can send them along to others who need it more than I do.

The absence of a question and request carries an underlying "Klartext", as they say in German (a clear and obvious statement that is never expressed in words, but is immediately understood by everyone involved). The underlying Klartext is that these other people need my money far more than I do, and since I have been lucky enough to have the opportunity to live in such a safe and secure country with this extent of food, conveniences, daily stress and video-on-demand, it is not even conceivable that I could be such a heartless bastard and not give a few dollars to those who are far less fortunate than I am.

The fact that the middle class is disappearing at a rapid pace and that those of us who are maintaining a tenuous grasp upon it are currently being victimized by every level of organized society, from finance to politics and beyond, does not seem to apply for her.

There is nobody going door to door where I live ensuring that corporate executives stop earning more than 200 times what their workers earn (or whatever the number is now), that the people at the top of the food chain stop plundering my society through their multi-million-euro bonuses and stock buybacks, replacing jobs with computers and artificial intelligence and decreasing the amount of food in the supermarket packages that stay the same size for the same price... nobody to make sure that they don't keep screwing me over here down near the bottom of the ever-narrowing spiral. No – in spite of my efforts to dig my trembling claws into the edge of the abyss to make sure that I am not one of the many who fall in day after day, I am the spoiled and ungrateful pig who has far more than is morally justifiable, and I owe it to – whoever – to make things right.

Five bucks will do it, just fine.

"I would rather not participate in that, actually", I say. It's a phrase that I have honed for such situations. It enables me to turn down the offer without being negative and disagreeable.

She has been nice so far, and I want to stand my ground without hurting her feelings. I don't expect this to go well – it never does – but I want to give her a chance. As the saying goes: innocent until proven guilty.

She's flustered. She received an answer she did not expect. She must inherently be used either to pleasant agreement and support or gruff rejection. Something between the two breaks the pattern to which she is habituated, and this simply does not compute.

As if my answer was unacceptable and, therefore, invalid, she says, "Well, is your wife at home?", craning her wiry neck to peer past me into my private residence without having been invited in.

"No", I say calmly. I never said that I was married, and I don't find that I owe it to this stranger to clarify the matter any further than that.

The crusader's mouth becomes a firm, straight line, and her eyes start to turn hawk-like.

"When will she be in?" The music is now entirely gone from her voice. I miss it, but I am no longer surprised when this happens in such interchanges.

At this point, there is a cultural conflict. The woman seems to be under the impression that she has run across a barrier to socialist progress and intends to go around that barrier by asking, "Well, if you don't want to donate money, is there anybody else in your home who will override your meaningless decision and give me what I want, anyway?".

I don't think she even realizes that she is being so rude. What if I live in a family of eight people; would she go through each family member one by one until she gets what she came for? If I have a wife who then comes to the door and likewise declines to donate, would the next request be, "Well, how many children over the age of 18 do you have who still live with you, perhaps in your basement like I've read about? Send them one by one to the door, until I finally get what I came here for. If that is not successful, I shall see if any of the younger children perhaps know where mommy and daddy keep their wallet and purse."

No means no, whether it's a young lady dancing with a drunken sailor on shore leave or a person in his own home deciding whether he wants to donate money upon request or not.

Such money-collectors usually appear suspiciously between the hours of 5 and 7 pm. Clearly, they know that this is the time when people who have just put in another long day of contributing to Germany's gross domestic product are about to tiredly lower their old bones onto a cushion and seek nourishment and, perhaps, a few moments of peace – an elusive goal which is interrupted because, after having produced enough tax contributions today to help the eastern states in Germany still recover from communism and to ensure that various forms of post-reparation reparations are still able to flow, I must put down my fork with the (now cold) asparagus and get back to work, because this lady has decided for me that I have more than my fair share already, and that it's time to settle accounts.

I wish her a nice day and close the door. Through the glass, I see her stiff, skinny form still standing there, tightly, ready to enact justice but not knowing exactly what to do.

I return to my well-earned asparagus, but I can no longer enjoy it.

Thank you, lady, for making the world a better place.

BING-boooong.

While I rush to the door, I look quickly out the window and see the bulky yellow mail truck, and I know that Internet shopping is working its wonders for me yet again.

I open the door.

It is a man who, in spite of his clean uniform and advanced technical equipment, looks like he might have lost too many bouts with Jägermeister over the years.

He opens his mouth and a gravelly "PO-oost" leaks out.

He says it like a crow moaning in late October. I imagine several of him perched in the branches of the tree in the front yard among the yellowing leaves, warning of the coming mail, impending doom, and whatever else might be ominous and unstoppable.

There is not one single muscle or tendon in his face which moves, twitches or shows any sign of life or functionality whatsoever. "Maybe his facial nerves are affected," I think. "He might have an illness. Then again, he might just be German."

He raises the device in his hand, I sign, and he leaves.

That is all.

This visitation occurs several times throughout the year. I imagine him going throughout the neighborhood, stopping at various doors and cawing his "PO-oost" to the citizenry.

Later that night, in bed, I rouse somewhat and am a little groggy. The wind is whistling sharply, and the boughs of the trees are clamoring and knocking against each other.

Perhaps I am still a bit asleep, but as I turn to look outside, I imagine that I see the face of that mailman in the dark, peering in at me through the window with his cold eyes, going "PO-oost", "PO-oost"..."PO-oost".

BING-boooong.

I look through the little frosted glass area of the door; it's a woman from the neighborhood. I've seen her around but I do not know who she is and we have never met.

As the door starts to open, there is a bright smile on her face, but as she sees me standing there, her smile suddenly melts into a frown of utter disappointment.

"Oh... I came to see Nadine", she complains – as if she didn't get the one of us that she wanted, and as if my existence in my own home is actually wrong. If she could file a violation with some state authority about the matter, it looks like she would do so.

I never regretted opening a door more in all my life.

BING-boooong.

I open the door and I see a child standing on the porch, alone. He has part of an old sheet over his head and shoulders, so that his face and half his torso is covered. From the knees down, his worn jeans and sneakers are clearly visible.

"Can I have some candy?", he says from under the sheet.

I have no idea about this one, I think to myself.

I run through all of the possibilities that might explain why an unknown child is standing on my front porch with a sheet on his head asking ne to give him candy.

I come up blank.

I calmly tell him no, that I'm not going to give him any candy, and he just stands there. I wish him a good day and as I close the door slowly, he turns away, dejectedly.

I look out the window in the living room and I see the boy across the street. He is hunched between a couple of cars, pulling off his sheet. Then, he just stands there, as if trying to figure something out.

After a while, it hits me. Today is the last day of October; that's Halloween in the USA. Some Germans seem to have vaguely heard something about it, but they don't really seem to understand it fully. I realize that this was apparently some protean attempt at Trick-or-Treating, but fully out of context.

… another international meeting of cultures gone awry.

BING-boooong.

"Hallo. I'm Ute, I'm your neighbor from down the street."

"Hi, Ute. You live here? Which is your house?"

"I'm in the other street", she says, turning behind her and pointing, "parallel to this one".

That's probably why I have never seen her, I think to myself. It's somewhat far away.

"We're having a party on the weekend…", she starts, and I think 'Great, that's a nice chance to meet some more of my neighbors', until she adds, "and we would like to ask if it's OK for our guests to park in your driveway."

After absorbing this shock to my non-Germanic system, which is used to a certain degree of subtly in terms of interpersonal matters, I ask "What's the party for?".

"Just friends", she says, and looks away vaguely, down the street.

There is a pregnant pause, and then it becomes clear that I am not going to be invited.

After a moment of adjusting to the blow, I tell her that I can't do that, since I have a car and I use the driveway myself.

She continues with "but we don't have anywhere else for people to park," as if that is reason for me to sell my car.

"Sorry, Ute, it's *my* driveway. You'll have to deal with your guests yourself."

She suddenly stares at me defiantly, as if I had somehow insulted her and she has categorized me as unacceptable and to be annihilated to the extent that is within her power.

She told me about a party that she was not inviting me to and then asked to use my driveway, even though I have a car parked in it. In other words, she was telling me, "We're having a party and we're not inviting you, but we want to use your stuff."

My rejection of her thoughtless request was somehow interpreted by her to be insolent. Her glare was an example of that frequent German attitude of "How rude of you to tell me that I'm rude!"

The party came and went, and I haven't seen Ute again since.

BING-boooong.

It's the chunky yellow mail truck again, and this time, it's that friendly young woman who has been making deliveries for a while.

"Package for you" she says with a carefree smile, as if she is giving me something that she made at home with her own hands, just for me.

After I sign for the delivery, she takes the pen and says, "Thanks" as if she means it, and then she gets into her truck and smiles to me once more before she rolls away.

A few days later, the doorbell rings again, just as I am moving a piece of furniture upstairs. I put the furniture in place, put my shirt back on, brush my hair quickly so as to be presentable and trot downstairs to the door.

It's raining out. It's the young woman from the post office again, standing on the porch under the little roof. She has another package in her arm, but as I put my hand out to sign, she still stands there, holding the package in place close to her for a few seconds, staring at me rather sharply with a firm gaze and an angry, pursed mouth. She looks as though she expects me to take that time to hate myself a little, and that without that, the transaction today will not be sufficient to her.

I took too much time to get there, obviously.

After finally receiving the package, I close the door and go to look out the window. The mail woman hops straight into her truck, pulls away and is gone.

'Boy', I think to myself, 'the weather in Germany sure is fickle'.

BING-boooong.

As I interrupt my preparations for my first New Year's Eve in Northern Germany, I think, 'It's seven o'clock at night. Who could that be?'

I open the door and behold a group of about seven children, who suddenly break out into song in perfect synchronization.

'How sweet', I think. 'I'm going to love it here.'

Then they hold their bags up to me. I look in, and I assume that they are not expecting me to take anything out and keep it, so I ask them what's going on.

"It's Rummeltopf", squeaks the leader, as if that's obvious to everyone.

"What's… Rumpul-dump?", I ask.

He seems to be amazed that he has to go all the way to the beginning of the matter and explain the whole procedure.

"Rummeltopf is when children go around and sing songs and then you give them candy".

I think about the boy with the sheet who had come once to celebrate a dysfunctional Halloween back in October, and I think, "So, they have their own thing on New Year's up here. And with song. Now that's the way to do it.'

"But I don't have any candy", I say. I have just moved in, and I certainly wasn't expecting the seven dwarves for New Year's Eve.

"But it's Rummeltopf. You *have* to give us candy."

I think about what I could possibly give to these children, as well as the others that will surely follow them at intervals over the next few hours. It will have to be something that I have a lot of. All that comes to mind is the pile of mushrooms in the refrigerator, an option which I quickly discard.

"I'm sorry, but I don't have any candy", I say. "I didn't know about Rommel-tub and I wasn't expecting you."

The leader looks around at the other kids in the group with a sense of significant mutual understanding, and after his head bobs up and his chin comes down, they start to sing another song, but this one is about how cheap I am and that I am basically a terrible person.

"Wait, wait!", I interrupt, "I didn't know about the candy. It's a mistake!" I am trying to explain my case to the jury, and there is a little bit of pleading in it on my side. I don't want to be scorned by the school children in my new neighborhood, and on New Year's Eve of all things, the time of fresh starts and new beginnings.

But there is no stopping them. They have their instructions, their cultural tradition and their fearless leadership. I am being mocked in song, denounced as a foul specimen of human life and a miscreant when it comes to matters of candy and German children.

I will clearly have to turn over a new leaf and catch up to the level of cultural knowledge of the local third graders, and I have exactly one year to do it.

'So this is how the Germans celebrate the start of the New Year up here', I think. 'They send their children out into the night to scold and insult their neighbors'. It seems somehow fitting, a part of a whole and a handing on of the baton to the next generation.

The doorway to German culture can be a tricky business.

Small Town Life

It's a beautiful little village, the town of Rucklingsdorf. It's not much more than a couple of streets, but the way they have been laid out, or rather grown out from the natural landscape around them over time, makes them quite picturesque.

Once the darkest grey of deep winter passes through the various stages of less oppressive gray week by week, on its way to that whitened gray of early spring, it finally breaks open intermittently into a pale blue that seems to offer a person everything that they could ever want in a sky, and which, in their darkest days somewhere in January, the residents had thought maybe wouldn't be returning any more this year after all.

It is on such days, when the air is so bright and pure, that the people in the neighborhood start to free themselves from the wintery isolation of their homes, which always starts feeling like it has lasted a bit unfairly long once the end of February approaches each year. In spring, though, they stretch and yawn and break free, like frogs that have been frozen in place in icy ponds to hibernate over winter, and now they (the Rucklingsdorfers, not the frogs) embrace that vocation to which so many of them devote the best part of their sunset hours for the next eight months or so – walking around.

If it doesn't sound like much, just walking around, that's because you have never spent an early evening walking around Rucklingsdorf at sunset, when the sky turns the color of pink chiffon, like a young woman's dress at a wedding party, and the birds perform their swooping, freeform ballet against the backdrop of the glowing cloudscape.

Not everyone comes out to walk around town at sunset during these months. In fact, most don't, but there are the regulars: young couples, retired people, members of a family meandering aimlessly together in a conglomerate, so slowly that it seems like they are standing still and just being moved along as a single mass on one of those flat escalators that you might find on the floor of some airports. The family members all look terribly bored on such walks, as if their minds have been numbed beyond slumber and they can't stand it another minute, but as though there is absolutely nothing that would ever stop them from settling into the challenge-less comfort of these lazy, traditional familial strolls.

Most other people just stay inside and watch TV, I guess, but some have developed this walking into a kind of custom, and I, on occasion, step out and join their ranks.

Tonight, it's still cool, a feeling that someone who has already experienced those oppressive, un-air-conditioned German summers learns to appreciate.

Down the next street, past the old water tower, there is a couple that is out for a walk. They are in their early thirties, and they are walking like couples their age often do when taking a stroll here: they are directly next to each other, holding their hands with a tightness that looks unbearable and inescapable; their heads are down, and they do not talk to each other.

They are not strolling, actually, as much as they are marching, marching in silence through the streets, as if they are either being pursued or are pursuing something, without being sure what it is, but not wanting whatever it is to notice them.

I watch them as they come from the turn of the road, past the old water tower, and nearly within greeting distance of me, and they have not said a single word to each other, looked up, or released their iron grasp upon each other the entire time.

As they approach, I greet them, and the woman smiles warmly to me, offering me an apparently heartfelt (and perhaps grateful) "Hello!".

The man's eyes dart up from beneath his dark brow, which remains lowered, like a flag after a national tragedy, and he seems to regret it somehow that his wife (or whoever she is) broke the wall and made contact with this, this… stranger.

I was glad to exchange a friendly greeting with the woman, anyway, and I continue on my way.

I walk past the little bakery, which has a little post office inside. By post office, I mean that the women who work there are also entitled to take and handle mail, in the little post office corner by the front window. They do O.K. with the basics: selling stamps, even registered mail, but ask them to tell you the cost of a package that is so wide and so long and that is destined to reach the United States within a week, and they will come to be visibly overchallenged, and not a little frustrated and somewhat aggressive in being asked such a thing.

The bakery is closed as I walk past it. It is only open from 8:00 to 11:30 in the morning, and then again from 1:30 until 3:00 in the afternoon. The baker himself must be either dirt poor or filthy rich to get away with such business hours. What the baker and the staff do in between those times I don't really know, but it has always struck me as rather inconsistent to see a "Siesta" taking place here in northern Europe. Perhaps they all go home, eat tapas, listen to Flamenco music, dance and clap in a circle, and take a nap in the corner under their sombreros until 1:30. Probably not. The supermarkets in the bigger towns are competing with each other to stay open later and later, a bit more each year, but the Rucklingsdorf Bakery and Post Office Corner somehow manages to get away with it, perhaps because so few people outside of Rucklingsdorf are aware of its existence.

On this wonderful spring evening, there is another couple, somewhere in their mid forties, out for a bicycle ride. As always, without one single exception, the man is riding in front, and the woman is trailing behind. I don't see any reason for this to be intrinsically necessary, especially in these days of alleged gender equality. Does he need to protect her from whatever might suddenly come across their path? Are their dragons? In Rucklingsdorf? Maybe a long, long time ago, but I think they would be on some reserved plot of land somewhere at this point in time, or maybe repatriated to some place like Lichtenstein (if that place is still hanging around. Did Lichtenstein even survive the financial crisis? Or did they just turn off CNN International in 2009, throw their heads back with a throaty laugh and pour each other another glassful of diamonds?). Anyway, the men are always in front on these bicycle rides, regardless of age, years of marriage, or any other relationship variable.

It's not that they start equally taking turns and one of them just buckles under with the years and finally says," Oh, what the hell, you go first. You're going to, anyway." No, they start this way, and they continue this way, year after year, until the end.

And you never see them riding next to each other ("What? That's impractical. There is traffic, and according to statistics from the German Vehicular Association…"). They don't smoothly change their speeds to be next to each other on a long straightway and exchange some comment, perhaps an observation they have made along the ride, a reaction about life, or just a warm smile and a look into one another's eyes on this glorious spring evening they are sharing, together.

No, they are in their set places, categorized and in order, covering ground as sufficiently as it can be done, so that they can finally get it over with. Perhaps this is a way for them to have the impression of doing something together without having to undergo the inconvenience of actually interrelating with each other. ("We would talk, if we could, of course, but we can't because we have to ride in single file. After all, as the German Vehicular Association said in its publication last month…").

What if the woman doesn't want to follow her husband and turn to the right again at his discretion, pass the big rock that says "Klempt 1982" in front of Ralf and Rita

Klempt's house, then left at the slightly larger boulder that brags "Stopf 1952" in front of Hildegard and Gustav Stopf's house, just like on every other bicycle ride before it since they have known each other?

What if she wants to turn left here and then head past that little brick house with the black Mercedes in front of it? You know, where Johan Johansen lives? She knew Johan back in their school days; they used to play together, and then later he was so impressive as the team captain in the youth football league, and he's done so well for himself now; his wife seems to be so happy whenever she is gardening out front.

Why can't the woman on the bicycle turn in that direction this time, to feel the wind in her hair, to feel free, to – her husband's right arm raises with pinpoint precision (she knows that he is doing it this way so that she will not possibly mistake it) and he throws his arm into a sharp, straight line, which ends with the very tip of his index finger. He turns right, and she looks at her husband's jeans leg rolled up on the side where the bicycle chain is; she slows down, just a little more than usual on this particular turn, and looks far to her left. Johan Johansen's Mercedes is shimmering in the orange of the setting sun; it looks illuminated, vibrant… sultry…

And then, the woman's head rotates slowly forward again and to the right, resignedly – and she follows her husband.

Just as the bicyclists fade away around the curve of Harglarck Strasse, a couple of old ladies pass them, approaching in my direction. There are a lot of old lady pairs.

In fact, there seems to be an incontrovertible rule in this town, almost an ordinance, that men socialize with men and women socialize with women. There are couples, of course, married or otherwise, but they have their own unique pattern of interchange (which arguably can be called anything but socializing), and their involvement with each other serves an entirely different purpose. When it comes to socializing, though, the gender lines are clear, and they are practically never crossed.

As the two ladies make progress (if progress it can be called), I see that they... yes, they are in fact both using what could only be described as Arctic walking sticks. These are commercial products that people hold in their hand and swing back and forth while they walk, almost like ski poles for the asphalt.

To say that such sticks are "used" is a rather controversial position to take. On one side of the argument is the viewpoint that, since nothing is particularly accomplished by swinging (or, such debaters would prefer to say, "carrying") them, the sticks are not really "used" in the traditional sense. Supporters of the German Arctic Walking Stick movement (and it *is* a movement, in terms of sheer number of participants alone if nothing else) would argue that the use of the walking sticks enables the walker to move his arms while walking, thereby offering an overall "workout" for the old ladies and men who generally employ them. It's science, it's logic (an appreciation of the rational arts that is not expressed while these same people sit over coffee and cake and gossip about the doings of their neighbors' neighbors, and what other people think about the mundane drama of these repetitive and rather foreseeable events).

Counterproof to this argument is the body shape of the proponents of this school of thinking; there is never a paragon of human physique seen walking with these commercial products. The stick-walkers always have one of the two general modern German body types: Type A (willfully gaunt and hungered) and Type B (obese and increasing annually, with their hands flopping at the wrists at those times when the sticks are not being carried). There are exceptions, of course, as to anything, but these body types cover the vast majority of cases.

The two women seem quite proud to be walking with their sticks. They do not at all seem plagued by the self-conscious feeling that they are doing something ridiculous in public. They even look as if they might say, "See us, walking with our sticks? Pretty smart, eh? Works the whole body. You don't have sticks? Why, how do you expect to keep your arms healthy? That's not a very efficient way to walk around the neighborhood. What's wrong with you?", and they might scowl a little in saying this. It is never said, though, just hinted at in their upheld faces as they strut past.

Maybe it has something to do with an inbred need that the Germans have to march.

Whatever it is, these ladies look quite pleased with themselves and their Arctic walking sticks, and as they pass, they take it upon themselves to greet me. After I return the greeting, they respond like a factory machine running on its loop for the thousandth time without any need for updated programming, and they say, "Beautiful day today."

I state my agreement.

"Not like that rain we had last Thursday!", they say, and they each laugh, as though they have found precisely the most fascinating and creative thing that could possibly be said in passing a neighbor on such a pleasant day as this in the lovely town of Rucklingsdorf.

I agree that it did, in fact, rain last Thursday, and I move on.

The sky is changing from its chiffon pink to a blend of orange tones, reminiscent of burning fireside embers. It's a particularly beautiful display tonight.

I follow Misthaufen Strasse and come across that couple in their thirties again. The man is still looking down, and he seems terribly agitated with the fact that we will be passing each other again. Their hands are still clenched together as before ('till death do them part, I suppose). I smile to his partner and she smiles back, but we leave out the greeting now, since it seems like it would be peculiar to repeat it at this point.

As she greets me, his eyes flick somewhat maliciously at her.

Maybe at home he writes love poems to her or cries when he sees bunnies scurry across their yard, I think.

Maybe he beats her.

I don't know.

I listen as long as I can after they have passed me, just to check, and they do not exchange a single word the entire time.

I pass the Golden Mule, where all of the social events, club sittings and town meetings are held. Anything that happens in this little village has its official debut here.

For such a little town with such a minute population, there is a stunning amount of clubs and associations. The German "Verein", as they call it, is a phenomenon without which German society simply could not hold together.

All people are, in spite of themselves, to varying degrees human, in the end. As such, everyone has a basic need to socialize and be together with other members of his species.

This is where things get a little thorny for those humans who happen, simultaneously, to be Germans.

Germans can't really just be together with people. There are certain psychological abilities that this personal intimacy requires that just come naturally to others, and to some people these skills are in abundance. There are some people who you can run across in life (mostly in more temperate climates) who, upon meeting a person for the first time, just interchange with them as though there is nothing else that they would rather be doing at that particular moment. A certain personal trust develops, a sharing, and a natural pleasure at being together, just because the other person is the way they are and you are the way you are, and they actually enjoy the experience.

This is not the case with the Germans. It's not that they refuse to do it, per se; it's just not really an option for them.

If two Germans who are strangers pass one another in such a town as this, there will usually be a greeting, neither warm nor cool, but rather void of any perceptible temperature, and it will be left at that.

If the two people recognize each other as neighbors but do not know each other long, there will be superficial chat – almost exclusively about the current, recent or approaching weather conditions – and that will be all. Talking about the weather is safe, it's easy. There is no exposure of the self – of what a person thinks and feels. There is no danger, no risk – and so there is no fear that something uncertain can result to shake the German sense of order and psychological safety. As a result, the chatters are safe – but they never really live, and there are a lot of missed opportunities.

The chatting will be conducted with a veneer of warmth and friendliness, with a smile and perhaps a laugh, and it will almost immediately be brought to its conclusion (Hello – There are weather conditions today – Goodbye), almost as though the end is sought after as a kind of moment of satisfied escape, an escape from a successfully handled necessity of communal living that they know they need but would really rather do without, if they were to be honest about it.

During these superficial interchanges, it is as if the people are still standing in their houses behind their windows with their curtains pulled back just enough to be able to peer out fully at the others with as little of themselves being viewed by the passersby in return. The Germans do this from inside their homes, too, but even once they leave their houses, this mindset remains with them; since they are outside, though, they need to have some other way to hide, and so they hide psychologically in these mundane and superficial chats about impersonal trivialities.

It is almost as if everyone outdoors here were walking with a portable circular rod on a pole, suspended above their heads, from which a set of drapes hangs (like when people get dressed up for a costume party as a person taking a shower, and they carry their little portable shower around with them as they circulate amongst the other party-goers). It is as though when the Germans see someone who is rather new to them, they close the psychological drapes around them as tightly as possible, peek out, and say "This snow, huh?" with a big smile, and then dart their heads back behind the drapes, frowning and shaking, clinging desperately to their drapes, perhaps even sweating a little, before anything dangerous or unexpected happens between them which they might have to... have to... handle emotionally (AAAAAHHH!!!).

The Germans are really rather psycho-emotionally handicapped.

As a result, when the locals in Rucklingsdorf pass each other by and chat exclusively about the weather, there is an undercurrent of anxiety and fear, one which they are apparently so used to that they seem to not even realize it, like a person clenching their fist day after day, until, purely from habit, they come to think that this is a normal state to be in.

To an outsider looking in, though, the madhouse characteristic is glaringly obvious.

Still, these people need to socialize, whether they like it or not. Now, if someone is related to you, that's OK, because it's safe. You know them, they know you, you know what to expect and there is no risk involved; there is also no novelty or creativity involved, of course, since everything is essentially foreseeable and follows its pre-established pattern, but that is a small price to pay for such a valuable German commodity as psychological security, so they pay it gladly and stay in their groups.

Aside from relatives, another option for inclusion in their social circles are friends from childhood. In this case, the two people first met when they had the brain capacity of seven-year-olds, before they knew that there was so much involved in human relationships that would turn out to be beyond their skill level; and before they knew enough to run away, trust had already developed, and it stuck.

So, relatives and friends from childhood. In other words, inclusion into social groups among Germans is based upon sexual intercourse: either somebody in my family has had sex with somebody in your family (for example, my mother's father had sex with your mother's mother, so we are cousins), or your parents had sex at least in the same year that my parents did it, so we were in the same grade in school, or were playmates in the neighborhood. Then, we can trust each other, somewhat; we can have coffee and cake together and talk about what the neighbors do, don't do, should do, or should not do (a good portion of these gossip sessions being all lies and inventions, anyway). Otherwise, without a sexual history to bond Germans into some kind of externally imposed and innate tribal membership, legitimate socializing just won't work.

That is where the German Verein or association comes in.

The Germans understand that complete isolation in their families and childhood friendship groups is not enough; after all, people need to pair up and make their own families, and that would lead to, well... incest... ahem, and, uh, Rucklingsdorf is, ummmm...

The psychological incest by which their tribal society functions is one thing, but they prefer to not take it past that point, if avoidable.

Anyway, against their will, if necessary, the Germans leave the security of their own homes and voyage into their many associations: the Volunteer Fire Department, the Youth Entertainment Committee, the Cards and Board Games Club, and so on. There, they are safe to talk and laugh with others with whom they are not directly connected through family or childhood; the reason is that they always have the safe excuse and escape that they are only there because it is Tuesday, 7:00 pm, Bowling Club Night, and if things get a little personal and it doesn't work out, well, they can always run back to the chatter of the association. "After all, I didn't come here to talk with YOU about my private life and concerns, it just came up because, because we are both here at this association meeting, that's all".

In this way, their countless clubs, associations and committees enable the Germans to relate with people beyond the social group they were basically given at birth, because they don't have to commit to any actual interpersonal responsibility. There is always the Verein safely imposed between them, like a dictator (uh-oh), and any contact they have with Verein members is indirect and, therefore... safe ("ahhhhh...").

In many other cultures, people normally become friends first and then say, "Hey, let's go out and do something together this weekend!" In Germany, the people have to (*have* to) start by doing something in public together, for a long, long time, and only *then* might they consider becoming friends afterwards.

It's all backwards (and, in German, the word for "facing backwards" is, coincidentally, "rücklings").

Now, once in a Verein, the members have the chance to try each other out, to take each other out for a test run before buying, to sniff each other up and down like dogs before deciding if they are a good fit for each other. And after so many hours verifiably dedicated to some sort of externally sanctioned communal activity, in public, in front of other people, where it is safe, then, and ONLY then, someone might, perhaps, consider asking you to show them how exactly you prune your roses to make them grow so well, and while you're both together in the garden a few days later, I don't see why we can't have a cup of coffee, and perhaps a little cake (what kind of cake do you like? Oh, really? Me too! We should do this again sometime... just to make sure that I am trimming my roses the right way, of course). And after a couple of years of this neurotic tango, you've got a friend for life – if you want it.

And in Rucklingsdorf, The Golden Mule is the nexus for this founding of future dynasties and lifelong bonds, which are as strong as iron, steel, whipped cream and powdered sugar.

The "Mule", as the locals are prone to calling it ("Did you hear what happened in the Mule last Friday?", "If we need a place for the meeting, why don't we just do it in the Mule?", "Someone has to clean up behind the Mule; there's a lot of garbage piling up by the back door there", and so on).

There are a couple of children playing in front of the Mule today. The game has something to do with little rocks they have found. One of the kids is complaining that the other one took his turn, and he makes a pouty sound as if he wants to start crying, even though he's about 10 years old (German children tend to be a bit whiny).

Down the street from The Golden Mule a little ways is the town cemetery, and the headstones look deceptively soothing and vibrant as they reflect the pageantry of this sunset.

Ranging high above the other stones is the local war monument.

There are such rock sculptures in a lot of these little German towns, I have noticed, a fact which strikes a non-German (particularly an American) as rather strange. The inscription generally goes something like this: "To our neighbors, family and friends who we lost in the Second World War". Considering that, in spite of the many great individual Germans who valiantly tried to stop the mess in the first place, the German citizenry as a whole (including the people living in towns like this one) are responsible for starting that event and everything that went along with it, electing the leader who carried it all through, and (in some cases) were actually in the concentration camps performing the atrocities (after all, they didn't outsource everything to Luxembourg) – considering all of that, it seems grossly inappropriate to mourn for the perpetrators and not to acknowledge their responsibility or even the existence of the victims of the Holocaust or the members of the other armies who they killed and maimed after starting the conflict.

It's the same as if there were a guy in town that everybody always liked, and it turned out that he raped a bunch of women before being captured and dying in prison, in spite of his friends having tried to hide him out from the law. If the guy's old classmates were to then put a statue in the middle of town with an inscription that read, "In loving memory of our dear friend Jup", that would be a grotesque and stunningly insensitive insult to the guy's victims.

It's the same with these German war monuments. What's wrong with a new inscription on them such as, "To all those who suffered in World War II"? That basically covers all ground and will fit on a nice little plaque, that the Town Council can pay for.

There can even be a Verein founded to handle the procedure, just to keep everybody happy.

Just past the cemetery, the road leads on to a little clearing, through which a few cows can be seen, lazily chewing the grass. As I pass, they raise their heads in slow motion and look up at me, staring without saying anything, just like the locals and some of the children do here.

'They must be German cows', I say to myself.

After the clearing, there is that prim little house with the low stone wall in front of it.

I remember the first time I saw it. I thought, "What is that lawn covered with, some kind of new material? Perhaps a latex coating?"

It turned out it was the grass itself: the homeowner just cuts his lawn so meticulously that it looks like a smooth sheet, with all of the blades of grass as near to equal length as seems possible (in fact, beyond what seems possible); none of the individual points of the blades protrude from the group.

I tried this myself at home on the following Saturday, and I found it unachievable, because there are too many bumps in the ground. Then I shuddered inside, as one from abroad is sometimes prone to do in Germany: did that man actually level out his dirt so that it is perfectly even? That would make his glass-smooth lawn all the more improbable, since his property is set on somewhat of an incline.

Last autumn, as I was walking down this street, I saw something else that amazed me. The nearest sewage drain to this man's home is in the street in front his neighbor's house. Now, Rucklingsdorf is a very leafy little village; that's one of the things that makes it so charming. In late autumn, the leaves always accumulate pretty heavily in the streets and on the sidewalks.

At some point, once the pile has become large enough for the residents to think that the shedding of the trees is largely over and that the majority of leaves can be collected in one single act of efficiency, the people come out with their rakes and garden sacks and clear everything dutifully away.

In this case, even though there were still areas covered with leaves at different spots all over the village (since some people had already gotten around to it and others were still waiting, perhaps timing it somehow), this man with the meticulous lawn was apparently ready to clear his leaves away, although his neighbor had not yet cleared his.

What I saw as I passed struck me as a uniquely German solution: the leaves in front of the first house had been fully removed, and in the street in front of the neighboring house, there was a perfectly even column of leaves about one foot from the sidewalk, starting at the property line between the two houses all the way until it reached the sewer drain directly in front of the neighbor's door – where it stopped abruptly (the leaves were still filling the gutter from there onwards).

This, of course, allowed any rainwater to flow from in front of the first house along the gutter and down into the sewer drain, unimpeded by any leaves – with the "neighbor's leaves" left for him to collect himself, whenever he got around to it.

I assumed that there had been some kind of spat between the homeowners. After all, what rational creatures living at peace with each other would resort to such a thing? To my surprise, I later found out that they had never discussed the matter in advance – it was just something that the man took upon himself to do.

In some ways, that makes it even worse – and far more frightening. I wasn't sure if this was rude or polite of him. It seems like a peculiar mixture of both.

In a certain way, I have been on my guard in Germany ever since that moment, wherever I go, because if that is possible, what might they come up with next?

Anyway, that happened last autumn, and as I continue my walk on this lovely spring evening tonight, two men can be heard in the distance exchanging a hearty greeting with each other. They sound very glad to have met, and I can hear that they have stopped to chat a while.

There's a very nice quality to the interactions here among the people who have known each other for a long time. They seem as though they are happy to have run across each other and to stop and continue a kind of an ongoing dialogue they have been having with each other for years now, and that this is just the latest pleasant installment for them (even though the dialogue never seems to actually go anywhere).

The greeting that they exchange with each other is "Moin", which is a word that is as complicated as it is simple. It is the greeting used in the north of Germany, and on the surface, it just means "Hello". Dig a little deeper, though, and it becomes clear that "Moin" has many different meanings, depending upon the relationship between the two speakers.

If the two speakers are relatives or friends from school, the word means "I wish you a good day and I am pleased to share the earth with you, fellow human!"

However, if you are a stranger (in other words, not even an active member of the Fishing Club, The Shooting Club, or one of the other "Vereinen"), then when someone says "Moin" to you, it translates loosely as "Stay away", "Leave me alone" or "I don't know you, so your presence and eye contact make me feel uncomfortable, insecure and, therefore, essentially unsafe. There, I have greeted you, and that should be enough, already. Now GO!".

These reticent farmers have managed to stuff all of those subtle and complex meanings into that one, little, nasal word, making "Moin" a true linguistic marvel.

It's starting to get a little dark now, and the sky is turning a pregnant shade of blue. I continue on, past Müller's field (he's planting wheat again this year, and the shoots are just starting to show).

Up around the turn, I see that couple once again. They are still marching in synchronized rhythm, faster than a quiet stroll with your loved one seems to call for.

When I see him this time, I think of Dostoyevsky (there is a noticeable similarity). As to the woman, I notice that she has one of those practical German haircuts which makes her look like a lesbian. Is that why they don't talk, I wonder? Are all the women with those haircuts a little... I don't know, I'm just wondering.

As we approach, I look the woman in the eyes, she looks in mine, straightfaced, and we pass each other without saying anything this time. I imagine that she thinks there is no point in dragging our relationship out any further than we already have. We had a good thing while it lasted, but after a greeting and a second smile, it's time to move on. We're all adults here.

Or perhaps she wanted to cry, "Help!", but didn't dare and needed me to just read the desperation in her eyes.

I imagine the intense awkwardness of passing them for a fourth time tonight, and I turn back. I reach my front gate, go in the house and shut the door behind me.

"It was a beautiful day today", I think to myself. "The ladies with the Arctic walking sticks were right."

At the Book Store

If you drive about a half hour south from Rucklingsdorf along the state road, you'll come across the town of Klarp, which is noticeably larger while still being charming.

Like most German downtown centers, the shopping street of Klarp is always a pleasure on a sunny afternoon. It is timeless, with its cobblestone and brickwork streets and the tasteful second-story architectural flairs of the buildings curving along the pedestrian ways.

In between the cobblestone and the second stories, though, there is one chain store after another, just like in any other modern German town or city. For someone who never looks down or very far up, there would not be much difference between this particular town and another one on the other side of the country, and it would be hard to know exactly which one he is in.

This can save a person a lot of money on vacations, since, instead of traveling to a charming, upscale village by the seaside, a person anywhere in Germany can just as well go into his local town center, shop for cheap clothing made in Thailand, eat a Döner, and tell everyone what a wonderful day he had in X (filling in the name of most any sought-after vacation spot in Germany that is sure to inspire jealousy in the people who look at one's social-media page).

Walking along the main shopping street one day in Klarp, I pause by a book store and, ever imagining that I will find in such a place some group of young, wild-haired intellectuals in threadbare clothes plotting a bouquet revolution in the corner as they lean about by the international literature shelf (although this turns out never to be the case), I enter the shop.

Past the circular displays of colorful paperbacks, I see a countertop with glass casing at the back of the store, separate and distinctive, as if it should be behind a green velvet curtain.

As I approach, I see that it is filled with various items and mechanisms of metal and glass which, if you try really hard, you *could* imagine needing in order to perform the delicate act of reading: there are black and white marble spheres fixed onto grey marble blocks (book holders for the sophisticated, apparently, or for those living in areas prone to earthquakes), magnifying glasses in velvet cases, and bookmarks made of various shiny metals (I use a scrap of old paper, myself).

Among this display of luxury and libertinism, I spy an object, or rather, it spies me. It is a golden pen, as slender as a finger, and when I pick it up and handle it (like a primitive island inhabitant admiring a seashell on the beach), I see that it also includes a flashlight. Yes, entirely useless, more so than marble balls, I suppose. Nevertheless, I am enthralled, and I decide to inquire about its purchase.

There is a young woman, thin and alert, busying herself with moving some items around on the shelves and then placing them back where they were. She is doing everything a bit faster than it seems to need to be done, if it needs to be done at all, and she strikes me as a person who needs to keep herself busy and distracted from who knows what.

I look at her long enough for her to know that she is being watched by a customer… if she wants to know it, that is.

Germans have a tendency to be able to separate themselves personally from all that is human about them, if they choose to do so. It's a little like a hedgehog freezing in place and just waiting for an intruder to approach its sharp quills.

When purposefully ignoring someone, most other people would look as if it bothers them to do so, as if it is something they force themselves to do against their will, but Germans seem born to the occasion in this regard; they don't always do it, and they can be very friendly, but woe to thee who incurs the German Wrath.

A German can stand directly next to someone, perhaps even right in front of them, and express absolutely no signs of recognizing that a human being (or even a valuable life form of any kind) is present in that space.

I think if a German felt that they had reason to do so, they could stand trapped in an elevator with someone nose to nose for three hours and (if the German has decided that he has reason to take offence in the other person or judged that everything and everyone in the entire situation is beneath him), the other person would leave the elevator after having been rescued by the fire department and say, "God, we stood nose to nose for three hours and he didn't even talk to me. I felt so devalued." If the fireman would then turn to the German and ask what he thought about the other person that had been trapped in the elevator with him, such a German in such a mood might say, "What other person?".

Similarly, I stand on one end of the counter in this book store a mere two meters from the saleswoman who has taken it upon herself to ignore me, although she clearly has no legitimate reason to do so. I wonder what I might possibly have done to offend her into this cold and dejecting behavior, but instantly remember that we have never met. In fact, I would *like* to meet her, because I want to ask her about the slender gold pen with the flashlight in it.

A colleague from another department comes up and asks her something work related, and my unintended nemesis responds attentively and civilly, even with a certain degree of comradery to her.

"So, it's somehow selective", I think. Perhaps it has something to do with her not wanting to be in the position of serving another person.

While many Germans who work in retail are very friendly and give the impression that we are all just a few degrees away from an ideal world in which everyone just gets along with each other fabulously, some of them seem to be under the impression that they are actually supposed to be in a royal court being waited on by bowing servants while deciding whether they should have another fine chocolate plopped into their mouths for them, but that there was some mix-up somehow and they instead ended up here in a shop, with "those people" demanding things of them.

The German brain is an amazing thing. God knows what's deep, deep in there.

I stand at the counter and wonder why she doesn't just come over and offer her assistance without my having to force it, and it is in such moments, more than any, perhaps, that I miss being in the United States, where I would suddenly be greeted with a faux-warm "Hi, there"(spoken high and musically, like by a thrilled cat), and approached by a saleswoman with a self-sacrificing smile intending to do her best, by glory, to please her customer.

"Excuse me, I would like to ask you about this pen, please", I offer.

Some time goes by, in which she has found enough leisure to dust a cloth across the top of a pile of boxes a half dozen times before turning more or less in my direction, as if she has already had enough of me and my impudent demands at this early stage.

I am suddenly thankful that we are not married.

She stands in front of me and looks down at her blouse, fidgeting with it as if she has found an unwanted thread that does not belong there (I look. There is no thread).

"Ja?"

That is all I get.

Not "Hello, may I help you?", or "Greetings, fellow human. We are all rocketing our way through this universe together. It is truly amazing that you and I happen to be here together in this same place and at the same time, and I thoroughly appreciate sharing this moment with you!"

No, just "Ja?" (imagine it in a deep, gravelly tone, like you might hear on the phone after dialing the wrong number at three in the morning).

"Does this pen come with refillable cartridges?", I chance.

She looks at me without making eye contact somehow, pauses, and then fumbles around in the counter below her for a brief while. When she comes up for air, a small box with a drawing of what looks like pen cartridges on it is before her, somewhat slapped onto the counter top.

That is all. There are no words.

The atmosphere is that, considering my previous question and (perhaps) the diagram on the box, any further statement would be excessive, and that she will not be sinking to an act that is so far beneath her as to respond with so demeaning and servile a statement as "Yes, here it is!". After all, what member of the royal court in the 1800's ever said "Yes, here it is" to a mere member of the public rabble?

She looks vaguely over my shoulder into the depths of the store, but with no evident interest in what she sees.

Whatever she is doing, she is making a lot of effort to go about it.

She just waits for me to make my foolish, little decision about the pen, so that she can carry on and be done with it, and, though I would have given in to the pressure and spoken during my first few months in Germany long ago, I now just stand there and look back at her for a few seconds (this is not my first regal German saleswoman) until she says, "Well?"

"I'll take it", I say, feeling a sense of cultural victory at her response, not only for myself, but for all of my brethren from every country who have stood before such German sales clerks before me and for all of those who shall do so in years to come. I feel a timeless connection with them, in spite of this isolation from the other human who is standing so coldly in front of me at the moment.

Then, the procedure begins.

She puts the pen back into its former place in the showcase, takes out a box from behind the counter (one which is long and slender enough to perhaps contain another iteration of the very same pen in which I am interested, but maybe not) and places it in the center of a piece of wrapping paper that she lifts from atop a pile on the counter.

She then retrieves a small box of (apparently) cartridges, holds it up for me to perceive it, and waits. I look at it, have a series of thought about her as well as the entire occurrence, and decide to simply nod, hoping that I have not just agreed to purchase a little box full of heroine.

She responds wordlessly by placing the little box next to the larger one, re-centering the two as one shape in the middle of the wrapping paper, equidistant left-to-right and front-to-back, and then her fingers move like ten tarantulas performing a St. Vitus dance, folding and creasing the wrapping paper at perfect right angles, rotating the parcel as needed (I swear I can heard a faint, mechanical "Whirrr" as she does so), somehow holding everything in place with the tip of one finger while she flicks a piece of tape off of a dispenser with a move like that of a switchblade, and seals the products in what I can only describe as the most perfectly wrapped bundle on God's green earth. It would make Santa Clause weep and go into early retirement.

The precision with which this package has been wrapped stands in a directly inverse proportion to the amount of humane interrelation that this breathing specimen of salesmanship across from me has exhibited throughout the entire procedure. I feel efficiently and duly serviced, but as though I am expected to pick up my clothes from the floor and leave, without a word and without ever looking back.

"Thank you", I say with a defiant warmth, fully expecting the resentful look that I receive for it in return.

She just stands there.

"Anything else", she states (not asks, but states).

When I say no, she turns and disappears through a curtain behind her.

I have no idea what she might do next in that room behind that curtain. Does she raise her skinny finger to scold small bunnies and tell them that it is all their fault? Does she break down and weep, or does she perhaps just stand there motionless in the dark, frozen and waiting for another customer to switch her on again?

At home, I spend a couple of weeks enjoying my new golden pen with the flashlight in it. I look at everything that I can look at with a flashlight in a pen: inside medicine cabinets, under the bed, I check my tonsils more than once, and I rejoice when something falls behind a shelf and I need some thin object to reach down there and provide just the right amount of illumination.

A few weeks are spent in this state of consumer bliss, and then, suddenly and with no warning, I push up the little button on the side of MY slender little pen and... and... and the light does not go on.

I switch it on and off, on and off repeatedly, more out of a sense of lost love than anything rational. Ultimately, after a period of mourning, nothing is left to me but to face the harsh reality that my... my slender golden pen with the flashlight is... no more. At least, it is a shadow of its former itself.

I spend some time trying to convince myself that I can carry on with it as it is (after all, I can still write with it, I tell myself), but after a while I finally can not believe even my own lies, and I realize the truth... it is over.

I go downtown again, enjoying the city's ancient charm as much as ever. I pass the ice cream shop with the giant, two-meter-tall plastic ice cream cone by the door, and I walk on to the book store and turn in.

The other customers are all peacefully going about their interests, browsing quietly, and there is a pleasant fluster of light laughter to the side of the store between a clerk and a customer who is just taking her change and turning away with a smile.

I head to the back where the display case is. Nobody is there at the moment, and I feel a little tug inside of me as I notice the gold pen on display, the very same one that... no, don't, I tell myself. I'm here on business.

"Can I help you?", comes a friendly voice from behind a handful of books passing by.

"Yes, I bought this pen and it doesn't work anymore, unfortunately."

"I'll call someone for you", she says, before smiling warmly and then leaving.

'It's a beautiful world', I think to myself. 'A beautiful world'.

After a while, a dark figure appears briskly behind the counter of pens and magnifying glasses.

Our eyes lock.

She knows.

In that instant, she knows.

It's that one, the Englishman (again, I'm from the United States) who bought that pen. She has been requested by me to come to the counter. She seems to sense a problem, as if there is going to be a conflict. As if it is not over.

"Ja." (Again, no question mark).

"I bought this pen the other day" – (I can see in her eyes that she remembers and thinks the introduction to be superfluous and wasteful of something) – "and the flashlight doesn't work anymore."

I leave it at the facts. It seems the most promising approach.

"Do you have your receipt?", spoken as though she is hoping that I don't, at which point, all bests would be off.

I unfold it before her, silently. I know my adversary, I know her type, and I am prepared.

She scans it thoroughly, her eyes darting back and forth, as though looking for a sign, any sign.

Then she pauses and, with a tight, crooked, self-satisfied smile that I resent tremendously, she says "this is past the two week return period", and flicks her hand with the paper back at me, like a 10-year old girl saying "WRO-ooong, I win!". It is the happiest I have seen her yet, though it is a bitter happiness.

All Germans know about the two week return period. It might as well have been chiseled in between the first and the tenth commandments. It is that valuable, and that incontrovertible. Anything, but ANYthing, can be returned within two weeks: fair game, sealed deal, no questions asked. After that, depending upon the kind of product, a company might have to fix or replace the item if it is broken or defective, but *only* if it is broken or defective, and *only* if the customer is not at fault. According to those rules of the game, if a salesclerk can prove that the product is not *really* malfunctioning through any fault of theirs or that it is working well enough to hobble and puff along out of the store, then forget about it. Sorry, sucker, you bought the mule. We had no idea that it was diarrhetic.

Then why doesn't every store clerk just say that the product is fine and that no guarantees will ever be upheld?

Munich, that's why. Because, besides the beer tents filled with puking tourists during Oktoberfest, Munich is also the heart and soul (so to say) of the German insurance industry, and the German insurance industry includes legal insurance.

In that delicate balance between upholding a product guarantee and telling the customer to shove it, there is the knowledge that any customer might just have the foresight to have taken out legal insurance. Then, every store owner knows that it is his insurance against theirs and, indirectly, every moody, rainy-day store clerk knows that her boss will not like it if she gets the store in the middle of a legal battle with someone's big-daddy in Munich.

So, when I stand face-to-face with her royal highness the book-store clerk, we both know it starts as an even battle. She has the self-assuredness and casual disregard that comes from being the gatekeeper, the pronouncer of the almighty "It Shall" or "It Shall Not Be Done", and the pleasure that I am entirely at her mercy to this extent – a mouse in her coiled talons.

I, on the other hand, either have the Munich mafia behind me, or I am bluffing, and she will not know which is the case until it is too late. She knows this, and this conflict between the taste of the approaching victory and the fear of the dreaded fall into the abyss is palpable in her eyes.

Why such people make things so difficult for themselves I do not know. Either way, it is clear that if I can lay out a good case, she will have no choice but to send the pen out for repair or to exchange it (at her whim and mercy, of course).

The receipt clearly shows that I have missed the two-week exchange period. And the battle begins.

"But it doesn't work", I proffer (the first, quiet rolls of the kettle drums).

"Do you need to buy another cartridge?"

Trying to evade the repair by tempting me into another purchase – 'You're a sly one', I think, 'I'll grant you that'.

"No, it's the flashlight. It doesn't go on any more."

"The battery might be dead. Maybe you need to buy another one. There's a dollar store right down the street"; she says, looking out the door and pointing, somehow, straight and to the right at the same time, with her whole torso leaning forward towards the door.

She is showing me the way out. She wants me to go, but I am not going to back down so easily.

"No, the battery is fine. The product is just no good. I would like my money back, please."

And then, the gatekeeper hoists the drawbridge – but tauntingly. She raises her arms in unison with remarkable slowness, expanding her rib cage, like a bird of prey swelling and about to take flight. Her hands trace the outlines of a ballet maneuver as they circle and cross in front of her breast and then insert themselves, like the crescendo of a tragic opera, into the deep pits of her arms, forming a barricade.

She stands, stoic, stiff, strident, as if harnessing a genetically inbred trait from a grandmother who might have similarly stood before a Russian tank, alone on a cold, windy hilltop so many years ago.

She seems to think herself quite an impenetrable force, this skinny, bony little sales clerk with a black-and-blue mark by her left elbow. I laugh at the presumption of strength in such a meager specimen.

When a German is in this state, like that of a swelled-up frog or a blowfish, their fantasy of their imperviousness is beyond all contact with reality and proportion. They actually seem to think that just because they twist their face into a sour scowl and expand their upper body, the other person will cower, whimper and run away, bobbing their little red balloon on a string behind them. They do not grasp that folding one's arms is not a strong logical counter-argument. Moreover, they don't seem to understand that a threat of physicality of any kind is meaningless in a society of laws – although when this ritual is performed by a skinny little thing in a cheap blouse, it is all the more laughable.

From atop her horse with the streaming banners and the flowing, regal cloth, she drawls a sentence that is more like a judicial sentence than anything else, one slow word at a time.

"Hooow do YOOOOU knoooow… that the BAttery… is not DEAD?!" She places a sharp, pathological accent upon her final word.

Again, this is not my first week in Germany, nor is it my first time buying cheap crap in a shiny casing in a German store and having to return it.

I have prepared for all contingencies.

The battery – it's such a foreseeable escape route.

I reach into my pocket and pull out a little battery tester, unscrew the golden pen casing, insert the battery, and let the "beep" of the full battery declare my victory.

I remove the battery but hold it there, as if ready and willing to insert it again and again, to produce "beep" after "beep" until the sales clerk is ready to tear at her hair and declare her submission to reason in a fit of madness.

She grabs the pen from my hands and stomps back behind the counter, where she cholerically pulls out a form and starts scribbling frantically upon it.

The form has the word "Repair" printed in bold letters at the top.

"A repair will not work", I say. "There's a problem with the design."

I now take a different tack and try to appeal to her sense of reason.

I remove the casing to expose the mechanism.

"Do you see this little piece of plastic?", I say, pointing at it. "It's too thin. It doesn't hold up after the button is pressed a couple of times."

Her eyes gleam, like those of a thief who hears the police sirens when he is cornered and then has one last, desperate, hopeful scheme.

"You must have pressed it too much."

She doesn't look up. She is bluffing, and she knows that I know it.

"Show me where in the instruction manual it states the amount of activations or the degree of pressure."

She is visibly nervous. In the face of a well-structured sentence and a sound argument, such people become highly unsettled.

The awareness of her position as the gatekeeper is in mortal combat with the ghost of the Munich legal insurance industry, and the battle is visible in the depth of her eyes.

She stares at my face; she looks me up and down; she looks into the store again for some sign of help, then at the pile of boxes behind the counter…

… then finally, her tight pupils dilate, and it is over.

She turns despondently to a block of paper, scrawls some symbols into a form there, and then r-r-rips the paper from its block.

Then, she clicks unharmoniously at the cash register keys until the drawer spits out at her. Her fingers lick up a few of the colorful European bills, and she hands them to me, together with a few bits of gold.

I thank her. She looks away. And it is done.

The Germans' German

It's generally agreed that the German language is, to put it mildly, complicated.

Having mastered the challenges presented by their own native language, the Germans seem to view this complication as a sign of their superior intelligence, while people from other countries can tend to reach a different conclusion altogether.

When Germans talk about their own language to foreign speakers, the Germans usually smile proudly (and somewhat condescendingly) and say "Deutsche Sprache, schwere Sprache" ("the German language is a difficult language") – as though they, who have been "to the manor born" do not have any expectation that the mere linguistic peasants from other countries, with their cute, little, easy syntax, will ever manage to climb the jagged mountain of German fluency.

It is true that foreign speakers often make certain mistakes with the little details of the language, regardless of how high up the mountainside their struggle might have led them. However, the Germans seem to view this as evidence that they themselves are more mentally advanced, because they can do something that others just below them on the mountain find unachievable.

The question that the Germans overlook in this categorizing and hierarchical viewpoint is the following: why is there even a mountain in the first place, and why must it be so jagged?

If a person (or even an entire society) has to travel from Point A to Point B, is it intelligent to take the road that travels over one pointy ridge after another, avoiding avalanches and plummeting precipices as best one can, or to take the path with the least bends, shaded from the hot sun, following the principle that "the shortest distance between two points is a straight line"?

In this case, who is smart, the person who puts themselves through unnecessary and avoidable travail just to get to the same point that is otherwise reached by countless other people on a regular basis, or the person who takes the more practical route and arrives at the same goal anyway – refreshed, with more energy, and perhaps not driven neurotic in the process of getting there?

All of these excessive complications in their own language are just another example of the Germans getting in their own way by hyper-focusing upon unnecessary detail.

The clearest example is the fact that Germans have so many different words for the single English word "the".

There are six words in total, all of which mean exactly the same thing: "the". Having arrived at that point of overcomplication, though, the Germans are not content to stop there and sit on their intricately woven laurels.

And so somewhere in the dark, stormy past of whatever happened over the centuries to make these people turn out the way they are, it was decided that those six words would change even further, depending upon the exact place they have in the sentence.

"Six words for one meaning? *Just* six words? Are you sure that's enough? Why, what if we run out? Without precision, there is not enough security, so…"

"OK, why don't we… let's see. Ah! I've got it. We'll take some of those words and use them, with the same exact spelling, to replace the other of those words when they are in different sequences in the sentence!"

"Brilliant!... but what the heck are you talking about?"

"For example, we say "der Mann" for the man and "die Frau" for the woman. But what if we make everyone say "der" again only in those cases when something is *given* to the woman? Then, instead of "*die* Frau", they would have to change everything around and say that they are giving something to "*der* Frau".

(There is the sound of mad laughter).

"Hahahaha! What a great idea... and in how many different ways should we do that?"

"Uhmmm..", says the ancient Germanic king from his bulky wooden throne as he counts on his fingers, "how about… how about twelve?", he says, looking up suddenly with a devious look in his eyes.

"Fantastic!!", the court eunuch erupts in ecstasy. "Twelve different words for the same meaning? That's brilliant, your highness!"

"Yes, I know", he says, slowly stroking his wild, grey beard. "*NOBODY* will be able to understand it – unless they are one of us!"

And then the mad king suddenly chugs another liter of fermented honey wine, spilling much of it down his wiry beard in the process.

Why did it have to come to this? The Dutch have a lot in common with the Germans, and even though they were not able to be content with a single word for the idea of "the", they had the good taste to at least limit the selection to a total of two: "de" and "het".

That is at least digestible.

But twelve different versions of the word "the", with each of them overlapping and being used to replace each other, like Scrabble tiles on game night in an insane asylum?

Seriously, people.

For those who are not among the initiated, the German language articles start out with an already excessive quantity of three: der, die, das.

Like bacteria in a petri dish, they instantly expand and multiply to six different words, depending upon the place they have in the sentence: der, dem, den, des, die and das.

And to nudge that rusty, pointed dagger a little deeper through one's brain, just to make sure, many of them are used to replace each other, depending, again, upon that valuable Germanic commodity: ORDER.

As a result, "die" might become "der", and "der" sometimes changes to "den", while "den" is one of the many other forms of "die", and so on, and so on, and...

Now, game night in the madhouse has turned into an hysterical free-for-all of musical chairs, performed by those who have apparently forgotten to take their crazy medicine.

Is this what makes the Germans so generally uptight and anxious – being children and undergoing the psychic stress of having to figure out these hyper-focused details from what the people around them are saying? After all, before a child can get to the point that he can finally understand that his caregivers are not actually saying, "Why don't we just *eat* the baby?", he has already needed to undergo such an initiation right into his own linguistic culture that there can be no turning back for him, ever again.

In that light, it would be an act of compassion for their own sake, as well as for the sake of the children, if the linguistic professors and the talk-show panel politicians were to agree to just change all the articles to "dat" and be done with it.

Some individual Germans have already inaugurated this process of linguistic simplification on their own, anyway, a sign that some from amongst the clan see that a change needs to be made.

Let's be honest – if that had been done years ago, nobody would be missing the other eleven forms of the word today. Think of the brain capacity that would be freed as a result, mental energy which could then be devoted to endeavors that are far more worthy than just figuring out what we are trying to saying to each other.

After so many generations of the mysterious and inexplicable early demise of their patients, doctors around the world finally woke up one day and stopped using leeches to cure patients by sucking the blood out of sick people. In honor of that act of tragically belated reason, why can't this progressive step of refurbishing the German language also be taken, for the wellbeing of mankind: for the Germans themselves, for others who deal with them and, if for no one else... for ME?!!

On top of all that, there is the hodgepodge of the different endings for all the adjectives, which is really just like throwing all the puzzle pieces up and the air and shouting, "Go!".

Germans, are you kidding? Are you really just toying with the rest of us? Do you really just speak a casual version of Italian at home amongst yourselves when nobody is looking? Be, honest – you can trust me, I won't tell anyone.

It's just too much.

And that's just the *grammar* – but the Germans don't stop there. No, no – the Germans take that same disregard for efficient and considerate thinking and apply it to their vocabulary, with every chance they get.

Let's look at the word they use for the English word "chimney" (see how succinct and compact that is, Germans?). Their word for "chimney" is "Schornstein".

OK, it's a little heavy on the tongue, and it sounds like anyone who says it is already highly inebriated, but it will do.

But watch what the Germans do next. They reach into their bag of fanatical vernacular and just start smashing other words onto that one, one after another, with apparently no rational end anywhere in sight.

As a result, "Schornstein" (chimney) becomes "Schornsteinfeger" (chimney sweep), and with a little spit and hope, that extends into "Schornsteinfegermeister" ("*master* chimney sweep" – that's the guy who had no problems early on pronouncing the word "Schornsteinfeger").

Now, if all of those highly skilled professionals were to decide to congregate, such as to exchange professional knowledge and to have a generally wild time in Las Vegas, they would attend their "Schornsteinfegermeisterversammlung" (a convention of master chimney sweeps), and if it were successful enough to be continued annually, it would morph (as if of its own volition) into their "Schornsteinfegermeisterjahresversammlung".

Of course, along with all of the heavy drinking and questionable rendezvous, a convention is not a convention without someone taking the meeting minutes, and that valuable document would be entitled the "Schornsteinfegermeisterjahresversammlungsprotokoll" (a word so long that it would not leave any room on the page for the actual ins and outs of the meeting itself).

Just in case you were wondering, the guys who are on call in case the chimney sweep is not available could also have their leaders at the top, their annual conventions and, of course, the recordings of their annual conventions' minutes. That document would be (get ready, now) the "Stellvertretenderschornsteinfegermeisterjahresversammlungprotokoll" (the meeting minutes for the annual convention of deputy master chimney sweeps).

That's nearly a full sentence in most other languages.

How can we ever have world peace when some of us are thinking like this?

Honestly!

Even a lot of more common words are just smaller words smashed together, as though with two heavy fists.

For example, the Germans say "umgehen" where English speakers might say "circumvent".

"Umgehen" is just the rather blunt fusing of "um" ("around") with "gehen" ("go").

We English speakers also have the option of saying we want to "go around" something, if we choose to, but we can also select the more elegant "circumvent" (which comes from the Latin "circum", meaning "around," and "venire," meaning "to come").

Now isn't that lovely?

Why does everything in Germany have to be so damned *practical*, at the expense of any trace or silhouette of beauty?

No, Germans want to have as few vocabulary words at their disposal as possible, so they can be done with the otherwise bothersome process of speaking.

You can sometimes get the impression that there are really only six words in the language, and that the Germans just hack them up and stick the parts together wildly here and there, like arms and legs on Frankenstein's body.

And I don't think it will surprise many Germans when I say that the German language is not a particularly graceful form of expression.

It's all those consonants, sometimes simply stuck together one after another, as if someone just found them laying around in a dusty pile in the attic and said, "Oh, what the heck, *this* can just as well be a word, too".

Look at the word "murmeln" (appropriately enough, it means "to mumble"). Just feel how the tip of your tongue moves on your pallet as you get to the end of that word there. It's like you're trying to scrape some peanut butter off of the roof of your mouth that inadvertently got stuck there, somehow.

And yes, you guessed it… the Germans go on from there: they say "murmelnd" when they say that someone is "mumbling", and no matter how clearly and distinctly they might pronounce it, the coincidence between the sound and the meaning is eye-popping.

Why not speak a little bit more like the Italians, the Spanish, the Portuguese – even the French, who are so creative with speech that they leave nearly half of every word to the imagination instead of speaking it all outright?

You could do it in your own way, but come on, Germans – soften things up a little.

Does it have to sound like someone is performing the Heimlich maneuver every time we ask a person to pass the salt?

Even if someone finally manages to get a handle on this wild horse of a language, the Germans will only begrudgingly ever acknowledge the other's accomplishment.

Most Germans assume that a person is either completely fluent or absolutely incapable of speaking their private language whatsoever.

There are exceptions, of course, but often, the moment you say "des Hund" instead of "des Hundes" in talking about his dog, no matter how long you might have been pontificating in advance upon the subtle glories of the animal and its likeness to a Grecian god, the German will suddenly begin to speak in monosyllabic utterances to you – as if you are all at once standing in front of him with a cheap suitcase covered with airline stickers in one hand and a German phrase book in the other, asking "Wh, wh, where ist det toilet?".

Germans generally don't grasp that in between beginning language skills and perfect fluency, there are countless degrees of difference, all the way along the scale.

In other words, at least when it comes to foreign language skills (and, I would argue, in other matters, as well), the Germans usually grasp black and white, and don't realize that there is a multitude of different shades of colors available on the pallet.

If they ever do welcome you into the club of fellow speakers of their rocky, stocky language, you will definitely have to be able to recite poems of Friedrich Schiller by heart long before they accept that you can, in fact, order your own coffee at the counter without your receiving demeaning linguistic assistance from them.

And even still, no matter what your accomplishments with German as a foreign language might have so far been, there will still be *certain* Germans who suddenly (and suspiciously) lose the ability to understand what you are saying – even if you have already been discussing the future of the European Union with them for 25 minutes – just because you are a foreigner.

Being "able" to understand what "a foreign speaker" is saying and "wanting" to understand a "foreigner" are sometimes two very different things in Germany – not always, but it happens, and, in my experience, with an unpleasant degree of frequency.

There is a type of person in Germany who does not particularly feel so cozy with the idea of foreigners sharing their air, and they are in contrast to those many members of the German population who are considerate and more welcoming to people of other countries, on one level or another.

If you sound as though you are an English speaker, the less internationally minded of the Germans (again, not all of them, but a certain type, and you *will* meet them here), so as to prohibit your access through them to the German language, might start to talk to you in broken English, the message being, "You, foreigner, to whom I am supposed to be friendly (so as to show myself and others that I am not a Nazi) but who I actually despise, because you make me feel uncertain and insecure, are too stupid and helpless to be able to understand our highly complex language, which only the superiorly born-and-raised Germans (uh-oh... here we go again) can understand, of course, so I will give you the benefit of speaking with me, but only in my highly insufficient use of *your* native language".

In other words, "If I judge, contrary to all evidence, that you are not capable of speaking our language sufficiently, it is entirely appropriate for me to speak yours, regardless of how poorly I might end up being able to do so – that is, even if my English is far worse than your German".

If, in such cases, the foreign speaker politely informs his local conversant that he should speak in the German language, since they are (after all) in Germany, such a type of

German will often then *begrudgingly* speak in German, but will only resort to words of one or two syllables, stating them with syrupy slowness and, in some cases, shouting them somewhat, as if the foreigner must inherently also be deaf (along with any other congenital defects which the foreigner might be assumed to possess; whether such a less open-minded version of a German also unconsciously imagines the foreigner to be infested with bugs of some peculiar kind is a somewhat open question).

This kind of extreme German, like a regular German on steroids, often starts out with a mock-friendliness, talking somewhat like a parent to a slow-witted child. If the foreign speaker then informs him that there is no reason to talk so slowly, to speak with extra volume, or to limit the dialogue to basic vocabulary and isolated sentence fragments, though, the foreign speaker can expect this more narrow-minded version of the German populace to display signs of being offended, as if finding it rude of the foreigner to question the native's hospitality towards this other specimen of human life that is standing before him.

In such a case, this cruder version of a German has fabricated for himself a justification for finding the foreigner to be unsatisfactory, even though the German's negative judgment of the foreigner results from nothing more than the foreign speaker simply rejecting the deprecating treatment he has received from his cultural host (or, from his likewise tax-paying neighbor, depending upon the case) as well as the extreme German's own expectation that the foreigner should accept such treatment, as though the foreigner is actually in a lower social cast, like in India, and has no right to expect equality.

Again, this does not describe all Germans, or even most of them, but it has happened to me often enough in day-to-day life (on the bus, when buying bread, and so on) that it is certainly a poison in the wine that is worth being on the watch for.

It's hard enough to deal with a foreign language, whatever the case might be. Regardless of my own personal accomplishments in the language, such as they are, I have stumbled along the path a few times, myself, without any hindrance from outside.

I once wanted to purchase a few erasers for my mechanical pencil. The shop clerk was very friendly and thoroughly helpful. She led me to the section in the store where the little box was that contained them, and then she asked, in complete innocence, how many of the erasers I would like to buy?

It's a mechanical pencil – you never know how fast those erasers will be used up. And since they were rather hard to find, I said to her, "I don't know, four or five… let's make it six!", glad that we were in this thing together.

Her entire attitude changed in an instant, and I had no idea why. It turns out that the German word for "six" sounds, mysteriously enough, exactly like the German word for "sex", and so, in my linguistic innocence and lacking a particular subtlety of the formulation of that precise German sentence, I inadvertently suggested to the pretty shop girl who was helping me with the little rubber erasers, "Let's have sex!".

She was not pleased.

If she had been, I would have been even *more* surprised at her reaction– since I had only been on the lookout for the little erasers.

She collected the six erasers from the little box, transported them with a brisk, tight walk to the counter across the room, placed them in a little paper bag for me and handled the transaction – and the friendly lady who had so kindly asked me the question in the first place was no more to be seen.

I thought of trying to explain myself, but I didn't want to make matters any worse.

Then, of course, there was that one particularly cold winter a long time ago. I had gotten a bit sick, and I went to the drug store to find something for my stuffed nose.

Looking through the shelves, I came upon the tea section, and it caught my eye: "Verstopfungstee".

"Well, 'Verstopfung' means a blockage, some sort of clog", I thought. "Besides, people drink tea when they have colds all the time."

"*This* is the right product for *me*!", I concluded.

It turns out that I was close– oh, so very close. Verstopfungstee *is* against a bodily blockage of a certain kind – and I spend the entire evening on the toilet, paying every so dearly for my simple mistake.

Misunderstandings between myself and the German language have not always resulted from my side of the relationship, though.

In some parts of Germany, there are big fields with flowers planted row after row; towering sunflowers reaching to the sky, multi-colored gladiolas, and an array of other wonders. And in front of them all, there is a little metal box with a small slit in it, with a few simple little serrated knives hung up at its side. The idea is that people come and cut their own flowers from the rows in the field, and then put the appropriate amount of coins in the little metal box, according to the price list that is posted there. This simple little agrarian institution is a marvel of trust, not to mention of public safety (due to the knives), but it always works fantastically.

One day, as I was holding a fist-full of thick, fuzzy sunflower stalks in my hand, a man walked up to the field. We looked at each other and smiled, and after I said hello, he said to me, "Asdfoa iweur oawd slja poeiur, het?".

It was a question, and it was in German dialect.

Instantly upon hearing the sounds, I noticed his missing teeth and the earth tones of his worn clothing.

What he said sounded like a random constellation of guttural ejaculations, and I could not be entirely sure that the man was not suffering from sore sort of bodily or psychological malady.

German dialect is not really German, per se. It's like a hearty sausage made of various unidentifiable ingredients that dimly resemble language.

Basically, if you were to take the language of the Netherlands, the language of Denmark, with perhaps a hint of Swedish, and grind them together in a meat grinder, just to the point to which everything is slightly integrated but there are still big chunks remaining, the result would be something that tastes and smells rather similar to German dialect.

When the man in the self-cut flower field started to speak to me, I ran through my memory of every single German language test, study guide and audio recording to which I had exposed myself to date, and I came up dry. I had been prepared to use German on a business level and in universities, but I was woefully unprepared to talk to a local while cutting flowers in the dirt.

So, foreign language in general, German grammar, German vocabulary, the sound of the German language and, occasionally, even some of the Germans themselves: it can be enough to make a foreign speaker want to just start drawing colorful pictures and handing them out to other people in order to express what he wants to say – or perhaps want to start learning a slightly more accessible language – like Japanese.

A Little Surprise

The sounds of seagulls calling to each other on the beach and the metal clanging of a sailboat mast fill my head. There is also the sound of something heavy being dropped, and then dropped again, as I wake and realize that I am in bed.

As the nautical scene fades away, the sounds are still there. I'm not sure why or what is causing them.

With some groggy, early morning effort, I realize that it's Saturday.

My girlfriend is there in bed next to me, and as she awakes slowly, she has a look as though her sleep has been intruded upon and wants to know why.

"It sounds like it's coming from outside", I say.

The clock says that it's a little past 9:15.

"What is it?", she asks, as much to herself as to me. From the way she says it, her question seems more to be "What on earth could that sound mean to us, and are we safe from it?"

The sound is becoming louder, fuller. It seems as though it's coming from everywhere, all at once.

Then, as I wake further, the sound starts to break up into different, identifiable parts.

"That sounds like music", I say, now all the more confused about it.

I pull on some clothes, stand in the doorway, and try to hear from which direction the sound is coming, and then I go there.

It leads me to the front window that faces the street. I look out, and I can't believe what I see.

It's a little parade, coming down the road towards us, but it is the smallest parade that I have ever seen.

As it makes its turn off Sockgasse Avenue and onto our street, it becomes clear that the parade only consists of five people.

There is the drummer, of course, and someone playing a high-pitched pipe ("the seagulls", I think to myself). They are joined by a person playing a glockenspiel, as well as a trumpeter.

In front of them, there is a man marching with the very utmost of pride in his assembly. He is carrying a big stick of some kind, with some sort of feathery material spraying out at the top, and he juts his stick up into the air and then pulls it down back into place in synchronization with the heavy, even drum beat.

My girlfriend has gotten up and has found her way to the window. Her hair is still messed up from the pillow. She squints her eyes and looks out, and then she turns to me and we both smile quietly to each other.

It's the Rucklingsdorf Poker and Bridge Club, having their parade.

They are all wearing some sort of casual uniform, or at least the same color clothing, but it's of a material that looks festive, like felt, and which would not be worn in daily life.

There are no other bands, no cars are driving slowly in front of them, and there is a noticeable absence of anybody trailing behind them in support.

Nothing.

Only the five members of the Rucklingsdorf Poker and Bridge Club, who have taken it upon themselves to state to the community in this way that they are an organized unit and are quite proud of it. They seem to think that rousing the other members of the community from their sleep on a weekend to express this pride is entirely within reason and not at all inconsiderate.

As they carry onwards, the music continues, and it's not bad, for small-town parade music. They hit all the notes, and they keep on beat with each other. Now and then, the pipe gets a little shrill and the trumpet is a bit wobbly, but it is clear that these guys have been practicing for this event, that they have been planning it.

They have been planning to wake the neighborhood up on a Saturday with shrill high notes from a metal pipe while banging on a bass drum.

They must have been preparing for this in their free time for months: evenings after work, on weekends, whenever they could find the time.

"That's Karl Grossbauch in the front", my girlfriend says, smiling easily and looking out the window at the entire spectacle, as though she is watching a bunch of puppies behind the glass in a store.

"Don't they have anybody else?", I ask rhetorically.

"They must have some family members", she says, "or some other friends."

"Something", I say.

Then I think to myself, 'If this is how it is, what if I go out next weekend with a little snare drum, a pair of cymbals between my knees and a kazoo and march through the street, all alone, as the sole representative of the "American Association – Rucklingsdorf Branch"? Would the locals welcome that show of pride early on a Saturday morning when they might otherwise be sleeping in?

I watch the five guys in the parade as they march past.

"Do you think anybody else knows this is happening right now?", I ask.

"I don't know", she says.

Then, my girlfriend and I turn to look at each other again for a moment, her smile starts to expand, and we break out laughing, buckling over there in front of the window.

"Let's go have some pancakes", I say.

"Yes!", she says excitedly, and we leave the Rucklingsdorf Poker and Bridge Club parade to march off into its glorious destiny.

On Vacation

Vacation is usually a chance for people to relax, to shrug off that yoke that we have to carry day after day just to keep ourselves going, perhaps to set the bar of our standards a little lower for a little while, and to generally take a break from the stress and tension that is involved in just being who we are and holding it all together.

This is not so for the people of Rucklingsdorf, or for any Germans, for that matter.

When Germans go on vacation, they bring themselves visibly and noticeably along on the trip.

What they need is to take a break for a while from actually being German, and there is no psychiatric couch that is strong enough to withstand the sheer force of that weight.

The problem is that, if Germans were actually able to not be "so German", even just for a little while – if, even for one, brief moment, they could loosen up that tight ball of steel and anxiety into which they have coalesced – then they would probably never want to go back into the psychological confinement of their previous Germanic existence ever again; they would start wearing more colorful clothing, singing spontaneously in public and cooking with more garlic, and they would no longer produce moving metallic parts and hoe their wheat fields as efficiently and effectively as before, and then where would they (or even the entire relatively civilized world) be?

No, it's good for us that the Germans never stop being Germans. After all, somebody has to pull the cart (after the

Americans take the idea of the cart from someone else, improve it, market it efficiently in affordable units, and convince everyone to go into debt buying it).

We need the Germans as they are – yes, there could be improvements made to the model, obviously, but it is unfortunately a package deal. Whatever makes them complain to the management that the walls in their holiday apartment are too creaky is the same source, the same precarious balance between id and superego, between self-gratifying impulse and externally imposed responsibility, from which their productivity springs. The Germans – take them or leave them; we have no other choice.

Being German comes at a tremendous cost to the Germans' own well being, though.

This is nowhere more evident than when the Germans turn the page in their agenda and see that it is the scheduled time for them to go on vacation.

You can spot the unique species of "Germans-on-vacation" immediately. Although the husband-and-wife couples generally do not interchange with each other anymore than they do in public in their colder climate, the groups of older German woman alone on vacation always seem to be having a fabulous time together (perhaps because their husbands are not there and they can finally relax a bit, at least to the extent that any of them ever actually do so).

This contrast between the behavior of the married couples and that of the groups of women (when traveling and otherwise), together with the women's rather abrupt hair styles, honestly makes me wonder if German women generally have a culturally disproportional tendency towards, let's say, wishing they could leave men out of the equation altogether, if the world were one of less taboos – regardless of whether or not they actually do anything to follow through with it in their private lives. They just seem so glad to be in the company of women their own age, and so different when together with their own male partners. Then again, given the way German men are, perhaps the women just find that they have no other choice than to find their social fulfillment in the company of other German women.

Whatever the reason is, groups of German women over thirty who are on vacation always seem to be in the middle of a party. They laugh, they chat freely, they smile happily, they are interested in everything that is going on around them: on vacation while in their groups, German women of this age group are clearly at their best.

What is noticeable about these parties, though, is that they are exclusive parties to which only these particular German women are invited. They might all chat together with a souvenir vendor in Florence, or laugh out loud together with a waiter in Athens, but they are comfortable because they are together in a clique with other German women, who think, behave and dress the way they do.

This is not really letting go; it's letting go *within the group* but it is not taking a break from the group in which one is deeply integrated.

It is that integration, that set of habits and behaviors, from which the Germans so desperately need a break, and you can't step beyond your boundaries if you carry your boundaries around with you, in every Croatian restaurant and on every Portuguese street car.

Man or woman, though, the Germans seem enraptured with the *idea* of being in the warmer, more southern countries. They seem to love playing southern European for a few weeks, pretending that they, themselves, could, if they wanted to, if there was sufficient reason for it, and if it would not very much impede their productivity once they get home, be as relaxed and casual as their neighbors in the more temperate climates.

When Germans go on vacation, it's like the pig who built his house out of brick (which the Germans often actually do, by the way) taking a few weeks to stay at the other pig's house who built his house out of straw; at the straw house, there is espresso (which the pig from the brick house incorrectly calls ex-presso, correcting the owner of the straw house who correctly pronounces it "espresso"). There is dancing in public (without any club membership or tickets involved). There is drama.

The Germans want to be free, but in the end, they have to produce, and to be responsible.

How do they resolve this dilemma?

They invent the conception of their "southern European soul".

Germans do not intend to ever stop being Germans, and they couldn't even if they wanted to. They need to feel a sense of letting go, though, and to believe that they are not *really* trapped in the cage that their compartmentalizing brains makes for them.

To balance these two internal demands, they remain as responsible, self-controlled Germans but convince themselves that their *soul* is really free and loose; it's just the requirements and necessity to be responsible in daily life that is imposed upon them *from outside* that makes them this way – that makes them *have* to be this way.

Otherwise, they too would be loose and carefree. They too would run with the bulls, gather in the town center and laugh raucously while throwing handfuls of tomatoes at each other for hours (without secretly wondering meanwhile which detergent would most effectively be used to get the tomato stains out of their casual off-white vacation trousers once they get back to the hotel room).

"Inside, we are free and easy-going", they tell themselves. "It is only *on the surface* that we are firm and punctual. After all, that's the best balance, isn't it? That's how everyone *should* be. That's what makes us Germans special, that's what makes us… well… really *better* than everyone else" …and there they go, being German again.

They just don't get it.

This fantasy of their free southern soul is evident in many of the names that they have been giving their children for the past few generations. A visitor to their country is initially surprised to hear so many first names that sound as though they belong in warmer parts of the continent: Manuela, Marta, Rita – until you find out later that the name is sometimes a shorter version of their official name, like "Rita" actually being an abbreviation of "Holgeritha", as though they are really named after a character from a Richard Wagner opera, but that their parents wanted the illusion that they are still on their three week vacation in Barcelona.

This is how the Germans are on vacation.

And the people of Rucklingsdorf are no exception…

———————————

Matthias wakes at 6:00 a.m. in his vacation apartment on the Baltic Sea on the east coast of Germany. He had set his watch to "vibrate" so that he wouldn't wake his wife Kathrin.

Actually, he had been lying awake since 5:00 a.m. waiting for the watch to vibrate (so that he wouldn't miss it and oversleep).

He hauls his large body with difficulty into a sitting position on his side of the little bed. He still reeks of nicotine from the day before.

He is in his early forties, and he looks very much like an ogre from the dark ages: he is gargantuan in height and girth, slow-moving and apparently inattentive, with beady little eyes that seem too small for his fleshy face, and he has constellations of black warts of varying sizes under his eyes. The skin on his face is covered unevenly with purple blemishes and little red bumps, and there is a thick mound of fat on the back of his neck.

The first thing he does is unroll the pair of clean, black socks that he has placed upon the nightstand and puts them on. Then he sticks his feet into his leather sandals, which he bought to prepare himself for this relaxing holiday near the beach.

In the bathroom, he pulls on his shorts and combs his hair over his bald spot. Then, he picks up two fresh, white towels from the pile on the counter, unfolds them, slowly refolds them one after the other so that their corners are even with each other this time, sticks them under his arm and heads to the door.

Even though the holiday apartment is in Northern Germany, the walls behind him are painted in southern European pastel colors (although these colors are not present in the natural environment of this region). The kitchen is decorated with framed watercolor prints of brightly-illustrated French baguettes and of steaming coffee cups with Italian words scrawled in elegant, flowing italics across them.

It is doubtful that the French and the Italians decorate their own homes with pictures of products from their local supermarkets. It is also not likely that there are many holiday apartments on the beachside in sunny Italy where the walls are decorated with pictures of German export machinery, or photos of a flowery field with "Schmetterling" (the German word for butterfly) boldly emblazoned in pointy, black Gothic letters across the surface.

The apartment has a soothing atmosphere of lightness and easy joy.

Through this bright scene, Matthias walks with a hunch, his arms stiff and lifeless at his sides, as though his entire body has frozen into place over the years. When he moves, he doesn't walk so much as he lifts one foot slightly, shuffles it forward, and then lets the entire weight of his corpus fall mercilessly upon it (there might just as well be a resounding drum beat and a vibrating bass note from a tuba as he takes each step, with the ground shaking and the children weeping in fear and foreboding for miles around).

There is absolutely nothing pastel about him.

Matthias makes his way down the narrow staircase, rocking slowly to and fro with each step as he does so.

Then, he lumbers out to the pool area in his shorts, his sandals, and his black socks showing through them. Nobody is there at this early hour, and he selects two chaise lounges that are near to each other and well out of where the sun will fall later (even though they chose this vacation spot so they could spend "a little time in the sun this year", as his wife told their guests, to which he nodded and grunted at the time, hunched over his cigarette at the table).

There at the poolside, he then unfolds each towel and places one on each of the chaise lounges. He looks at the result for a moment, and then he bends slowly and reaches with difficulty for each towel again and ruffles them up a bit with his stubby, smoky fingers, rather strategically, so that the towels seem as if they had been casually strewn there in a moment of frivolity.

He then turns and lumbers back up the stairs and into the bright, colorful holiday apartment. The bed frame squeals as he gets back into bed with his wife, secure in the knowledge that he has unquestionably reserved the two chaise lounges for when they are ready to go sit by the pool after breakfast, regardless of how many other tourists might want to use the chaise lounges in the mean time.

After all, rules are rules – even on vacation.

A Social Visit

The Schmalztupfs have been invited over. My girlfriend has asked them to come for dinner, and so I play along as part of the deal.

I had met Rüdiger Schmalztupf a couple of times in town. He seemed, well, very German. He was the kind of guy you would rely on to handle your taxes, but you would never expect him to look at you jelly-eyed afterwards and say to you, "Can I have a hug?".

As the minute-hand of the clock clicks into its place for the hour of seven p.m., the doorbell rings.

"Fascinating", I think to myself.

It is Rüdiger's ring, certainly: distinct and self-assertive. He holds his finger on the door-bell, to be sure that it has functioned sufficiently, and then holds it there a little longer than necessary – long enough to be intrusive to anybody who has not already appeared at the door, through a fault that could only be attributed to themselves. In this procedure, the "Bing" is dragged out against its will before the "bong" is permitted to finally catch its breath afterwards.

The ladies greet each other, their seeing each other clearly being the reason for the event. Rüdiger shakes my hand, as factually as such a thing can be done, and as though it is a very, very important event that is occurring here this evening.

"This is my son, Üorg", he says, waving a hand in that direction.

"HiI'mgladtomeetyou."

He is in his mid twenties and he speaks with an amazing velocity, the way young German males tend to do. Perhaps it is the accumulation of testosterone that they have not yet learned to categorize and compartmentalize at this early stage in their development. Whatever it is, it takes a lot of effort to decipher what he was saying, where one word breaks off and the other begins.

"Hello", I say. "Excuse me, but what was your name again?".

"Üorg", Rüdiger bellows.

"Yerg?", I question.

"Üorg", Üorg says.

"Irg?"

"It's 'Üorg'", Rüdiger's wife, Frieda, says (again, rather factually), pivoting towards me.

"Org?"

"Üorg, with umlauts", the boy explains.

I am thoroughly confused, and I wonder again why Germans seem to embrace the urge to name their children after sounds that someone might make when choking on a chicken bone. Perhaps it is the sound that the woman made at the moment when the child was conceived.

We enter the living room. While the ladies chat, like water finally flowing after a plug has been released from the bottom of a bucket, I look at Rüdiger and can see that there is an assessment occurring.

To warm things up a bit and to forge some sense of togetherness, I look for some similarity between us.

"I see we have the same taste in clothes", I say.

He stares suddenly at my green cashmere sweater, which happens to match his. Then he grabs for it with both hands, and his meaty fingers rummage it up out of my jacket (I had just come in from the back yard), and he says, "But YOURS has a HOLE in it."

He is noticeably relieved to have discovered the whole, of which I was unaware until now, since it was no small, and which would naturally have been made much larger due to Rüdiger's excavation procedure.

"I'm glad you could come tonight", I say anyway, using "Sie", the polite form of the German word for "you", which is used to show respect.

"Oh, I think we can use 'du' with each other", Rüdiger says, changing to the word for 'you' that is used among close friends and family members.

'Really?', I think to myself. But, when in Rome...

Rüdiger starts to slowly approach a painting on the wall. It is one that I made, of an ocean scene with the light reflecting off of the tips of the waves, with that light matching the color of a bird in the foreground. I'm quite proud of the result.

"Did you make this painting?", Rüdiger asks.

"Yes", I respond, with quiet pride.

"...I thought so", he murmurs, in a deep, gravelly tone, as if exposing a disappointing discovery behind his hand to someone next to him on a jury's bench.

He looks away from the painting, as if he is done with it forever and sees no reason why anyone should want to return to it.

'The whole evening', I think to myself.

The son seems young enough to perhaps not yet have had his own proclivity in the arts fully replaced by the concerns of industry, so I ask him, "Have you ever been to the museum in Kargburg, Yourg?"

"Actuallyit'salittlefarforme."

"Sorry, but could you talk a little bit slower for me? My German isn't quite perfect yet."

"Oh", he laughs, self-effacedly, as though embarrassed at his error and more than happy to concede.

"Isaidit'salittlefarforme," he continues, with absolutely no change in his high-speed performance. "It's fifty two point seven kilometers from our house, and I don't have my own car yet." He mentions the data like a computer spitting out a printout across the room.

I buckle a little inside at his happening to know the exact distance in kilometers (and perhaps in centimeters?) to a place that he has never visited.

"Do you plan to get one soon, Yourg?", I ask.

Frieda pivots to me again and says, "It's Üorg", clearly aggravated at this point with my inability to grasp something so simple and obvious.

In chatting with Frieda about home decoration, my girlfriend mentions that I am currently redecorating the little corner upstairs that I use as a sort of office.

"Is that so?", says Frieda to me, crossing her arms in preparation for something or other, "What color are you going to paint it?"

"I was thinking about a nice blue", I say, glad to be reminded about the nice blue at the moment.

"You should try light grey", she informs me. "We painted our living room in light grey", she says, flicking her head over to more or less where Rüdiger is standing.

"Grey? Well, it's a rather dark corner, and I wanted something a bit more festive."

She stares at me for a moment. Then she turns to my girlfriend and tells her, "The grey in our living room has really made the black in the furniture stand out," extending her own torso a bit higher in the air as she says it.

'My God', I think. 'There's black furniture?'

The ladies talk about different colors and then Frieda turns back to me, still with her arms crossed, and says, "The grey has really made all the difference." It is a response to something my girlfriend said, but Frieda decided to direct the statement at me.

She stops talking and is staring at me. I stare back at her, observe her body language, and say, with a factuality I have adopted from Rüdiger, "I'm painting it blue".

I decided then and there about the blue.

She glares at me as if she would like to pounce, like a hungered mountain lion, and to rip to shreds anything about me that is not the concept of painting that corner gray.

She then seems to have a vague and subduing recollection that there are laws, that there is a federal constitution, protected freedoms, perhaps the American military, and… she retracts her nails and cowers moodily in place, as though there is a dark cloud rumbling above her head, threatening to burst at any moment and yet not daring to do so… not just now.

We go into the dining room and sit down to dinner.

When I ask the son if he is working, he mentions that he is studying engineering. I ask if his friends are as interested in mathematics and data as he is.

"Yes, moreso, even," he says with pleasure. "Sometimes, when we want to go somewhere on the weekend, instead of saying the place, we say something like the year when the building was built, or the speed my friend would have to drive to get us there in an hour, and the others have to guess what the place might be!"

He says this with evident glee, like a crazed child licking a lollipop and noticing that it is the one with the extra sugar in it.

"And then we all laugh!", he says, laughing himself to pieces, in a unique moment of, what for him, must be total release.

I look at his parents, Rüdiger and Frieda, in turn, and wonder what they have done all these years that he has come out this way.

I open the red wine, and ask Frieda if she would like some.

"Yes!", she harrumphs at me sharply, apparently angered that I have cornered her into a position in which she has to say something affirmative to me.

"Yarg?", I ask, hovering the bottle in the area above his glass and awaiting his decision.

"Yesplease", he says.

Rüdiger is eyeing the transaction, and then he says, "Red wine is good for the heart, Üorg."

"Yes", the son replies, "the most capillaries are to be found in the human face, where –"

His father interrupts him with tired patience, as if it is a habit to which they are all accustomed.

"Üorg's older brother just had his second heart attack", the father states.

He waits for my girlfriend and I to nod compassionately, and he then proceeds.

"Dirk is in banking. He's manager of his department", Rüdiger adds, with a mixture of quiet, stoic pride and a sense tragedy. "He had his first one soon after he turned 30."

'What happened in these children's home?', I wonder, as if I want to call someone to save them… although I know that it is too late at this point.

"He's really dedicated to his job", Frieda adds. "His wife says that all the time."

" Rüdiger, would you like a glass of wine?", I offer.

"Yes, please", he says, watching the red fluid cascade into his cup, and clearly anticipating the pleasure that awaits him.

He smiles as he lifts the glass to his thick lips. A quick moment after he tastes the wine, he retracts the glass and the sides of his mouth pull back like those of a disappointed Calvinist. He then places the glass down and pushes it just perceptibly a small distance further away from him.

"It's too sweet", he pronounces. ""Do you have anything else?" He lifts his torso somewhat and I watch his head careening back and forth, while he tries to peer into the wine collection on the shelf behind me.

'Germans', I say to myself.

My girlfriend handles the matter and places a second bottle and new glasses on the table, and after a further tasting, approval is declared in due time.

I continue drinking the original wine from my glass, even though it actually is too sweet for a dinner wine. "I like it", I say, in support of my girlfriend, who had selected the original wine in eager pride the day before, as well as to strike a blow for civilized hospitality.

The conversation turns to politics, society, and various events in the news. Regardless of the topic, Rüdiger is not at a loss when it comes to having and stating his opinions, as well as clarifying that any others to the contrary are misguided.

Then, just out of curiosity and to confirm whether I have read Frieda clearly so far this evening, I ask her what she thinks about the color of the walls there in the dining room. She glowers piercing into my eyes and tries to continue driving that dagger deeply into my brain… but I don't let it through.

Üorg states what he estimates the length and width of the living room to be, and he says that he finds the proportions to be quite suitable. As the conversation changes, Frieda sits there, angrily loathing me in silence.

I turn to my plate and enjoy my Rouladen and potatoes with the thick brown sauce.

After the main course, my girlfriend and I take turns bringing in the dishes, bringing out the dessert, and talking with the guests.

The son mentions that he has an interest in chess. He describes the various opening moves that are possible (all of them, in fact, in order of imperviousness), as if relishing in the abstractions of the art of war.

Trying to align my interests with those of the other party, I ask him if he knows when the game of chess was invented, expecting to be promptly illuminated as to the subject.

He looks up from his dessert into the air, seems to come up with nothing, and then stares at me. He has been a rather positive, agreeable person up until this point, but he suddenly looks shaky and uncertain, as if he is losing his footing upon his foundation. In his eyes, a defensiveness suddenly grows, which is just as suddenly followed by a look of unmanageable aggression. Then, in the very next fraction of a moment, he looks guilty, as if aware of how he was reacting to me, deeply regretting both this and the fact that he had lost his otherwise tight grip upon his character.

His father informs us that he and Üorg play chess from time to time, and then Üorg, as though in an effort to make up for his moment of collapse into his darker side, says, a bit overly chipper, "Yes, I play about three times a week. I asked my girlfriend to play, but she said that she doesn't like to."

So, the chess engineer has a girlfriend. I wonder to myself how their romance could possibly be. I imagine them in a moment of intimacy, with the door closed, making love, with the girl's voice starting with a quiet little "Oh" of surprise, followed by another little "Oh", slightly louder and higher than the first, pursued by another expectant "Oh", and then... nothing.

'Stalemate', I think. 'In three moves'.

The dessert is finished and the guests seem contented to be adding to the cloud of smoke that they have been collectively producing in our home for the past hour or so.

There is a comfortableness in such moments, after dining with the locals, that stands in stark contrast to practically all other forms of their company. Perhaps that other part of them is subdued by nicotine, like Dracula is by sunlight.

The coffee cups are emptied, the ashtrays are filled to overflowing, and Rüdiger, Freida and... their son maneuver to the entrance hall. Handshakes are distributed all around (well, nearly all around. Frieda makes sure that she is conveniently just out of reach as our turn comes) and our guests make their exit. Standing outside the door, Rüdiger turns to us and says, "We have to do this again sometime."

Upon hearing this, I have a surging impulse to immediately slam the door and bolt the latch, but I resist it.

As the Schmalztupfs finally leave, I remember that much of what I have to do in Germany can be handled electronically and over the Internet, and I am, for the first time this evening, truly happy.

At the Supermarket

The supermarkets in Germany are an oasis in an otherwise crumbling era; they are a reminder that, as our society collapses internationally into its next dark age, the German supermarkets will be the last to go. They will remain heroically and steadfastly (if not merely out of uninspired habit) as the last bastions of good taste and civilized daily living – as if, thousands of years from now, six-fingered space-creatures with mysteriously shining foreheads and enlarged finger joints will dig up an ancient, naturally-preserved loaf of bread from the bakery department of a site where a German supermarket had stood hundreds of years before their time and, recognizing the high qualities of the glorious loaf, place a hologram of it in one of their hovering museums. Surrounded by a laser-protected display case, the loaf – with its crispy crust, its tender inner heart, and just the right flavors of salt and yeast – shall result in the future space creatures holding our epoch in a far higher esteem than these times actually come even close to deserving. After all (the futuristic space creatures might think), how bad could a group of people be who produced bread that is as deeply satisfying and wholesome as this? (I imagine that whatever amount of bread was sold in the 1930s in Germany was, ironically, also of high quality).

Eager for my latest adventure at the local supermarket a few towns outside of Rucklingsdorf one Saturday, I turn my car into the next lane of the parking lot, and while casually looking for an available space, I suddenly come face to face with that regular component of a German "Einkaufstag" – the multi-jointed row of shopping wagons protruding, in a swaying line, out from their covered hut, as if forming a drunken, prehistoric snake, daring all who pass, taunting the would-be shoppers with the snake's thriving body, and biting fang-like scratches into the cars that creep daringly by.

There are other supermarkets in other countries, also inhabited by humans, where such shopping-cart snakes simply do not exist. It is somehow in the power of human beings elsewhere to manage and afford to send a worker out who distributes the carts so that they fit into the various storage huts, without these wiry behemoths impeding the progress of shoppers (and, thereby, the flow of the national economy) as they do.

After all, a tremendous amount of effort and planning goes into creating a supermarket, all to attract customers via the shovels full of money that is spent on advertising. Finally, from all the people who throw away the shopping leaflets that they receive in their mail, a select few have actually decided to come to this particular supermarket in this particular town and spend their money, in order to help their overworked and under-attended family members to have nourishment enough to survive for yet another weak – and the German supermarket manager, as if in one of his misfired efforts at "out-of-the-box" thinking, decides:

"I know what I'll do! I'll use the shopping carts to create physical barriers between the customers and the entrance doors, so that the shoppers will not only have trouble driving through the parking lot, but will have the added challenge of completing a sort of obstacle course in actually maneuvering around the carts once the shoppers leave their cars and attempt the circuit on foot. That way, the customers will *earn* the right to shop in my glorious supermarket. Otherwise, any random person might come in, and they might not have the skills to appreciate the wonderful qualities of the goods that I am selling."

This follows upon Friedrich Nietzsche's concept that "only the strong survive". Particularly in a country that is centered so steadfastly upon the production, purchase and flaunting of expensive automobiles, if a person does not possess the driving skills to navigate around protruding metal gratings that sway in the breeze, then they certainly do not deserve to receive food and drink in order to survive.

Why, it's a question of evolution and an increase in the quality of the species. If it were not for these shopping wagon snakes in the parking lots, the quality of the German race would begin to plummet at a record pace. We should all be grateful that these supermarket managers do not send workers out to break up these monstrous wagon-chains, for the German children would then, through lack of challenge in their environment, grow to be weak-minded and of a lazy character, and never be able to become the German engineers who supply our world with all kinds of twitching machines and lethal sports cars.

In fact, without the added challenged that these lengthy barricades of shopping carts present to the average German citizen in day-to-day life, the future generations of the

German people might not have the inner strength and the harsh, jagged gusto that is needed to differentiate at will between the German grammatical articles of "die, der, das, den", etc., and Germany would become a society where the people either babble gutturally and incoherently to each other without the use of organized grammar, or they would all be forced against their will to start speaking a simpler and more pleasant language (I believe Esperanto is still available, at a good discount).

In spite of the challenges placed upon me by my environment on this particular Saturday, I make it into the supermarket once again, feeling the due sense of honor at this accomplishment against all odds. As if by a wagging finger and a scowling face, however, I am soon taught by German society to not sit too soon on my past accomplishments in the parking lot; in order to ensure that I keep my alertness razor sharp, the manager of the supermarket has been so considerate as to place a standing metal sign reading "We Care About You"(in English, naturally) directly in the entranceway.

There is, of course, a knot of customers consisting of people trying to enter the store, others trying to exit the store with their purchased goods, still others trying to return shopping carts near the entrance, as well as the drivers who are trying to tenderly but defiantly park in the close-up spaces into which this knot of hungry and wayward humanity is pouring. It must have taken several meetings and numerous attempts of the supermarket leadership to have finally identified precisely that location at the entrance where this loving expression of forward thinking and human consideration would block so many customers all at the same time.

It's a compliment to the German people that they handle such congestions of movement without any interpersonal conflicts or apparent inner stress. None of them ever seem to have a problem with such a hindrance; they seem to quietly accept its presence merely as another necessary burden of modern life (although it is absolutely *not* necessary), and might even be satisfied about the international and progressive characteristic that their local supermarket shows in placing this particular sign in this particular place.

On the other hand, this also appears to be yet another example of the "Führerprinzip" in action: if the person a step above on the hierarchy does something, it must be blindly obeyed without it being questioned or countered. That's something that makes me worry here any time I see it put into practice, or rather "activated".

The knot of customers is bumbling spasmodically along, but it's working out, in its own dysfunctional, third-world-country kind of way. It takes extra effort, though. Germany is no place to relax and simply go about your day. Thank you, German supermarket managers, for ensuring that I stay on my toes and do not let myself go. In what condition would I be without you?

Since the sign is in English (as part of that ever-present effort by the German business world to seem international and not at all stiffly limited by their own Germanic tendencies), I also wonder how many people in this small farm town (most of whom have never travelled past the neighboring farm town, which is exactly like it) even understand what is stated on the sign. The concept of advertising is that it just grabs your attention without your thinking about it, as subconsciously as possible. The moment that accessing the Internet with your portable phone in order to translate an advertising slogan is required, the very purpose of a sign is no more.

A piece of Stonehenge could just as well have been imported from England and placed there to block the flow of movement: it would have been equally ineffective and international, causing about as much unnecessary chaos, but with at least a bit of rural charm.

Upon entering one of the higher-end German supermarkets, there is instantly the sensation of abundance and quality. Here, anything that a person with middle-class taste desires (in other words, selective but not too refined) is available, and there are enough brands of each item to cause a Soviet-block resident from the 1980's to stand before the shelves with glazed eyes, immobilized from his inability to decide from amongst the various options for his purchase of stuffed olives.

Along with choosing from among the various tubs of flavored, spreadable fat and the multitude of sliced animals that are available, as always, I am interested in buying a bottle of red wine on this particular Saturday. As if they have studied my own personal habits and tastes through countless market research, there is a small selection of wines from Southern Europe in a display right by the entrance. There might as well have been a sign saying "Stuff to make you feel more fancy than you actually are in reality"; this selection works its magic upon me, as always, so I select a bottle of wine and go on my way, satisfied that I have one less item to search for on my list and that I am therefore one step ahead in my life.

Then, after moving along past an item called "Sülze", wondering what exactly it might consist of and why anybody would find the consumption of the product to be an addition to their lives in any way, I happen to come across the actual wine section.

Now, I'm a person who is not unfamiliar to living in a foreign country, learning a foreign language and adapting to other ways of thinking. Within this wide range of possible variations of how things can be done by other people all over the world, though, a certain degree of practicality and logic is expected. For there to be two completely different sections in different parts of the store where the same product is displayed is simply not rational.

I know, I know… a very stiff German with rimless eyeglasses, no facial expression and absolutely no modulation in his voice might answer, "But the first section is for fine specialties, and this section is just for wine." I understand that, but according to that same principle of (dis)organization, there should also be wine displayed by the fruit section, since wine comes from fruit, after all. Likewise, in a Germanically organized supermarket, there should also be wine sold next to the orange juice, since they are both beverages which result from a certain pressing procedure. Moreover, why is there not also wine sold by the laundry detergent (in other words, in the "pourable liquids" section)?

For a society that prides itself upon being hyper-organized, this tendency, which is common in nearly every supermarket throughout Germany, is an example of over-categorization getting in the very way of organization itself. It is stunningly inefficient in its efficiency, since a person has to look at various sections at different places in the store in order to make a single purchase, sometimes returning again to the previous place to return a prematurely selected item. Why not just hide the wine that I want under a sofa cushion like an Easter egg?

This dysfunctional thinking that results in hyper-attention to putting everything in its proper place leads me to imagine someone with a compulsive disorder who is counting all the tiles in the flooring and then, when one is missing, has a nervous breakdown.

In other words, for a society in which "There must be order *(Ordnung muss sein)*" so that the people can feel a sense of security and peace, this failed attempt at creating order (and, instead, actually creating chaos by doing so) is a sign of a people's need for something that they are not capable of providing themselves.

The Germans desperately need order, but they place one product in three or more different places in their supermarkets, because they are not able to decipher the one single place where it would be most suitable. What happens when this mental approach is applied to politics, schooling, or something really important (like the sequential presentation of desperate performers on "Germany's Next Top Superstar")? When the German mind cannot create order, the result is "Deutsche Wahnsinn" (German insanity), and the people start to get stiff, tight, and accusatory. Look at this organization of products in a German supermarket, and you will have a piercing insight into the very dark depths of the German psyche!

Braving this realization, and since the people in the supermarket apparently still feel enough sense of order to go quietly about their shopping without escalating to a crazed state, I continue on, past the little section of Italian goods, which include some frozen pizzas and, stunningly, yet another assortment of wines (I know, the "Italian Stuff" section... I get it, I get it...), along the display of oriental items (they always have their own place, segregated from everything else that is German and belongs freely), the "Gifts for Someone You Would be Warm With if You Were That Sort of Person" section, and then I brace myself for the endless voyage from one end of the frozen pizzas cooler to the other (yes, that's right... a second section for pizza. I took notice of that).

As I turn the corner, I see that there is currently only a single cashier open, with a long line before it. I go and take my place at the end, and after a while, there is some movement evident at the cash register in the next lane.

Oh my god! A second cashier is about to be opened, and a time will very soon appear in which this single line will have cause to split into two, with some of us remaining on the mother line (like on the Titanic), and others from amongst us deciding to break free and take our chances with our uncertain final placement on line at the new cashier.

There is a palpable sense of intensity in such moments. Body posture stiffens a bit, and in some cases, hips leave their temporary, diagonal position of disinterested and unwanted leisure and enter their horizontal position in preparation for conflict and war. For those pioneers who are in the throes of deciding whether to take the risk and break away or to stay in the comfort of the safe and familiar, this shifting of weight is the sign of who among the group shall, in a matter of minutes, become one's challengers.

There are laws, and then there are just the ways people do things in a certain region of the world without having to be forced to do so. In such a situation, when a new cashier is being opened in a German supermarket, what *could* happen is this: everyone could simply agree implicitly with one another that whoever is first in the original line has first choice, and when that person chooses to remain where he is, each of the next individuals, in sequence, then decides (with no pressure from anyone else) to go or stay. There are some civilized shoppers in Germany who function according to this principle, and I, as a member of society and a contributor in my own small way to the course of human history, am ever grateful for their good taste.

Amongst them, however, there is so painfully often at least one "jumper", the guy with a bag of bland white bread, a can of tuna and a bag of imitation gummy bears (the cheap knock-off kind) clutched precariously in his fingers, who INSTANTLY surges like a raging tide alongside of any other individual ahead of him who has clearly stepped out of the flotilla of the original line to enter the stream of the new one. It is a matter of life and death. Thankfully in such moments, the Schützenheims (the German shooting clubs) have to lock up their guns after use, so this conflict of changing lines at the supermarket is an event that is essentially sure to be free of any tragic outcome worthy of graphic news coverage. However, it is a reminder that not all of us have decided to sign the social contract and to keep the well-being of the group in mind at all times.

After waiting a beat in time for my predecessors in the first line to make clear their intentions (not without a certain sense of fraternal love for them in this instant, in which we all had to face a mutual decision and decided to work together instead of against each other), I step casually out of the row and head leisurely to the next one. Suddenly, like a dark cloud the size of Russia shuttling from one corner of a sunny sky to the next and casting a pall across the heavens, a giant "jumper" appears from behind and to the side of me. From his thick, amorphous form and his choice of groceries, it seems as if this might be the most physical exertion that he has made all week. There is no bodily contact made, so officially, he has enough space to pass by, as long as he runs at a desperately rapid pace and prevents anyone before him from occupying the space if they choose to do so.

He could have chosen peace, like the rest of us upstanding members of society, but no – he has chosen combat, he has chosen war, he has chosen unregulated capitalism. He has destroyed the covenant upon which our civilization is based, he has drawn a decisive and unmistakable line in the sand, and has stated "I don't care who amongst you has family members at home who are ill, elderly, or decrepit, or whose children with you in line are doing everything they can to hold it until they get home. 'Tis I or thou, you are either with me or against me. If you are so weak as to not make the effort like I have, then you deserve to remain left behind, whilest I reap the sweet profits of my entrepreneurial energy. Hear ye, hear ye, I shall thrive!"

And then, there we are: two guys standing on line in a supermarket, next to each other. His hips start to leave the horizontal plane and slant in lumbering boredom as he waits for the people ahead of us (who meanwhile have entered the line from the other aisle) to be served. There we are, two warriors (or one wayward warrior and a Saturday shopper) at a distance from each other that would normally be dangerous and uncomfortable among adversaries, but which now matches the distance of our groceries on the conveyor belt as they move along. After an awkward pause and a tense silence, he quickly reaches for the little dividing bar and, after some nervous fumbling, places it clumsily between out items.

Then, I speak.

Nobody ever speaks in such situations at German supermarkets, and this is one of my small contributions to human history.

"Thirty seconds", I say to him, calmly and rationally. "You have saved about thirty seconds in your life by rushing up here the way you did."

He pretends to be invisible. I assure him that he is not by adding, "and now you have to stand there anyway."

That is all; it is said with quiet steadiness, and there is no aggression... but he knows. And a place a few steps behind us in line suddenly would have been a lot more comfortable for him than his spot atop the mountain, where the wind blows the coldest.

While waiting, I pass the time by looking around. Most of the other shoppers use shopping carts, but there are a couple of them who had decided to walk past all of the rows of carts as they entered the store and now stand cradling their goods in their hands precariously like a baby that they are in danger of dropping.

This always amazes me: people know that they are going shopping, and in the process of doing so, they know that they are going to collect a series of items and will inherently have to carry them. It's one thing to see a college kid do it while he's getting a couple of beers and a bag of chips; he's learning (after all, that's why he's in college). Why, it's even comical. Once a shopper has lived past the age of 30 or so, though, he has most likely purchased nutrition for himself before and is familiar with the process, and in spite of his years of experience in this regard, he still ends up standing there juggling his cold container of Haagen Daas and his fragile bag of nuts.

In the other line, a man is placing his items from his full shopping cart onto the conveyor belt. Right after he starts, the old woman who is next in line starts to approach the end of the conveyor belt with a presence that would make a policeman suspicious if he were to see it on a city street at night: she looks alert while making the effort to avoid any eye contact, and then she starts to move cautiously forwards, as if driven against her will by an urge that is greater than anything that schooling and religion might have tried to instill within her. She then starts putting her hand into her little basket, pulling out her products and putting them on the conveyor belt with surprising agility.

Meanwhile, the man in front of her is far from finished emptying his cart; he has many more items to go, but as the conveyor belt is moving, the old lady's things start to chase his, thereby filling the spot that he would have needed in order to put the rest of his items in place. There is an awkward moment when the old lady hesitates, apparently hoping that the obvious will not in fact come to pass, and when it does – when it becomes clear that she has unequivocally encroached upon the conveyor belt space of the man in front of her – the rapid ritual of recompense and shame begins in her moving her items back on the conveyor belt, one by one – starting with the items in the front line and jumping over the other ones into the space that become free at the end of the line as the conveyor belt moves on.

It is like a reverse game of remorseful chess, in which the only goal is to make one's pieces run away from contact with those of the other party.

Like in most competitions between man and machine, the old lady is not spry enough to free sufficient space for the new items of the man in front of her in this way – perhaps it is a question of age; perhaps in her younger years, she possessed the agility to perform this peculiar supermarket chess game and, if not to win, then at least to hold her own against the competition.

If so, those days are now past her, and she apparently no longer sees any option but to use her bare forearm and shove all of her items backwards on the conveyor belt (though only doing so to the minimum extent that she seems to think necessary to rectify the calamity that has, to her surprise, been unleashed). Her little shampoo bottle gets knocked and starts to topple off from the conveyor belt, and she is forced to make a very graceless and desperate move in order to save it from its plummet. This is the situation she has created for herself: she is deep into it now, and there is no turning back.

In the end, the man in front manages to empty his goods onto the conveyor belt (thanks, largely, to his piling his goods on top of one another like building blocks and squeezing his produce into the area that the old lady behind him has deemed to make free for him from the space that she has seized).

It is because of this event happening to me a few times and my noticing the cultural pattern that I began early on to enter supermarket lines with my body first, trailing my shopping cart close behind me on line and using it as a moveable barricade between me and whoever was next in line behind me.

Normally, the presence of the cart between us is sufficient to prevent the psychopathology from being set loose in the first place; often, there is a look of tension in the eyes of the next person behind me, who moves, ever so perceptibly and as if by habit, to place their items on the conveyor belt before I have finished laying all of mine down; then, they suddenly realize that my cart is protruding past the end of the line and keeping them at a palpable distance of a good meter from where they want to be.

I even find it necessary (and advisable) to do this when I am the first in a new line and the entire conveyor belt is open ahead of me like an endless black highway, with the big metal cage of my shopping cart serving the purpose that should be served through the self-control, consideration and patience of the next person in line.

But then again, this is Germany. It's like the BMW drivers on the highway; wherever they are on the road, they evidently imagine, "Yes, the place where I am is good, but if I could only get to that one next space a few centimeters ahead of me sooner, then this urge in me would be satisfied and the wolfman within me would be quieted until… OK, got it, and now the NEXT space, and the NEXT, and if only… grrOWLLLL".

The entire time this event is taking place on this particular Saturday in this particular German supermarket outside of Rucklingsdorf, the old lady and the man in front of him do not make any eye contact, recognize the existence of each other or enact any amount of human interchange whatsoever, in spite of the fact that they have been performing this Freudian ballet together in front of the entire supermarket clientele, who have nothing better to do but to silently observe it.

There is movement ahead of me. This is it – I'm up. The "jumper" who ran in front of me is finishing his purchase and, likewise, avoids eye contact with me as he leaves (there's a lot of effort spent in Germany on the purposeful avoiding of eye contact. The amount of energy expended in this way is so great that, if invested productively otherwise, there would be a marked increase in the German gross domestic product).

As my turn comes, the cashier presents me with a greeting which shows that she is trying to sound heartfelt, but after so many times she just can't any more.

It reminds me of prostitutes that I have seen in the windows of Amsterdam, who had a look that expressed both a boisterous "Glad to see YOU, big fella!" as well as a simultaneous, exhausted and world-weary "Please watch your step as you enter the ride, sir".

Looking at the cashier, I am filled with tremendous empathy for her. She is not spending her time at the moment painting pictures of French landscapes, and I doubt that she is composing a final stanza to her latest poem while the machinery goes "Beep. Beep beep... Beep" below her.

As always, I then wonder how often she regrets not having made more effort in her school years.

This thought is followed by my wondering how many people throughout Germany, all over Europe, as well as in China and Uzbekistan and Ecuador, also sit at such cash registers and have to offer the same kind of greeting to custom after customer, with the fear that if it doesn't seem welcoming enough, they might get fired.

She tells me my total and there is a pause while we wait for my bank card to be processed in the device. In this moment, I am both grateful for her that she has a chance to be free for a few seconds from the entire economically suppressive web in which she is sitting, while I also feel a sense of operatic tragedy in thinking that, at such moments, she does not have the distraction of the hand movements and the beeping machine and has to just sit there and be fully aware that this is her life: today, tomorrow and the day after that.

I think of Bob Cratchit, the worker who slaved for Scrooge in *"A Christmas Carol"*, and then of computer programmers and other workers who labor away in isolation for hours at a time.

Then my thoughts shift and I think of the German expressionist painters, who vomited color and feeling from inside like nobody else could, I think of Goethe and the sufferings of his young Werther, of the German economic miracle of the 1950's, and I think, "Is this what it has come to, after all?"

I hear the cashier say "Kassenbon?", I say yes, and the receipt is ripped out and handed to me. Then, she looks at me and says goodbye – we make eye contact, hold it, and exchange a cordial smile. And then I think, "Ah, after every 45 seconds or so, she has a warm, human exchange with one person after another. During hundreds of moments each day, she breaks that barrier in the world between strangers and herself, that barrier which exists between so many of the customers on her line at the supermarket. That's not so bad for her, after all. At least, it's something."

Yes, I realize of course that maybe she is required to do this in order to keep her job and that she might hate these countless moments more than every other part of her day.

It *is* a distinctly non-German thing to do, holding eye contact with a stranger. Still, she makes a human connection, even if it *is* against her will – and that is more than can be said for many people in little towns like Rucklingsdorf.

These are very emotionally conflicting moments for me at the supermarket cashiers', in any supermarket. The joy, the sorrow, the regrets, the yearning for them to join together in union and break their chains and shout "Now we are free! Release the champagne!", and the tragic awareness that there will be no such revolution, and that the rich guys at the top are just turning the screws tighter and more efficiently day by day.

I leave her there where she was sitting (again, the image of the prostitute in Amsterdam comes to mind) and move to the shelf by the window when I take a few minutes to put my groceries in bags. I am always, without exception, the only one to do so. Nobody in Germany seems to have discovered the convenience of bagged groceries. I have never once in all my years here seen it done by anyone else. I want to spread the word to them, like a preacher in an old-time medicine show, and convince them of the benefits of this way of functioning. Then, I remember, I am far away in a world where they have done things differently for centuries, and that such habits do not break easily, if ever.

I go back out into the parking lot. It has started to rain. I pass German after German hunched at the back side of their cars, putting one item after the other strategically in its place in the car trunks (they apparently have their system), all the while with their practical haircuts getting wetter and wetter in the cold, dark rain. They are all wearing thin shirts, with no jackets and no umbrellas (Germans don't wear jackets until the dead of winter, when they all mutually consider that it is no longer a sign of weakness to give in, and they don't grant themselves the luxury of umbrellas – they just suffer and bear it. After all, why get a good umbrella wet when it's not absolutely necessary?).

I see that look of bitterness on their faces, and wonder why they do not learn and change. Surely enough of them in this village have seen me using grocery bags to the point that they could chat about it over coffee and cake with their family members and the members of their various organizations and associations, with the word spreading like gossip through the grapevine, and little by little, there could be progress.

But no – there is Germany, and the people stand alone by their exhaust pipes in the cold rain and put their items from the wagon into the car, from the wagon into the car, like robots.

Do these robots ever rust in the rain?

Even when there is a married couple enacting this ritual, there is no conversation, no laughter, no joy shared between them.

I get in my car filled with high-quality groceries, turn on the Frank Sinatra CD, sing along about love-gone-by, think about the tragic cashier, the anarchistic "jumper", the rainy-day robots, and I roll on into another rosy German sunset.

The Coffee Klatch

Elke is just putting the good cups down to finish her table setting. She is expecting her cousin Clothilde at 3:00 this afternoon for coffee and cake (every Thursday, coffee and cake with Clothilde at 3:00).

This afternoon, though, Elke is feeling a little differently than she normally does as the event approaches. Her cousin asked if she could invite another woman to the coffee klatch, someone who had just moved into the neighborhood and with whom Clothilde had developed an acquaintance through their time in the local Music Appreciation Association – which, for all intents and purposes, was really just another coffee klatch, with the exception that they put on a CD and let it play once through until it runs out in the background while they chat; moreover, they have a secretary, who always starts the event by a reading of the minutes from the previous meeting (which usually consists of a recitation of the name and the year of publication of the CD they had played in the background during their previous meeting), so there is more of an air of formality about it.

Actually, the new girl (Sabine, who is in her thirties) moved into the town of Rucklingsdorf over a year-and-a-half ago, and she spent a majority of this time trying to attach herself to the community through one club and association after another, but she always sensed that, after the meeting was over, she would not be hearing from the other members until the next meeting, and that there was really no sense of progress on a personal level.

That was how it went until she began to participate as an "Associate Member" of the Rucklingsdorf Music Appreciation Association. Official Members have to pay an annual fee of 50 euros (in order to cover the cost of acquiring a few new CD's once in a while, beyond the ones that the respective host just brings down from her own shelf upstairs, as well as to more generally have a reason to draw a distinction between Official Members and those who are just Associates), and the other Official Members don't think it is quite right that Sabina should have to pay the fee, for a while anyway, since the others have decided that she is still new in town and must have other expenses to cover, from her move and all (again, from over a year-and-a-half ago). The time might come, perhaps, when Sabina will be paying her fee and will become an Official Member, but that time has not been assessed to have arrived just yet.

Even though Sabine is still just an Associate Member, Elke's cousin Clothilde started taking a fancy to her little by little. 'That's the way Clothilde is', Elke thinks to herself with a little sigh, as she repositions the little dessert plates in their places, twisting them slightly (even though they are circular in form, so it doesn't really make any difference).

Clothilde is one of those Germans who seem to have stepped out of a Grimm Brothers fairy tale. She is heavy set, and she lives in one of the low grass huts (officially, the "Reetdachhäuser", so they actually have roofs made of reeds) that are to be found in the village.

She also wears a kind of clothing that is more of a felt wrapping, sometimes with an extended collar that looks like it might grow into a hood in certain weather conditions (if a few secret words are pronounced over it), giving her the look of a monk or a goodly witch. She orders the clothes from a catalogue that is targeted to those who have a penchant for a particularly tactile wardrobe, flowing garments, warm earth tones, charms, and various knick-knacks that often have a somewhat medieval characteristic to them.

And Clothilde *is* goodly, nobody has any doubt about that. Those close to her often call her "Clotschen", which is the diminutive form of the first part of her name (in English, it would be something like "the little clot"). This is what her mother used to call her when Clothilde was a child. Once in a while, upon hearing this, some playmate or other would sometimes call her "Klößchen", which is German for dumpling. Some of the locals who speak a form of language that is vaguely between high German and a primitive dialect still today pronounce her name a bit similarly to this teasing word from her childhood (intentionally or otherwise, or perhaps something in between), so at one point she just decided to accept it as part of fate and began to respond when people called her "Klößchen".

When she was a young woman, she started to develop a penchant for all things new-age, and after she had been married for a while, she had her husband Detlef put up a sign in front of their reed house declaring to the population that she provided "Wellness and Spiritual Healing" services (actually, he spelled it "Welness" by mistake, with one "l" missing, but most people didn't know the difference, and the majority of those who did just attributed it to Klößchen "creativeness". And of course, some just didn't care).

Over the years, there came to be a few competitors in the neighborhood offering similar services (or at least having a sign out front stating that they do), as a result of which Clothilde ended up adding a little colorful swirl, a kind of sparkling, effervescent spiral, around the partial word "Welness", so as to make herself stand out and to show that, whatever any of the others might claim to be doing, she was the real thing in this village, and everybody should make no mistake about knowing it.

Her interest in the new girl in town, Sabina, is based upon Sabina's condition as the outsider, and Clothilde finds this characteristic of great interest – "enchanting" is the word that she uses in order to describe her new acquaintance to others.

Now, that doesn't mean that the new girl has her path cleared for her entirely. After all, Clothilde is German, in spite of how she might otherwise carry on… uh, that is… how she might otherwise be. There is an undefined quantity of hours that Sabina has to perform in her chosen Verein before she is ever (if at all) to be considered entitled to cross that iron threshold between "them" and "us", "in" or "out", and she is just barely on the cusp of having fulfilled that requirement.

There is a primitive tribe living on an island off the coast of the civilized world somewhere, and they have been cut off from society for so many centuries that they don't wear clothing in the modern sense, their language is intelligible to no one outside of their clan, they still paint their faces in different colors and designs and they have no contact with anyone beyond the limits of their isolated world. A few times, strangers have tried to intrude upon the tiny island and interchange with the local inhabitants – and it did *not* go well (at least, that is what is surmised from the remnants of shredded button-down cotton shirts that have floated up to the mainland over time).

In many ways, Rucklingsdorf is very similar to that tiny island nation. And here is Sabina, a German from a different state, trying to break the seal upon their tribal world. The fact that she is from the same country is not sufficient – for the locals, there are still more things that are different and unknown than there are certainties and similarities, and so they consider her to be a dangerous mystery.

Clothilde has an attraction for dangerous mysteries, in her own hazy sort of way, so after a year-and-a-half and well over seventy hours spent in the Rucklingsdorf Music Appreciation Association, she took it upon herself to ask her cousin Elke if perhaps it wouldn't be nice to invite that "charming" woman from the association to have coffee with them one of these afternoons.

Elke suddenly stiffened in place a little more than usual as the suggestion was presented, and, knowing her cousin's ability to wear a person down by kindness (and who knows what kind of other powers that she might actually possess), she begrudgingly agreed. After all, the vague criteria of about 70-or-more-hours in an association had been nearly met, and the intruder was being vouched for, as required. Elke wouldn't have invited her, but there was really no way around it now.

The bell rings, making Elke twitch a little, and as her visitors are welcomed in (or, rather, as Clothilde is welcomed in and her guest Sabrina is pulled along in the current), the three of them stand for a little while in the living room, not far from the entrance door they had just come in through, and exchange a few basic words of greeting, drowning themselves in polite formalities while avoiding any personal commitment.

"So", Elke says to Sabina, "You've started at the Music Appreciation group", as if asking for verification, just in case.

"Actually, I've been going for over a year now", Sabina says, with a big smile and a pleasing tone, subconsciously aware of her having to be more obsequious than usual in this, her entrance onto the next level.

"Well, then, you're no stranger to a nice slice of cake and a good cup of coffee", Elke says, giving in and being sociable while stating absolutely nothing of any meaning at all.

"Yes", Clothilde says placidly, "we've been known to conjure up something pleasing now and again."

"Well, let's all have a seat, then", Elke says, as if mistaking this for one of the association meetings.

Along with the spotless china with the tasteful but simple blue design along the edges, there is one small cake, just enough for the three of them, with each of the guests being able to take a peace home with them, like a kind of parting gift. There is also a plate of cookies of diverse kinds (from the discount supermarket, but the ones with the regal imprints of horses and crowns on them, so that they are suitable as guest cookies). There is coffee cream, a full pot of strong coffee (with another ready in the kitchen as backup), a bowl of freshly prepared whipped cream (Elke had showed herself to be quite a force in the applying of the whisk to the cream earlier in the day) and, of course, the little porcelain jar newly filled with sugar.

The ample spread for the coffee klatch is in stark contrast to the snack of one dry, pointy, rectangular piece of Knäckebrot (basically, "crunch bread") and a thin slice of slightly smelly cheese that Elke had allowed herself about halfway between breakfast and the arrival of her visitors. The Knäckebrot is similar to what in other countries would be a cracker, but it is more abrasive and dense, as though pressed compactly between two fists of steel until every remnant of moisture and lightness of being has been strangled out of it... and then it is sometimes sprinkled with a few seeds before it is thrown into the oven, just in case. It can be quite delicious, actually, but you have to be ready for it. It has a tendency to resemble the last ration left from the otherwise empty shelves of an underground bunker.

All formalities having been handled, the "Quatschen" (chatting) begins. It is superficial without exception, in terms of thought as well as feeling, with the topic jumping from one second to the next, and no one single idea being retained or developed to any sense of maturity, usually with one sentence being interrupted to interject another, which is of no greater value than the first.

"So", Elke begins, since she is the host and, besides that, the type that always begins these things. "How are things going with the Music Appreciation group?"

"Just fine", chirps Clothilde. "Oh, Elke, this cake is fabulous! Are those almonds?"

"Yes, I got them yesterday when I went to Frevelskirchen. I had to mail a letter. Did you see that the Jansens have a new car in their driveway?

"Yes", her cousin says in turn. "That's their son. He's visiting from school for a few weeks."

"Beautiful drapes", erupts the new one, Sabina.

"Why, thank you", Elke responds (well placed, Sabina. One small step ahead). "I got those right after I came out of the hospital."

"Elke had to go to the hospital for a few days last year because of a skin irritation. It got pretty severe."

"Yes, I couldn't stop scratching. I was scratching for weeks!", and they all laugh, regardless of the absence of any humor. When the laughter starts to simmer down, Elke flicks her chin over her cup, in the direction of the window, and says, "Look how well the forsythia is growing this year."

"In a little while, it's going to take over that side of the house", Clothilde says, with a sense of ominous warning as she sips her coffee.

"How long is he here from school?"

"Who?", her cousin asks.

"The Jansen boy."

And for this, Sabina has invested over a year-and-a-half of her free time and waited for someone to vouch for her.

Thank God the coffee in Germany is so good. Otherwise, I just don't know.

That's how the conversation goes, anyway, until the quatchers come across the main reason for the encounter: hashing over rumors – rumors about anyone and everyone who does not happen to be present at that particular time (which might, in fact, be a reason why so many German women appear at so many coffee klatches: the tradition might be carried on as an act of self-defense).

"Oh!," Elka introduces, as if just happening to accidentally remember something, and as though she had not looked forward to this coffee klatch for the past five days since the event supposedly happened just to talk with her cousin about it, "did you hear that Lars Jansen might have – how shall I say it?", Elke looks up into the air above her for the sake of a dramatic pause, tapping the pads of her bony fingertips together with a devious, wry smile on her face, "dipped his hands a little too deeply into the cookie jar at the office?"

"Do you mean that secretary?!", Clotschen gasps, leaning forward, with a smile on her face, clearly hoping that it *is* about that secretary.

"NO!", Elke blurts, as if taken aback by the suggestion and not wanting to destroy, rather only to play with the mouse a little bit, "I said his *hands!*"

"Oh", her cousin says as she sits back, looking at the floor, clearly disappointed.

"What did he do?", the new girl, Sabina, asks her host.

"Well", Elke resumes, after sizing Sabina up for a brief moment and deciding that she herself is glad to be telling her rumor to any interested audience one way or another, even if it *is* to someone who has merely almost met the requirement of the 70-or-more hours of Verein activity and been vouched for, and nothing else. "Do you know Wenke Sorenson?"

"Sure", says Clothilde, countering Sabina's blank look. "Her husband works at the truck rental shop with Lars Jansen. No!," Clothilde shouts, as if it has just dawned on her. "Do you mean…?"

Elke is already nodding her head up and down slowly in affirmation.

"That's right", she says, as if she has just won a contest of some kind, except that the trophy is all dripping with evil, "Wenke Sorenson told Katrin Altnagel that her husband told her that there were one hundred and seventy two euros missing from the cash register on Friday, and that was when Lars Jansen was on shift to close up for the night."

"Did the husband see him do it?", Sabina says, enjoying being welcomed into the workings of the inner circle of the town like this, although making the beginner's mistake of ladening the conversation down with something as burdensome as evidence.

Elke shakes her head, more at Sabina's naiveté than at the fact that there were no witnesses.

"No", Elke says shortly, "but Katrin Altnagel said that right after Wenke's husband had counted the money, he closed up the shop, and Katrin said he told Wenke about it right away when he got home… and Lars *did* order the steak platter on Monday night at the Fundraiser dinner at the Golden Mule, didn't he?", allowing insinuation to fill in the holes where a verifiable argument would have otherwise been.

The obvious possibility that Wenke's husband might have just miscounted the money without recounting it seems to conveniently elude everyone, from the husband all along the chain of gossip to Klößchen and her new acquaintance Sabina.

"Do you really think he took the money?", her cousin asks, a bit sadly for Lars' sake.

"Well, Wenke Sorenson seems to think that her husband thinks so."

That's it, then. No matter what really might have happened, the reputation of Lars Jansen is now tarnished, and for good. The chain of gossip is too long for anyone really to follow, and so the judgment has simply been decreed.

Luckily for him, there is gossip and rumor like this about basically everybody in the neighborhood, so they are all essentially even in the end.

There are even a few rumors floating around the village about Elke, and she is planning to try to send her cousin out to a few targeted coffee klatches around the neighborhood to find out exactly what the details are supposed to be.

And, of course, there are more than a few rumors floating around about "Klößchen", what with her "mood crystals" and her "ways", but nobody places any importance upon what they hear about her. The opinions about "Klößchen" had been made up a long time ago.

In Rucklingsdorf, rumor-churning and gossiping are not seen as an immoral way to handle other people's reputations and to devalue one's own use of time; it is instead the art that these people wield: Mozart had the piano, Napoleon had his soldiers and terrain, and the Rucklingsdorfers have… well, each other, and there are no other puppets that are more pliable and that serve more efficiently for their given purpose.

Though by no means alone in the vocation, Elke is particularly fond of manipulating rumors – hearing them, passing them along on their way, altering them to her taste and convenience, whatever her schedule in the week and the willingness or gullibility of her listener at any given moment makes room for.

Elke is in her thirties, only a little older than Sabina, but she could easily be mistaken for anywhere up towards the region of sixty, depending upon the lighting. She has already started to wear her hair in that style that is distinctively German, which women who support or defend it describe as "practical" (not graceful, beautiful, endearing – but practical, like a marriage of convenience: "It's not exactly a happy marriage, but it's a practical marriage").

She is also particularly tall and rail thin, as if she has not discovered that the Turkish immigrants in Germany have long ago imported with them that marvel of their cuisine: the Döner – pita bread overflowing with spit-roasted meat, various sauces, and a little touch of heaven (among the grease and fat, of course). Elke sticks to her Knäckebrot, where she feels safe.

The interest in the "news" about Lars Jansen fades somewhat (since the women at the table have basically gotten about all they can out of it at this point, before more reconnoitering occurs) and it is filed away for future use.

Sabina presses another morsel of cake free with her little cake fork, while Clothilde pours a little more cream in her coffee, lifting her index finger as she circles the creamer once, twice, and then taps it quickly over the cup, as if performing a magical spell.

Out the window, there is a man walking his dog, and across the street, there is another man who just stops where he is, turns towards the other man and silently follows him with his eyes, staring: a German "Glotzer", a species that is common in this region of the world.

"Look, there's Gerhard", Elke mentions, seeing them. "He's out with his dog again."

"Did you hear that they want to build a street to the highway in Frevelskirchen?", her cousin asks, as if informing her of some heinous act she has read about in the news.

Here was a topic that needed to be addressed. Not in detail, per se, but in the full of its effrontery.

"Can you believe that?", says Elke, "As if we don't have enough people driving through Rucklingsdorf already", she says, and she throws a sharp, silent glance at Sabina over the rim of her coffee cup as she drinks.

"I don't see why they think we need another road in the area", Clothilde says, pouting defensively. "Who knows what sort of traffic that's going to brew up."

Elke puts down her cup with a decisive "clink".

"That's what I told Dagmar Schimmelfuss at the meeting of the Pig Breeder's Association last week", Elke says, "and he agreed." She relays this information with her head raised high, nodding it a little, her eyes closed into rectangular slits and slowly crossing her arms in front of her chest, as though this shared opinion with a local has settled the matter fully in terms all of the finer points of justice. Her cousin nods in agreement, and Sabina, the intruder, just looks from one to the other.

"It's not like it was", Clothilde says, in agreement with her cousin's agreement of her own viewpoint.

"That's right, Clotschen", Elke says, using the diminutive form of her name to show support and endearment.

At this point, the two Rucklingsdorfers are of the opinion that they have explored the matter from every possible angle, and the final judgment is that a connection to the highway is just a silly waste of valuable time and hard earned money, a suggestion made by people who don't know any better, people who don't know as well as they do.

What the two homeowners neglect to take into consideration is the fact that an access to the highway nearby would make their town more desirable as a place to live, which, in turn, would drive up property values. As a result, this single change that would be made for them while they sit passively on their backsides complaining (backsides which, in some cases, are themselves steadily expanding as a result of so many cream toppings in one coffee klatch after the next) – this single change would mean the difference of tens of thousands of euros for each of them in terms of property value – for nothing, and all in the name of progress.

But that word is a foreign word here in Rucklingsdorf, where the local residents stare steadfastly and directly into the center of their plates and do not dare or bother to look over its edge, as the German saying goes. They do not notice anything that goes on beyond it, in complete confidence that their full and unlimited knowledge of everything that is occurring within the limits of the edge of their plate includes all knowledge and information that is of any relevance to anyone with good, common sense.

Sabina wipes her mouth with a napkin and then clears her throat lightly.

"Actually", she says politely, "that road will save me a lot of time driving back and forth on my work days", as if the rationality of this contribution were an addition to this particular dialogue.

Elke looks significantly at her cousin, and Clothilde looks down at the saucer that is beneath her raised cup of coffee. She dabs a chubby finger at a last, remaining crumb in the center and then pokes it into her mouth.

Farewell, dear Sabina. It was a nice year-and-a-half, while it lasted.

Sabina works a few days a week in a doctor's office about 45 minutes away. She has to commute on the country roads, since there is no other option. In the mornings, after she makes sure that her kids are on their way to school, she often gets stuck behind a tractor, moving at what can best be described as a spritely jog, a pace which does not help other people behind them keep up with the demands of modern civilization. The other day, the tractor in front of her was hauling a tall, wooden trailer, and when the tractor came upon a bump in the road, a big, dark-brown clod was joggled free from atop the steaming pile that was being carried. The clod soared up, with the unencumbered grace of a bird taking flight, and landed with a loud "FLUMP!" on Sabina's windshield – through which she no longer had a clear view of either the charming country road, the tractor in front of her, or any possible oncoming pedestrians.

The two cousins don't see the benefits for them as well as for the workers in town (including their husbands) that a new access road would most certainly provide. They would find it better for the drivers to continue to be showered with cow dung rather than undergo any signs of progress and change in the form of a connection to the highway.

It's a tight, tight circle, the edges of those plates in the town of Rucklingsdorf.

"Well, we'll see what they do over there", Elke mumbles disagreeably.

They all sip their strong coffee. Clothilde takes the time to eat another cookie and then, after looking at the remaining pile briefly, quickly transfers another one onto her plate for later.

"Oh", Elke suddenly remembers, "my husband said he saw yours on Saturday, and that they had a good talk about something."

What happened was that Elke's husband was going out to put a letter in the post box on the corner, and he ran into

Clothilde's husband, who was passing by. They greeted each other, with a tone as though the event was a very pleasant surprise, indeed, and then Elke's husband looked up and said that he thought the clouds were starting to come in a bit heavy from the west there. Clothilde's husband looked up likewise, and said, "Yup, looks that way." Then they shook hands, said goodbye in a tone of gratefulness and appreciation, and went their separate ways; Clothilde's husband walked on in the direction that he had been going, and Elke's husband returned home, having forgotten to mail the letter in the rush and excitement of the social event.

When he got in the house, Elke asked, "So, did you mail the letter", and he said "Nope!" with a big smile, and he told her everything that had happened with her cousin's husband, which is how she found out.

"Those two have gotten along with never a problem between them for as long as I can remember", said Clothlida.

"Your husband Dagmar is one of my favorite cousins", Elke says, smiling approvingly.

"I know", the little dumpling says, proudly, "He was always more easy-going than our other cousins."

Sabina stops sipping at her coffee and looks from one of the women to the next.

Then her curiosity becomes too much for her.

"How closely related are your families, anyway?", she ventures.

The two cousins suddenly look away from her. Elke starts to realign her silverware more evenly with her place setting, and Clothilde decides that this is the right time for that extra cookie.

In Rucklingsdorf, the subject of who is related to whom and how close these relations are, exactly, can be a touchy subject. Depending upon how far back the match in question goes in the family tree, there are some cases in which nobody mentions the matter directly or ever clarifies any question that may arise, avoiding the issue with a lot of changes of subject and clearings of throats. Perhaps they aren't even sure themselves, but there have been stories over the years, and now and then, there is a particular relative who either behaves in a rather peculiar way at a given social event or makes a particularly foolish, life-altering decision that negatively affects a few of the people in his inner circle, and those questions arise again in people's minds, only to remain unspoken.

Accordingly, Elke clears her throat, freeing a little piece of Knäckebrot that had been lodged somewhere, in defiance of all the coffee.

"Uhhh...did you see that new cashier at the supermarket?", Clothilde spits out desperately.

"YES!", Elke affirms, with evident gratitude. "She's Turkish, isn't she?"

"I think so", her cousin adds. "Her kids go to the same school as Lukas and Johanna, don't they?"

"Ja", Elke says, sipping her coffee.

"Are your kids friends with them?," Sabina asks.

"In school, you know, they do a lot of things together, and they see each other a lot on the playground."

Elke thinks of a time when they she went to pick Lukas and Johanna up from the playground because they were all going to visit Elke's parents together. A few teenagers came up and the young Turkish boy ran immediately to them and starting chatting excitedly with a big smile on his face. The one he was talking with returned the boy's warmth and interest, and Johanna told her mother that it was the boy's older brother.

Elke remembered how the three teenagers looked: they were extremely coiffed, with highly self-conscious hairstyles (even their eyebrows looked stylized). Their Levis were painfully tight and there were a lot of gold chains and rings to be seen everywhere. From the way they moved and reacted to one another, it was obvious that each member of the group was highly focused upon whether the other members liked his coif, his jewelry, his eyebrow landscaping, etc.

"Well, he's a wonderful boy!", Elke adds after the recollection, as if daring anybody to challenge her statement.

"Yes!", her cousin adds, also a little too eagerly, "I hear the whole family is very nice!"

Elke looks at Sabina for her to please say something, but Sabina just adds, "I've never met them."

Elke turns away from her, disappointed, and adds, gropingly, "I hear the father is working in… I hear the father works somewhere."

Clothilde looks up suddenly and reflectively with a sharply fixed gaze into the air above just her head, as if trying to see something there.

"Yes, I suppose that's right", she says, with an unnaturally shaped smile.

After a pause, Elke adds, "I hope they feel at home here."

"Me too!", Clothilde almost shouts.

"I think it's nice that they have come here", said Elke.

"Me, too! They have every reason to come here. It's nice that they're looking to have a better life for themselves!", Clothilde says, looking with wide eyes directly at her cousin, who returns the stare in equal intensity.

Then, Elke sees that it is Clothilde's eyes that dart first to the photo on the wall. Next to the pictures of Elka's smiling children and a glamour shot of a radiant Clothilde and her husband, there is a frame that displays an ancestor of theirs who is not long deceased. He is standing with a severe firmness that is matched by his tight facial features. There is a military correctness noticeable in everything about him, as well as a piercing, cold look in his eyes.

Elke turns slowly to look at the picture too, as if drawn to it against her will, and Sabina notices that the eyebrows of the two cousins raise in turn, as if questioningly, remorsefully... and then, in turning their heads back to the table, the eyes of the two cousins accidentally meet and they exchange a quick, uncomfortable look before just as quickly turning their heads away from each other.

"Well, would anybody like some more cake?", Elke says in a tight, high voice, and when she looks at the cake and notices that all of it has been eaten except the two pieces that are left for the guests to take home with them, she scowls at it, as if it has let her down.

"Maybe just one more of these cookies", Clotschen says. "They're so small."

"Sabina", Elke commands, "Have a cookie!"

Sabine looks suddenly at Elke and, without thinking, takes a cookie and holds it over her plate. After a moment's pause, with Elke still staring at her, she then places it in her mouth and holds it there, without chewing.

The TV has been on, and after a little period of awkward silence, they all turn in that direction.

It's a reality show, and there is an American family being shown on a trip through Aachen. When one of the parents is interviewed, it is clear that he has started to learn German, but he speaks it with such a strong American accent that it displays absolutely no sign of cultural adaption in his style or manner. When he says "aufregend" (the German word for "exciting"), he pronounces it with a heavy, slow Texas drawl: "Eeeooowf-raaay-guuun".

The television scene switches to the family walking up to the cathedral, and the woman screams shrilly in excitement at how "awesome" it is. At the coffee table in the living room, the shoulders of the three women all twitch a little at the unexpected scream.

The reality show closes with the family gathered at their selected place of refreshment in this center of European history and culture: the American coffee shop chain.

Sabina looks at the other two, lifts her eyebrows and shrugs her shoulders, and the others agree.

Maybe there's hope for Sabina, after all.

A Train Ride

In the telling of human history, there are infestations, plagues, viral epidemics – and then there is The Deutsche Bahn.

The Deutsche Bahn is the main company that operates the overwhelming majority of the trains throughout Germany. It is the only company that offers such a tremendous portion of this service upon which so much of the population is dependent, and so its victims – that is, the passengers – have no realistic choice in the matter.

And The Deutsche Bahn knows it.

The Deutsche Bahn is like an iron and steel mafia: they know that they can largely do what they want, everybody else knows that they can largely do what they want, and the members of the population mostly just go about in acceptance of this unequal balance of powers, avoiding it when they can, and bearing it when they cannot.

Yes, there are meetings of politicians and there are talk shows with semi-intellectuals in jeans who discuss and debate the matter (after all, this IS Europe), but nothing changes substantially (again, Europe).

After the Sunday panel discussion in which members of the different political factions debate the management of the train system and discuss the various implications of its insufficiencies, the local train platform is often filled on Monday morning, yet again, with two or more carloads of passengers who have not been picked up by the trains that have been delayed, yet again, one after the other – as if there is a giant sinkhole in Germany at a spot where each and every one of the train lines has to pass through, and one train car after the next just keeps falling into it, like lemmings – into the great sinkhole of The Deutsche Bahn.

"You don't understand", one of the semi-intellectuals from the panel discussions might say, smirking arrogantly at my foolish innocence, since he really grasps the whole situation in its entirety, and I am just a mere novice in the subject. "There are many different lines in the train system, and their tracks are not all improved yet, particularly in the east" – it's been over thirty years now – "and the degree of complication in synchronizing so many components on this level of logistical management, particularly in consideration of the external pressure that is placed upon costs and budgeting, can inadvertently result in"…

.. and meanwhile, the wet, shivering workers on the platforms are delayed from contributing to the German export industry yet again.

How can this happen in a country which is known as the epicenter of logic and orderly functioning? A country to which people walk for thousands of miles across desert lands controlled by murderous warlords, just to arrive here, to learn the language, to find a job, and… to have to arrive late to work because the German train system just can't pull itself together today.

Sometimes when a person wakes up, no matter what they do with their hair, no matter how many handfuls of mousse or gel they lather into it, there is still a lock of it that simply juts out disobediently, refusing to be tamed. Brushing the hair just doesn't work out and there is really no hope for it until the person gives up, goes about their day, goes to sleep at night and takes another shot the next morning. In these moments of cosmic and cosmetic torture, an American will say that he is "having a bad hair day".

After an underslept German commuter has spent an extra hour standing on his train platform in the morning, being told by the announcement that his train will be delayed again, and once he arrives late to work for the fourth time this month, he can tell his boss that the worker is having a "bad train day today."

When a train is delayed in Germany, the passengers are informed about it by recording of a female voice over a loud speaker. The voice is friendly, gentle, but in the end it is still just another cold-hearted piece of German machinery – it presents an allusion that "We, the Deutsche Bahn, are nice, we are beautiful, stylish even, perhaps scantily clad; come and let me whisper this message in your ear, just for you; we are peaceful and not at all aggressive, and you shouldn't become aggressive, either, no matter how long your train is delayed this time. Bye bye, my special friend. It's a wonderful day today."

After the message, I always expect to hear a little laughter inadvertently recoded at the end, as if the speaker with the beautiful voice turns to her coworker and says "These suckers", and they both chuckle wickedly. Then, I imagine her coworker picking up the phone and saying, "O.K., how many trains should be delayed *this* week, Mister Putin?"

From the entire group of commuters who are forced to arrive late to work due to these delays, aren't a certain percent of them those highly advanced German engineers we keep hearing about? Doesn't that make the entire situation rather embarrassing?

For those of us who rely upon this system for transport back and forth between our source of earnings and our place of sleep and security day after day, the Deutsche Bahn is a demon. It's method of functioning can remind a commuter of that ancient Greek myth about the liver that is plucked out by a vulture, only to grow back to be eternally plucked out again, forever and ever afterwards.

When a commuter has to stand on the platforms and wait for yet another delayed train, that means an extra ten minutes, twenty minutes, an extra hour of his life that is just stolen from him against his will, time he can never get back again.

How many hours in the lifespan of a passenger of The Deutsche Bahn are wasted like this? – time he could have spent with his little son or daughter, looking lovingly into each other's eyes as they play together, with trust developing, wellbeing unfolding in his offspring, instead of that look on the child's face when mommy puts the phone down, tells them, "Daddy will be late coming home from work again, sweetheart", and the child turns with two moist, hopeless eyes to the front door that doesn't open.

Then, the child feels neglected. He starts to have problems at school, his performance is impacted, he gets lower grades, he doesn't develop the skills to fill those scientific and research jobs that Germany is struggling to find young people to occupy.

And there it is, dear train passengers – the Deutsche Bahn is a danger to society.

Florian wakes to the frog croak sound of his phone alarm.

When he and his buddies chose it together over a couple of beers one weekend, he kept pushing the button to make it sound when they weren't looking, and they all kept busting out laughing. For a few weeks afterwards, they would each let out a loud "Croooooak" every time something happened that they thought was funny.

Right now at 5:00 a.m., it just doesn't have that same effect on him.

It's still dark. His wife Stephanie is asleep. She gets to sleep in until six, when she has to start getting the kids ready before she drives them to school and then goes to work herself, closer to where they live.

He has a nutrition bar and a quick swig of juice, because he knows that if he wants to eat breakfast, he would have to wake up and see the number "4" glowing blue before the other numbers on the clock's face every morning, and the young man inside of him who had always expected something glorious to happen in his life just couldn't accept that.

He takes a shower, in about half the time that he does on the weekend. The water is tepid, but too cool to really enjoy. He knows that if he makes the water too hot, the pores of his skin will open up, and it will just be worse standing in the wind on the train platform during these winter months.

He walks the twenty minutes from his apartment to the train station, carrying his soft briefcase with his office papers over his shoulder.

He remembers when he and Stephanie first decided to leave the little village of Rucklingsdorf and move closer to the city for work. When they looked at the apartment and saw how close it was to the train station, he said, "Isn't that great, honey?".

The wind is bitter today. As he walks, he has to lean in and to the left a bit with his torso, and then it is almost bearable.

Inside the garage of the yellow house, the dog that always barks when Florian walks past starts barking, and it's a little sharp on the young man ears this morning. He winces, and then again as the dog barks in rhythm.

Florian climbs the cement steps to the train platform and notices how many people are there already. It's more than the usual amount for his train, and he realizes immediately that some of the people are waiting for their previous train that has already been delayed.

He still has about three minutes, in spite of the wind this morning, so he stands where he is on the high platform and looks out at the sunrise blossoming over the farm down below in the distance. The cows are out already, and he watches them chewing the grass and shifting back and forth on their bony legs. 'It's beautiful this time of morning, even though it's so cold', he thinks to himself, trying to look on the bright side of things. One of the cows moos plaintively; the other one stops chewing for a moment and looks at the first one, and then lowers his head back to the grass. Florian thinks about his and Stephanie's plan to maybe buy a little house here in the countryside one day. The children can play in their own backyard, and they can have a peaceful –

– "Dear Train Passengers", the staticy announcement interrupts. The abrupt change creates a palpable and unpleasant feeling just under Floian's temples. "The 6:15 train to Smurzeldorf will be forty minutes delayed. Thank you for your understanding."

There are a few light grumbles to be heard on the platform, but that is all.

'I didn't give you my understanding', Florian thinks to himself: he hates The Deutsche Bahn a little more each time he hears this end to the announcement. 'They make me stand here in the cold, and then they just assume that I accept and understand it and am not pissed off about it', he thinks, becoming more aggravated with each passing second.

Cell phones are raised, and the rapid clicking begins of messages being sent, informing supervisors that the passengers will be arriving to the office late again this morning, sorry (together with that fear that goes along with pushing the send button, the fear that, at some point, the department manager will have finally run out of patience and will just turn to somebody else for that promotion).

'Thank you for your understanding', Florian hears again in his head.

The cigarettes come out now, almost as a consolation, and the passengers stand a bit more at leisure, shifting their weight from time to time. A man in a tie quietly makes a frustrated "Umph" sound to himself after reading a message he has received on his phone. A young woman's head looks up from the little plastic container of yogurt she has just opened, and after she sees what the disturbance was, she returns to her breakfast.

It starts to rain lightly. Collars are pulled up and people start to compact themselves towards the inner part of the platform, away from the edge. As the rain begins to increase, Florian walks to where the long bench is. There are a couple of spaces free, but they are just below the hole in the wooden roof above them, and water starts to splatter and collect on the surface of the bench. Now and then, a few drops splatter and land on the shoulder of the woman sitting next to the empty spaces, and the rain absorbs into the material of her coat.

Even after the second delay, everyone is surprisingly calm. They are clearly frustrated, and exhausted, but nobody seems to be agitated. There is no yelling, no complaints are raised, and there is no sense that they will start talking among themselves and unite their anger into a common voice, to contact those in power and demand change.

They just seem to accept it as an unalterable inconvenience, which is apparently why it never changes.

When the whistle of the coming train is finally heard approaching in the distance, the lady from the bench gets up. She has a wet mark on her coat where the rain had been accumulating on her shoulder.

The red, metal form of the train car pulls in front of Florian, blocking from him the view of the tranquil farm. A pair of tired eyes from inside the train slowly slides into its place, and for a moment, Florian and the commuter who had been passively looking out the window are suddenly and unintentionally staring deeply into one another's pupils – stranger's pupils – which are only a few inches away from each other on the opposite sides of the glass.

He hadn't even seen Stephanie's eyes this morning by the time he left the apartment.

As the doors open, it is clear that the train is already rather full and that there will be no seats. There is barely enough room for the new passengers entering the train to stand.

He finds a place, and then has to take a few steps closer to the other passengers to make room, but he can see through the window that there are still two people on the platform, and the Deutsche Bahn's customers squeeze closer and closer together.

The train jolts a little bit as it starts, and Florian has to suddenly widen his stance and flatten his feet like a wrestler to stop from being thrown off balance. He bumps slightly into the woman behind him, anyway, and he gives her an apologetic smile. They both raise their eye brows and make an expression with their mouths as if they are having trouble swallowing something bitter, an expression of the sentiment that they and everyone else there are all undergoing this thing and nobody is particularly pleased with it.

The countryside darts by outside, but Florian can only catch glimpses and slivers of it between the heads and necks of the other passengers as he stands in the aisle.

Sometimes, on those few days when he leaves work early, the train is rather empty, and he is able to sit in one of those areas where there are four seats facing each other in a square, the only passenger there. On these days, he takes out a book or just looks out the window at the landscape shuttling past, with his legs crossed like a gentleman.

He looks at where those seats are in this car today. The four people are sitting as upright as possible, so as to not press against each other. One of them is a young woman wearing a colorful wool hat. She's next to an older woman, and across from them are two businessmen. The businessmen are each reading newspapers, folded into tight little squares to save space. They look fortunate compared to the others who are standing, but they still have people bumping into their heads or suddenly grabbing at their seatbacks to catch their own balance as the train changes speeds.

Florian starts to notice the heat. Since it's winter, the train cars have the heat on, but it is always either completely off or turn all the way on. The Deutsche Bahn doesn't bother with anything as considerate as an intermediate setting. He needs to cool off. Because of all the extra passengers from the delayed trains being gathered together like barnyard animals in one confined space, though, Florian is squeezed in so tightly that he can't maneuver to take off his coat, so he keeps it on.

Before the next stop comes up, he starts sweating from the heat. He notices that the freshness of his morning shower has long faded and that he is soon approaching that point at which he would need another one, although there are no showers at his workplace.

He notices the time on a watch above a slender female hand that is gripping the back of somebody else's seat for support. He can only see the woman's hand and some of her forearm, and he notices that her fingers are clutching the seat rather tightly and desperately, sinking into the foam.

'It's only 7:15 a.m.', Florian thinks. 'How can a person's day be made so unpleasant in so short a space of time, and so early in the morning?'.

He starts to become aware that he is sweating profusely, and he wonders if he is going to have to hide the fact that he has perspiration marks under his arms once he gets to the office and removes his coat.

After a while, it starts to become hard to stand in one place for so long, especially with the floor of the train constantly shaking under his feet.

'Why is it like this?', Florian thinks. 'Why does it have to be like this?'

The woman with the colorful wool hat in the corner starts to rummage around in the striped backpack that she has between her feet. She pulls out a red thermal container, straight upwards and very carefully, as if it is a nuclear weapon and she doesn't want to set it off. After she sets it in her lap, she positions her hand over it with her elbows still tightly to her side, and she screws off the little lid, with her fingers making quick movements, like someone opening a safe.

'It's chicken soup', Florian notices. He can smell it after the cover has been open for a few seconds.

'Maybe she's sick', he thinks, since he cannot help but notice her as he stands there.

She starts to sip at the soup, as quietly as she seems to be able to, and the businessmen across from her start to look at her in turns. The older lady to her side shifts herself in the direction away from her as much as she can, although it doesn't make much of a different, due to the lack of space.

The young woman seems to not notice the people glancing at her from all over the car. She is clearly enjoying the comfort of her soup.

Florian remembers the nutrition bar and his glass of juice from this morning, and he feels his stomach tighten. It already seems so long ago.

After a few sips, the young woman in the colorful wool hat screws the lid on in reverse, slides the thermal container back down into its secure position in the backpack between her feet, and when she sees the one businessman across from her staring disapprovingly at her, she pouts a little at him in apology.

Florian remembers when he and Stephanie first moved into their apartment not far from the station. He was looking forward to taking the train to work back then.

'I'll be able to read while other people have to drive back and forth in their cars,' he thought back then, 'and besides, it will be better for the environment.'

He looks at the watch on the arm by the seatback and calculates that if he had driven today, he wouldn't even have needed to be leaving the apartment for another hour or so.

He remembers watching Stefanie's eyes as she woke on the pillow next to him last Sunday.

"Hello, Reiner!", he hears, and he sees the young woman in the colorful wool hat talking on her cell phone. Her voice is as loud as though she were outside.

As the conversation on the cell phone progresses, everyone in the car is displaying varying degrees of frustration with the woman. The two businessmen with the tightly folded newspapers across from her and the older woman next to her are clearly agitated, but are too physically close to her to say anything about it; they would then have to sit across from her after any confrontation for the remainder of the train ride, and the awkwardness this would cause keeps their frustration in check.

Her voice starts to escalate, as tends to happen on a cell phone when there is so much background noise. She is now basically yelling in the faces of the passengers who are in the seats directly across from her.

Finally, a woman from behind Florian just busts like a swollen boil and yells to her, "Oh, would you please just shut up!"

She has clearly spoken for everyone else on the train in doing so.

The young woman on the phone tells Reiner that she has to go, and then she puts her phone away and sits quietly in her place, keeping her elbows in, but otherwise as though she has done nothing wrong.

'It wouldn't be this crowded if they didn't have all those delays this morning', Florian thinks to himself. He realizes that the train company is not responsible for this woman's behavior, but if all these people weren't forced to squeeze in so tightly, she wouldn't be as intrusive as she is. She would just be 'that loud woman on the train today in the other seat'.

'After all', Florian thinks, 'there are always going to be people like her, but they don't have to worsen it by squeezing us in all so close together like this. It just makes it so much worse.'

He looks back at the woman he had bumped into earlier and with whom he had shared a look of comradery under stress, but there is no sign of empathy from her at this point. She has a glazed look now; all the muscles in her face are slackened, and she clearly can't stand the whole situation anymore.

The shaking in his feet starts to slow down, and he knows that they have almost arrived in the city.

Through the window on the right, he can't help but see that tall building on the opposite side of the station from the town center. It's the building with the windows that the hookers always lean out of, waving at the trains as they go by.

The first time he saw it, he thought, 'Wow, how friendly', then he saw another woman in another window, and then another, and he thought, 'Oh'.

He is amazed to see that there are already (or perhaps still) a few women on the job, waving back and forth from the isolated windows, slowly, with wide arm movements as if they were waving a flag, as the train pulls past them.

It seems strange seeing them there when he is just getting ready to start his day in the office, being responsible – behaving himself. He looks out the opposite window without realizing it.

As the train approaches the station, there is a controlled rush and rotating of passengers to position themselves in relation to the doors for the moment of exit.

There is the sound of scraping metal as the train slides to a halt, and as the doors open, there is a narrow but visible alley left clear among the new passengers on the platform. The passengers outside the train wait, with evident impatience held in check by a sense of Germanic duty, for the commuters in the train car to exit before those outside follow their own impulse to enter.

When Florian was in a city in the south of Europe on business once, he was on a train, and when the doors opened, he was compacted into a thick wall of people inside wanting to get out, and across from them was a thick wall of other people wanting to get in. After each group seemed to wait a second for the other to get out of their way, the individuals in each group started to just weave their way forward, into the opposing group, like individual fingers, or like the fish of two schools starting as a whole, breaking up to swim through each other, and then uniting on the other side, like an M.C. Escher drawing.

'It's different in Germany', Florian notices, and he appreciates this difference as he exits through the cleared alleyway, before the eager German passengers from the platform slip as quickly as possible in behind him the moment the number of passengers still exiting is small enough to fit through the cleared space.

He runs this gauntlet and heads towards the stairs.

As he passes a kiosk, he sees a few books piled up for sale. Among the romance novels and murder mysteries, there is a bright red book with the picture of one of the trains on it.

'Another book about how bad these trains are', he thinks. He bought one once, years ago, and read it. The authors had even established an organization to fight against the train system, with a website that showed where the latest protests were going to be held.

'The trains are so bad that there are even books sold in the train stations about how bad the trains are', Florian thought. 'How can it be this dysfunctional and still be allowed to go on like this? Why don' the politicians fix it?'

The sweat on his face from the overheated train car starts to feel cold on him now that he is outside. He shivers a little, hoping that it doesn't get worse.

As he reaches the stairs, he looks up at the big clock above the platform.

He still has to catch the street car to go up town, and then walk from there. He always plans extra time into his commute to account for train delays, but it's not always enough.

'That's it, I'll never make it on time now.'

When he gets home later that evening, his eyes look tired, his body is slumped, and he is sniffling.

He puts his soft briefcase down on the sideboard and then sneezes profusely, making his hair flop into disarray.

Hearing him, Stefanie comes from around the corner with her office clothes on.

"Hi... are you sick?", she asks, with concern in her voice.

"Yes", Florian says. "I'm sick of the Deutsche Bahn!" – and he is already thinking through plans to buy a second car.

Carnival

Those hot-blooded Brazilians, the wild, artistic souls of New Orleans, and – the Germans?

Yes, believe it or not, there is a festivity that is so unbridled and libertine as to be able to welcome the folk of all three of these diverse cultures into its throbbing fold – and that festivity is Carnival.

The lengthy Carnival season in Germany is appropriately referred to as the "fifth season", as if it does not really occur within the limits of reality as the Germans generally know and acknowledge it. In the Rhineland, Carnival starts in November – at eleven minutes, past the eleventh morning hour, on the eleventh day, of the eleventh month.

Leave it to Germans to schedule a precise time on a specific date when they permit themselves to finally loosen up and have fun.

This particular day is the day of their "Hoppeditz" – a mythical little figure who is a cross between a court jester and some sort of little goat creature, leading back to the pagan times in Germany (assuming that the pagan times in Germany can be said to have ended by now, of course). On this day, Hoppeditz awakes in the town square and emerges from a giant jug of mustard (depending upon each local custom and, I would assume, the current availability of mustard). The event is heralded with music, singing and, of course, the drinking of much German beer.

Then, there is a lengthy period of cold, grey winter, with the Carnival groups preparing for the big day, working month after month like drunken bees in the bee hives of their respective Carnival associations...

...and then it happens: the mayhem is let loose.

In February, the people gather in the bigger cities dressed like clowns, Vikings, furry animals, and with a large amount of men dressed like women in skirts and blonde, braided wigs (as if, suspiciously enough, they have been waiting all year to finally be able to display this side of themselves. "Because it's Carnival, of course. Not because I'm, uhhh... Who wants another DRINK?!!").

There are parades with giant floats, satirically mocking the politicians, who are portrayed with giant, grotesque heads, songs are sung in unison by the tens of thousands of people in the streets... and there is the drinking. And more drinking.

It is said that the most babies in Germany are born nine months after Carnival (again, notice their scheduled precision, even when it comes to the greatest act of human libertinism and indulgence). Considering the great concern over the pronounced decrease of the German population, if it were not for this excessive consumption of alcohol and public drunkenness, the German culture would apparently disappear from the face of the earth.

Along with the parades, there are also various celebratory events called "Sitzungen" – "sittings", in German, so named because the gathered celebrants sit at long tables together while they listen to live music, singing along with each other and, of course, drink.

Leave it to the reserved Germans to take such a raucous event and name it after the rather subdued event of "sitting".

Then, on Ash Wednesday in the spring, a straw puppet, often believed to be the poor "Hoppeditz", is brought to the public square, and, as has been the custom for centuries, the poor creature is encircled by the whooping and inebriated celebrants, blamed as a scapegoat for the sins that they themselves have performed during the Carnival season (and perhaps a few more that they still have yet in mind), and the figure is set aflame until it burns – an image which has numerous obvious parallels to the darkest moments of German history. It is peculiar that the people of this country exhibit such a deep-seated need to gather around a figure that they perceive to be weaker than themselves and mock it before trying to destroying it, preferably in flames – the Germans should really look into this side of themselves, before it gets out of hand again.

I remember when I took part in Carnival in Düsseldorf some years ago. It was when I was visiting the city, before I even imagined that I would one day live in Germany. We were lubricated at home with a suitable quantity of Schnaps (not liquor, but "Schnaps", a beautiful, peppy word which my wandering American heart just adored to hear). There was a sense of something great about to happen, a sense of anticipation of the wonderful... and I was not disappointed.

As we made our way downtown, *everybody* was celebrating, *everybody* was lighthearted. The police were noticeable casual amongst the wayward throng that they were there to control, and I thought how different they were from the police I had seen in cities in the United States during big parades – that attitude as though they were just *looking* to smash someone's head in with a wooden baton (if not worse), "Just gimme a reason!".

Not here on the sunny streets of Düsseldorf. It was as though the celebrants and the police were all glad to be part of Carnival together, and nobody wanted to do anybody any harm whatsoever.

As I walked among the crowd of these loose, free, happy Germans, I remember thinking to myself spontaneously, "You know, I could live here".

We made our way to a place on the sidewalk, and I thought, 'Whatever it is, *this* is where it is going to happen!'.

Everyone was jubilant, leisurely expectant of the beginning of the festivities. There was a contented and boisterous chatter that started to grow.

And then from down to one side of the street, there was a low rumbling – far away, indistinct, but clearly approaching us in this direction.

I looked at the others in the crowd, in my group, and they were smiling and laughing.

'So it's a *good* rumbling', I was glad to think.

And as the rumbling morphed into music, there were walls of parade floats expanding in size as they crept slowly closer, ever closer – the unhurried foreplay of an approaching parade float at Carnival can truly overwhelm the senses.

And then the singing began. It was a song that all the locals knew, and there was a unified roar of joy, of people raising their collective voice in song, singing lyrics about absolutely nothing of any meaning whatsoever, and which was therefore all the more liberating on this day of freedom from the dark, dank cage of winter and responsibility, this day of liberty into the multi-color, confetti world of Carnival.

And as the parade floats hovered before us, there was the ebullient, long drawn-out cheer of "Alaaf!" in greeting between the riders of the float and their worshipers in the street.

And then the throwing of the candies began, the "Kamellen". From high above us in the air, there rained down one colorful spray after another of individually wrapped candies, handful after handful, like expanding clouds of sweet polka dots thrown out against the pale-blue background of the sky – and the crowd went nuts. At that moment, there was nothing more important to any of us that grabbing one of these Kamellen from the air in its freefall, like reaching out and grasping a canary or a bright orange finch, or, if you were not so lucky, scrambling on the floor in eager desperation to salvage your moment of greatness and to be among the "haves" and not the "have-nots" of this glorious event.

For the Kamellen, these simple little candies, suddenly acquired a value that was far out of proportion to their actually day-to-day worth. If we bothered to stop a moment to look at this cherished marvel that we clutched in our hands, we would see that, in fact, it was nothing more than cheap, individually wrapped, sugary candies from the discount store, which anybody could buy at any time by the bagful for two bucks (including on that day, in the store just to our backs there on the sidewalk).

But this was Carnival – excuse me, Karnival. Why would anybody stop and think about the meaning of – why would anybody stop and think? We just got through a whole winter of sitting and thinking in dark, dreary rooms. Today was a day of JOY, today was a moment of BLISS, of, of – of SWEET CANDIES BEING THROWN TO US FROM THE GRATUITOUS SKY ABOVE, and all we had to do was to want them, to reach out into the air, and our hands were filled for us – and there was happiness.

Under such conditions, the value of these candies became momentarily and wildly inflated, more so than what happened during the Internet bubble of the late 1990's – even more than the great tulip mania of the Netherlands in the 1600's, when individual tulip bulbs reached a price that would pay for a mini-mansion on the coast.

Today, there were no such concepts as inherent value and marketability, not in this, the fifth season of four, when the boundaries of what was and what could be, what *should* be, became progressively blurry (perhaps from all the drinking, but nevertheless…).

Any yet, as invisible as all else that was not a Kamelle in these moments became, there was an inspiring sense of togetherness and sharing, without a single memory that anybody could ever be against another of his brethren, not his Karnival brethren – not here, on this patch of sidewalk, and not today.

Occasionally, some individuals amongst us were so distracted by the act of drinking as to not notice that the moment of spontaneous bequest was upon us yet again with the arrival of the next float. When this became clear (or at least clearer) to them, they would suddenly chug what they could from their red plastic beer cups and then raise them high up into the air with a loud "Alaaf!!", as if calling out for a blessing – and this blessing they did receive, as a hard candy wrapped in bright orange-and-blue paper landed with a great, sloppy "PLOTSCH" into their cups, spraying the crowd in their vicinity with the stale beer, like a benediction – and the anointed smiled gleefully with beer dripping down their faces at the receiver of the valuable Kamelle, happy for him in the great bounty of his newly found fortune.

As yet another parade float passed by, with all of us still in the wild intoxication of the Kamellen, a young woman on the sidewalk across the street looked out from amongst the throbbing crowd of humanity about her, and our eyes met – she saw me, I saw her, she smiled and I smiled back, and though I was already there celebrating with my girlfriend and had no other plans to the contrary, I realized, "Yes, *anything* can happen here today!"

Amidst the ecstatic thrill of this impulsive event, it is interesting to note that Germany is also known as the country of some of the greatest philosophical thinkers who have ever graced the earth – the masters of rationality – and on this day, I imagined Immanuel Kant and Arthur Schopenhauer stumbling together through the cobblestone streets of Düsseldorf, each wearing red foam noses and dressed in multi-colored balloon pants, with their arms draped casually around each other's shoulders, singing raucously and swigging beer from big tin mugs as they keep an eye out for chicks (hey, maybe it would have done them some good).

I sensed the vibrancy of the peaceful, happy crowd that I was a part of, and I thought, "I love it here in Germany!".

I remember all of this today, many Februaries later, as I sit in my easy chair in Rucklingsdorf and watch TV.

One of the many "Sitzungen" events is being broadcast: there is the uplifting, waltz-style music from the accordions, the quick and steady OM-pah-pah, OM-pah-pah from the drum set, the bright and festive colors everywhere to be seen – on the table tops, on the musicians, on the people's costumes, on the bunting and other decorations strewn and hanging freely from the lights above. There is that laughing and inebriation which tomorrow will alter the lives of so many individuals and the formation of so many family units for generations to come.

… and there, amongst it all, sitting at one of the drinking tables, surrounded by revelers on all sides, is the German "Sauertopf" – the "gloomy sour pot", a woman in her mid fifties, with a frown that is the exact inverse of a smile, so deeply plummeting that it is pressing the side of her jowls ever lower with each thumping drum beat. She was brought there by her family members, who bump into her as they dance together in abandon in the aisle behind her.

Among the joy and celebration, she sits, miserable, elbows on the table, her claws surrounding her giant beer mug, which is half empty and not half full, with the beer suds thinning and disappearing as they slide slowly and tragically down its sides.

Her mouth is painted all around with an oval of thick clown red, and there are big, orange-brown freckles dotted onto her face. And raging high out in a curve from atop her puffy, purple-and-green felt hat is an artificial sunflower, towering in place as it vibrates up and down to the music in spite of her.

She (or any of the countless other Germans much like her) might also be found sitting outside at the tables in front of street cafes on beautiful summer afternoons in Germany, with the jovial Italian ice cream vendors singing from under the yellow-and-orange-striped awnings as they plop scoop-fulls of colorful flavor into paper cups for the happy little girls and boys, who can barely wait in their eager expectation – while she, the "Sauertopf", the black vortex of joylessness, the perfect advertisement for psychotherapy, burns in her disgust and dissatisfaction so as to rival the radiance of the noonday summer sun.

And today, at the Carnival festivities, surrounded by the friends and family members who are nearest and dearest to her, amongst the room that is just busting with rhythm and sound and color and joy – she sits under the drooping flower on her head, and she lets the Carnival pass her right by – once again.

Euro Trash

Mr. Klumpf is sitting in his wooden chair with the good back support across from his open window, trying to make his way through the correction of another box of student papers in his apartment this Saturday morning.

His lives about 40 minutes southeast of his hometown of Rucklingsdorf, and the school is another thirty minutes away from there.

He's prepared to be busy until dinner, so he's got his cup of peppermint tea and a bar of dark chocolate on the little table beside him, as a small luxury to help him through.

He has six big, clear plastic boxes full to finish by the grading deadline at the end of the month, one for each of his German Literature and Language classes at the Berufskolleg where he teaches. It's a kind of school program that provides vocational preparation for office workers who didn't quite make it into the university. His courses are a requirement in the program, and none of the students are particularly excited about having to participate in them.

The quality of the student reports is horrifyingly low, and it's getting perceptibly worse each year. As he makes a mark to show that two broken sentence fragments have to be made into one complete one, he thinks about the student whose work it is.

'His father bought him a Porsche last semester', he remembers hearing one of the other teachers telling him.

While struggling to figure out what the student might actually be trying to say in the next paragraph, there is the sound of voices outside. They start and stop, but after a few minutes, they become a steady presence, and they increase in volume.

He looks out the window at the charming little park with the pond that is right across the path along his building. At the picnic bench which is right across from his window four stories down, there are three men sitting and drinking beer.

One of the men, the lanky one, looks gaunt and malnourished, the way alcoholics tend to. He has an unevenly shaved crew cut and a blurry tattoo of a spider web on the side of his neck. His T-shirt is black and faded, with the words "100% Schwarzarbeit" printed on it, referring to the illegal work that some welfare recipients in Germany do on the side without declaring it to the government. The shoulder of the T-shirt is coming apart at the seams.

The other two guys look rather shaggy, and the T-shirt of one of them has a faded skull-and-crossbones on it.

"Hmmm", Mr. Klumpf grunts lightly to himself, and then closes the window.

After returning to the papers, he soon notices that the sound of the voices outside is still coming through the window.

He gets up and turns on the classical music station to drown them out, and then returns to his chair.

With the window closed, the air in the apartment soon starts to become stuffy and uncomfortable, and after two more papers are finished, he realizes that between the distraction of the music and the sound of the voices that comes in audibly over it now and then anyway, he simply will not be able to concentrate on his work.

He puts his pen down, has a bite of the chocolate and a sip of tea, changes from his slippers into his shoes (the same ones he uses for work during the week, he notices unpleasantly) and goes downstairs.

He takes the steps just to get a little exercise after sitting all morning, and he goes outside and walks towards the men at the picnic bench.

They are still chatting and laughing with each other, but the one with the patchy crew cut raises a beer can to his mouth and peers over it as he watches Mr. Klumpf approaching.

"Hello", the teacher greets them in a friendly tone.

They just look back at him, as if not appreciating the intrusion.

Then, the one with the crew cut says, "How's it goin', dude?" is a deep, scratchy voice. He's missing a couple of teeth on the side.

After briefly recollecting his displeasure when he heard this same phrase in the hallway at school the other day, Mr. Klumpf says, "Fine, thank you".

Then, hoping for a smoother transition into his concern and finding none, he tells the three men why he is there.

"I live just upstairs there", he says, turning around and pointing at his window.

The lanky man with the crew cut takes note of which window it is, and then he takes another drink from the can.

"I'm a teacher and I have a lot of papers I have to correct today, and I can't concentrate with you guys talking so loud down here, unfortunately."

He says it to the entire group, but he realizes through instinct that the man with the crew cut is the leader among them.

The leader stares back rather defiantly at the philology teacher, before suddenly morphing into a light attitude and saying, "I'm sorry. We'll try to be more quiet".

Mr. Klumpf notices a slight smirk on the face of one of the other young men just before it disappears behind a raised beer can.

"Thank you very much, gentlemen", the teacher says.

He turns around and heads back to his apartment, glad to have found a peaceable solution to the problem, though doubting the sturdiness of the agreement that has been reached.

He settles back down into his chair again, and he is please to notice that he has finished another three papers without having heard any noise from outside.

'They're just a couple of raggedy guys having a few beers on the weekend', he thinks. 'That's not so bad.'

He takes the next paper from the pile, noticing that the box is still near the rim yet, and looks at the name.

It's the girl who always sits in the last row, looking at her cell phone. While he teaches, he notices her facial expressions rotating between boredom and sudden glee, followed by long bouts of boredom again as her finger swipes the screen, and he knows that she is looking at social media. He got her to put the phone down once or twice, but as soon as he writes something on the board and turns back around, it's in front of her again. The administration says that he can't do anything about it, because she has a right to be in the class and get her education.

After a sigh, like someone who has to carry a heavy stone up a mountain and is not looking forward to doing it, he begins.

Half way through the first broken sentence, there is a sudden pulse of throbbing music, overlaid with an eruption of hearty laughter through the glass of the closed window.

He looks at the straight, thin mark on the paper that his pen made when it slipped with the distraction.

The laughter rises again outside, all three of them together and then in turn, as the throbbing continues.

He stands up and goes to the window, where he looks with an aerial perspective at the men lounging across the picnic table. There's the radio, a big red and black box of a thing with oversized speakers.

To the right, he sees the street that runs along the park to the dead end where his building is. 'It's still and quiet everywhere', he thinks. 'Everywhere but here'.

He looks back at the men and the radio. From his perspective, he feels like he is in a military bomber, siting a target.

He taps with his fingertips against the pane of glass, like a bird in a cage, and the men just carry on without noticing.

Then he curls his fingers inwards and taps again, more forcefully this time, to be heard over the music, and the three faces look up in unison at the thin form in the window.

They take a few swigs from their beer cans and return to whatever they might have been discussing with each other for the past hour.

Mr. Klumpf taps again, harder and with the taps following more closely upon each other this time, and when the faces look up to him this time, he waves to them, to remind them that he is still there, trying to correct the papers.

The man with the crew cut waves back, wiggling his fingers at the man in the window, and the two other young men burst out laughing, banging their fists on the table.

Their leader looks satisfied with the reaction he has gotten from his buddies. The philology teacher just glares down at them and, seeing no other alternative, returns to his chair.

As he curls the aluminum foil back from the chocolate bar, he bites into it, with his upper gums exposed and his lip curled up tightly.

Then, out of desperation, he tries to convince himself that his circumstance is not as bad as it seems.

'Well, how long can they sit there, after all?', he tells himself. 'They're just chatting with each other and listening to that pounding music. How long can they stand it? Besides, what can they possibly have to chat about for so long?'

He remembers the two students on the left side of the classroom in Period 4 yesterday who constantly talked with each other, first every time he turned his back, and then even when he was facing the class, regardless of his having asked them several times to "quiet down".

'They'll finish their beers and go', he persuades himself, 'out of boredom, if nothing else."

He returns to his papers and concentrates as well as he can with the noise from outside.

After around 4:00 in the afternoon, he notices that it has been quiet for a while. He gets up and walks towards the window, adjusting the drapes a bit and sneaking a look out at the picnic table.

It's empty, except for a few crushed beer cans strewn about. The radio is gone, as well.

Filled with relief, similar to what he feels as he leaves the school and turns out onto the road to head home in the afternoons, he returns to his chair.

He sips his tea, convincing himself that it is more of a satisfaction to him today than it actually is, and returns to his papers.

The next morning, Sunday, he wakes with a burning in his eyes. He slept in, to take what luxury he could before returning to his work at the wooden chair, but he was awakened from the sound of voices outside the window and that pulsating electric beat.

'They're back', he realizes, his eyes wide opened as he lies there, suddenly stiff on the pillow, and he feels a sense of being trapped.

In the other room, he looks out the window and he sees them, and he sees that they see him, and he watches as the man with the crew cut and the spider-web tattoo turns leisurely away from the window back to his friends, with his legs crossed and his arm with the beer can draped casually across the radio on the picnic table, like a king holding court.

Mr. Klumpf prepares himself a cup of peppermint tea and sets himself to his day's work. He doesn't like having to work on Sunday, but the corrections have to get done in time and he has no other choice.

He starts in on the hour and a half of work that the hopes to complete before breakfast, and he finds it a constant struggle to concentrate through the noise from outside the window.

Suddenly, there is a high-pitched scream, almost like a long, drawn-out squeal. He gets up and looks out the window, and there are now two women there with the men at the picnic table. They are all drinking beer, in spite of the early hour, and they don't show any sign of leaving any time soon.

"They're expanding", he says out loud to the room, and then looks at the pile of papers that are barely below the upper rim of the clear plastic box.

Not through any sense of logic as much as out of desperation, he turns to the window and opens it and calls out to the party down below.

"I have to *work*!", he shouts at them, realizing that there is no longer any pretense that they are cooperating with each other and that they are now clearly in the position of being adversaries.

"So do we!", the leader shouts up over the noise of the music, with his hand cupped to the side of his mouth, his other hand with the beer draped casually across the radio again, and the whole crew breaks out in laughter, as if they were just waiting for a reason to do so.

The loud pitch of the shrieking woman rattles a nerve in his ears, and he shuts the window with a loud "FLUMP!".

"That's it", he tells the room defiantly, and he picks up his phone and calls the cops.

"Hello", he says to the voice on the phone. "I'm a teacher and I'm trying to grade my papers on a Sunday and I've got a bunch of – PEOPLE (he says sarcastically) outside my window drinking beer and making noise, and I can't concentrate on my work!"

When he stops, his realizes that his voice has been raised, but he hopes that the words "teacher" and "beer" will carry enough weight to get some results.

"We'll send a car, sir", he is informed, and he thanks the man on the phone, guilty at having raised his voice to someone who wasn't part of the problem and who was, after all, going to help him.

He returns to the wooden chair and he takes another paper from the pile. In spite of the firm support, he feels that the muscles in his back are tight from yesterday, and after squirming around for a while, he just can't find a comfortable position.

He's making some headway through the pile, despite the constant mumble through the window pane adorned with the sudden outbreaks of laughter and the loud shrieking.

He looks at the clock. It's been over an hour since he called the police.

"How long are they going to take?", he asks the empty room.

After another forty minutes, there is a ring from the street door, and soon after, a knock on his own. He opens it and sees two policemen standing there.

He feels reassured that so many have been sent to handle the situation, and he imagines the look on the faces outside when they are taken away.

After welcoming the policemen in and explaining the situation again, basically repeating what he had already said on the phone but adding "and you can hear that radio from in here", he points to the window and the policemen look out at the group down below at the picnic table.

Smiling to himself at the justice that is about to be unleashed upon his adversaries, he is surprised when one of the policemen says to him, "Do you have another room you could work in today?"

"Another room?", Mr. Klumpf says in disbelief, his voice tight and a bit elevated.

He feels his grip on the situation slipping, and he starts to view the policemen as more a protector of the other party than intending to do anything to break it up and send the drinkers away.

"No", he says, as if the facts will help swing the matter back around in his favor, "it's just these two rooms." He says it rather bluntly to them.

"We'll go down and talk to them", the same policeman says. The other one hasn't said a word so far.

"Thank you", Mr. Klumpf says, yelling it at them a little.

They leave, and he waits for a change to occur. The steady, bass thumping of the music is starting to match a pulsation somewhere in his head.

He steps tentatively up to the window, and he sees the policemen outside talking with the disruptive drinkers. He's surprised at how calmly it's going, as if they're having a nice chat together.

The main policeman gestures to the radio.

"Here it goes!", the teacher says out loud to himself, expecting his much delayed reward to finally be handed to him.

The man with the crew cut says something and the two policemen start laughing easily.

"It's like they're at a pub together", Mr. Klumpf says, astonished at what he sees unfolding outside his window.

They suddenly all look up at the window together, and he ducks behind the curtains.

Then, he sees the tall, gaunt drinker reach for the radio as if he's turning it down. The drinker turns back to the policeman, they each shake hands, and then there is a round of handshaking among the entire group, and the policemen disappear.

Mr. Klumpf opens the window quietly, imagining that he will not be seen doing it from down below, and he hears that the radio is still on, but that the pulsing is quieter now.

"What just happened?", he asks out loud to the room. "That can't be all they're going to do about it."

Then, there is the ring at the street door, followed soon by the policemen knocking at his apartment again, and they enter.

"We talked to them", the head policeman informs him calmly, "and they agreed to turn down the radio for you."

'Agreed, for me', the teacher hears, as if it's a favor, something that they don't *have* to do, and as though they could just as well decide otherwise. As if he should be *thankful* to them.

"What?", Mr. Klumpf says. He is in such disbelief that he's a bit disoriented as to how this could be the state of things.

"You should be able to correct your papers now", the policeman says, as if he has handled the matter successfully and restored peace to the neighborhood.

"Are you kidding?!", Mr. Klumpf says, visibly agitated. "They're just going to turn the radio back up after you go!"

"If that happens, you can keep a list of each time the music starts and stops, and it would help if you get a few of your neighbors to back you up in doing that."

"Who has time for that?!", he yells. "I've got this whole pile of papers to correct by tomorrow", and as he glances at the plastic box of the student's work, his head starts to throb a little harder. If it weren't for the disturbance outside, he would have been half way through by now. "How can this be allowed to happen?", he says, not believing that this can be the only option that he is presented with.

"We get a lot of calls like this", the policeman says, turning slightly to his partner, who remains silent but present.

"You get a lot of calls like this? Then, why don't you *do* something about it?" He realizes that accusing the policemen is not going to help him any, but he is now more disgusted with the sheer injustice of the situation than the actual disturbance itself.

"We can't do anything else about it", the policeman explains, as if he might like to but that his hands are tied. "They'll aloud to be outside and talk."

"OK", says the teacher, agitated by the minimization of the whole situation like that, "but what about the drinking, and the music?"

"They're allowed to have a drink outside if they want to, and they can listen to music as long as it doesn't disturb anyone indoors."

Mr. Klumpf is infuriated at this point by the irrationality, and he makes an effort to remain cool.

"But *I'm* disturbed by the noise. They're disturbing *me*!"

"The noise has to be above a certain decibel level, and they lowered it to a volume that's OK now."

The loop of counter-logic is becoming maddening to the teacher, and he tries to get some kind of rational response by rephrasing his question.

"But what happens if they just raise the music after you go? I don't have time to keep lists and organize a neighborhood watch program. What do I do *then?!*"

"You can call the department again, but it's really not going to accomplish anything. They'll probably just turn the music down when we get here, and wait until we go."

'So, they're not so foolish after all', the teacher thinks. 'They *know* what's going on'.

"How can this be allowed to happen?", he asks. "How can a teacher be stopped from being able to correct the papers of his students just because a bunch of drunkards want to sit outside his window and disrupt the neighborhood?"

The policeman shrugs his shoulders.

"These kinds of people are pretty smart", he says.

Mr. Klumpf's eyes tighten. 'Now I have to listen to compliments about these degenerates', he thinks to himself.

"Do they even work?", he challenges.

"We don't know about these particular individuals, but when we get calls like this, it usually turns out to be people living from Hartz IV", the policeman says, mentioning the welfare program in Germany for people who have not worked for an extended period of time.

"You mean welfare riders?!"

"Usually", the policeman repeats, "they are people who are living on Hartz IV."

"Do you mean that a teacher can't help young people become educated and to get jobs, all so that a bunch of welfare riders can be allowed to sit outside his window, get drunk on Sunday morning and disturb the neighborhood?"

"The system's not perfect", the policeman says, somewhat world-weary, apparently not without empathy for Mr. Klumpf's situation, and aware that the man who called them is now, for the first time, discovering the very tip of the system in which the policemen function day, after day, after day.

"It's politics", his partner suddenly says, speaking for the first time, as if it's important enough for him to get it off his chest.

The other policeman remains stone-faced, looking at Mr. Klumpf.

"If they become aggressive, or if there's any damage", the first policeman says, "call us and we'll be right over," almost as if he would be glad to be able to do something about it, at least for once.

Mr. Klumpf hears the words "aggressive" and "damage" and wonders how far this situation could escalate, how dangerous it could become for him.

"I'll do that", he says. Realizing that the policemen are not choosing to be passive, but that they are just as victimized by the system as he is, he says "Thank you for coming, anyway."

"You're welcome", the policeman responds, looking deeply into the teacher's eyes, still stone-faced, but as though grateful that the overall situation has been understood by someone else on the other side, glad that another person has perceived the dysfunctional net in which he and his partner are trapped.

After they go, Mr. Klumpf sits back down in his wooden chair, and even though he is far, far behind and does not know how he will ever get these papers corrected before the next batch has to be started tomorrow, he takes a minute to let the ramifications of the situation sink in.

He stares vacantly in front of himself into the empty little room.

"Society", he says out loud, as if it's a curse. As if he's answering a question someone has asked him.

Then his eyes regain their focus, and he turns to the little table where the chocolate is, only to see that there is nothing left of it, only an empty wrapper.

"Damn it", Mr. Klumpf says, not thinking about the chocolate any longer.

The Waiting Room

As I enter the waiting room for my annual medical exam, I see that the room is largely empty except for one old woman sitting in the corner.

We smile welcomingly at each other and I take a seat in the row across from her.

"Hello", she says, apparently eager to start up a conversation while she waits.

"Hello", I respond in turn, smiling back at her.

"I'm here for my gall bladder", she informs me, as though her exam has already begun right there in the waiting room.

"Oh?", I say, a little lost for words. "Well, I hear that the doctor has a very good reputation", I add, trying to think of something that is as closely related to her gall bladder as propriety will allow.

"Yes, I've been coming here for years already", she says.

It feels nice to have this friendly chat while we're waiting. It makes the world feel like a more intimate place.

We continue exchanging a few words back and forth, and I am pleased to see that the conversation is rolling along smoothly, in spite of my American accent and my shortcomings in speaking German.

We talk about the town, and how nice it is.

"Yes, I go shopping there from time to time, too", I say.

Then she pauses and looks at me, smiling.

"I have a *neighbor* who's Turkish", she says suddenly, as if doing me a favor of some kind.

She says it with an accent on the word neighbor, as though, since I am a foreigner and her Turkish neighbor is a foreigner, that is just as well the same thing (even though I do not look in any way Turkish).

In an instant, I wonder about this woman's parents back in the 1930's, about how she was raised, about how her own children and grandchildren have been taught to think...

...and I turn to a magazine to start reading an article about menstrual cramps.

At the Street Market

Up there at the end of the narrow, cobblestone alley, in between the massive grey stone of the Town Hall and the open, green window shutters of the old inn, the city's fruit and vegetable market can already be seen thriving in all of its liveliness and bounty.

The first thing that is noticeable is the crowd – the sheer quantity of people who have assembled here today, in this town square, simply because they appreciate good taste – because the fruit is softer and sweeter, and the vegetables are crunchier and more vibrant.

There are stands overflowing with meaty plums – such a dark shade of purple that they're almost black, with one cut open in half for everyone to see how good the plums are – that rosy, alluring flesh inside, glistening in the sunlight because they're so moist.

There are piles and piles of thick, green grapes by the bunch, imported from Italy and overflowing upon each other, like a boisterous family. The grapes are covered with a powdery golden vapor, and they taste like sugar and grace, as though you can already taste the wine that is cooked into them from the Florentine sun.

Next to them is the flower stand, just erupting with every single color that you have ever seen, and then a few more that you haven't. It's like a candy store, a happy dream, with the gigantic sunflowers, their heads as big as the heads of children, the proud tulips, so bright that they seem as if some mad artist came by and painted them with watercolors when you weren't looking. There is one deep, watery vase after another filled with life-embracing shoots and pedals, bright green and purple, orange and blue.

Along that row is the fish stand, with the aroma of fresh, battered fish being fried in the open air, in the little fryer in the corner. The battered fish is served on a flaky, little roll that is far too small for the big fillet of fish, which juts out on either side, just as far as the roll is long. It's completely impractical, and the juice from the fish drips all over the place – down your hands, into the cracks between the paving stones on the floor – but still, there's always a long line of people waiting in front of the counter where the fryer is. Everybody seems content to wait, because they know it's worth it: that warm juice that seeps out from the crunchy batter as you first bite into the fish – *your* fish, freshly cooked just for you, at the market today in the public square.

The array of cheeses, hard and soft, white and yellow and orange, some with herbs mixed into them, some surrounded by a rind of colorful, crushed flower pedals. The big round wheels with a wedge cut out, displaying the gaping holes in the heart of the cheese. The platters of cheese spreads, mixed with nuts, with honey, or dusted with spicy red paprika.

Today, there is a young couple who thanks the cheese vendor as she hands them a small sample, and the father hands it to the little girl at their side. As she tastes it, her eyes look upwards and to the left, as if she is noticing a subtlety in it, something she had never know existed yet, and the parents watch her and smile. And the cheese vendor watches her and smiles.

The little raised tables where people can stand in front of the potato pancake wagon and eat their crunchy potato pancakes with the apple sauce on them are nearly full; there's just one more spot, if you want some. You have to wait a little while, though: the man in the booth is chatting with one of his customers, and you're turn doesn't start until the other customer has said what he wants to say, and the man in the booth says what he wants to say. You might stand there for a minute or more, waiting. And then, after the warm exchange runs its course and comes to its natural end, the smiling face turns to shine upon you, as well, in turn, and you know everything is alright.

At the bakery wagon, there's a short line of about five people, and as everyone waits patiently, looking at the cakes and pies and rolls and loaves of bread, an elderly woman starts to appear from the side of the stand. She sneaks up, not looking at anybody, and she stands to the side of the first person in line, without saying a word. After the customer who is being served has his goods wrapped up for him in a cozy bundle and carries them away, like a fresh baby, the man behind the counter turns to the elderly woman with a welcoming smile and asks what she would like to buy today. Nobody seems to mind, and once she thanks the baker and they share a look of mutual gratitude, he turns to the next person in line, and the order is placed with eager warmth.

Our baskets are full now, with plump figs, two big bunches of the golden-green grapes, with scarlet red flowers jutting out on their bright green stems, the peaches, the fresh dessert squares with the yellow cream inside and the whipped cream on top.

We walk past the Town Hall, back down the cobblestone alley, pack everything in the trunk and turn out of the parking lot.

... and we drive back from the city, along the pastures, past the wheat fields, back to the little town of Rucklingsdorf, our senses full, our baskets overflowing, and we know that no matter what else happens, it's going to be a good week, again.

(Former) East Germany

When traveling through the states of former East Germany, not so far from the town of Rucklingsdorf, what is first noticeable is the general sense of apathy, the general sense that "this is not working out".

Firstly, there is an overwhelming proportion of walls in eastern Germany that have apparently never been painted – even now, so long after the fall of the Soviet Union, and in spite of about 25 years of additional funding through the "Solidaritätszuschlag" (the "solidarity tax" that workers in the west of Germany have to pay in order to bring eastern Germany up to speed).

Drive along the main roads in eastern Germany and you will see one dry, uncoated, porous grey farm wall after another, as if they have sucked away all the sunlight, and nothing which can radiate any brightness is left.

Everything else is a neglected olive green or faded brown, like yard waste.

There are no flower boxes with bright, red geraniums spilling out before the windows, no yellow half-timbered "Fachwerk" houses in meticulous condition to allure the eye of moneyed tourists.

Instead, there are the long, tin-looking farm storage units, which appear to be housing an abundance of dilapidation more than anything else.

In the town centers, you will not be able to avoid seeing the welfare housing blocks – miniature high-rise apartments which, at best, might have received a coat of plain white paint across their flat, rectangular facades which are institutionally void of any sense of adornment or visual stimulation whatsoever.

Inhabitants of these buildings will often be hanging out in front of the local discount supermarket, as though they have now come to replace the military guards which used to serve the purpose of border control and Soviet enforcement in the region.

In public parks, among the strollers and the people eating lunch, there are others whose bodies are crumpled hopelessly across the grass, who seem like they have nowhere to go and nothing in particular to do. It's a different look and body posture from that of leisure – like the difference between someone who is retired and someone who is unemployed.

Then, you will run across people who seem as though they have not smiled in decades, who appear to just sit around in one another's company, staring at your car going by, as if in a zoo, as though they have no intention to say anything to each other, since they seem not to have been saying much to each other so far.

There is no sign that people are generally enjoying the sense of being gainfully employed, of wielding their minds and bodies as only humans can and finding the satisfaction that results from such an endeavor. There is no sense that people expect for tomorrow, or even the next decade, to be any better than it has been going for them so far.

Instead, there is a rotting, a collective decay.

I remember being on a bus tour in Berlin through the remnants of the former East German regime. It was a patch of the earth that had been thoroughly encased in concrete, from top to bottom and side to side, like a person in a cement suit, with cement in their nostrils, their ears, with not a single blossom or tree, not a single sign of life, with the sky blocked out by thick, soulless buildings that were too close to each other, as if required to stand side by side, like strangers forced at gunpoint to live in each other's homes – a wall of walls within the former Wall that had surrounded part of Berlin. The entire vicinity was a standing monument to evil and despair, conditions still palpable as I passed by on the bus decades later. It was easy to imagine a camera on a pole, watching everybody, knowing everything about everybody, and the few who were writing down the names of some of the many. I had never before known the sense of the putrefying of human hope as I had seen in that place on that day.

And the countryside and towns of former East Germany look like a variation of this pale, bloodless theme, still today – like it *would* be in the western part of Berlin if nobody had picked up the broken bits of brick and stone and built them back into a thriving civilization.

It's nice that the wall came down and the soldiers went home.

… but now what?

How about some paint and a few flowers to start with? Then, we can go on from there.

Cats, etc.

When it comes to cats, Germans exhibit a surprising ease in their frequent and public use of the word "pussy".

Their nickname for the animal, which has exactly the same potent, double meaning as it does in English, is "Muschi".

German couples will be out for a walk and when the man sees a cat on the sidewalk, he'll just call out in German to the animal, "Pussy, pussy" as loud as he pleases, and his wife doesn't seem to think anything of it.

Once, when a neighbor from another country was gardening in Rucklingsdorf, another neighbor walked up to her and they started chatting. As she was crouching among her flower bed, her cat appeared beside her and rubbed herself on the woman's shorts.

"What a beautiful pussy!", the man bellowed from behind her, and the woman nearly fell over with surprise.

Sometimes on a warm summer night in Rucklingsdorf, a certain woman can be heard as she wanders through the streets calling for her cat by name, going "Meitzie, MIETzieeee", trying to bring it in for the evening.

When I hear that, I always expect her to be followed by some man with similar interests roaming the streets not far behind and calling out in a plaintive voice, "Pussy, PUUUssyyyyyy!".

The New Friend

It was another Town Council meeting being held at The Golden Mule, so the big room was being used tonight, and it was full.

Before the latest intricacies of village politics were to be unleashed upon us, there was cake and hot beverages, as a kind of a warm up for whatever was to come.

I took my slice of poppy seed cake and coffee to a free space at a table and sat down. Next to me was a man about my age who I had never met before, and after a friendly greeting and a smile, we got to talking.

"So, another Town Council meeting", I said as a conversation starter.

The man just shrugged his shoulders and pursed his lips, and then smiled to me, as if sharing a secret.

'So, they don't even expect anything from each other in the end', I thought to myself.

We got to talking about the weather, and then how the gardening was going so far this season.

"My wife and I just planted a new hydrangea in a shady spot by our walkway, and it's doing very well", he said, beaming with evident satisfaction.

"At least it won't be eaten by the snails", I said, and we laughed lightly together, sharing a common foe.

We enjoyed our cake and drinks, talking the entire while, smiling to each other and exchanging a pleasant chuckle here and there. We were clearly glad to be in each other's company.

After about twenty minutes, a disoriented rustling was evident at the table in front of the room, and he said, "It looks like the big moment is about to start".

We smiled again to each other, with a kind of warm gratitude. Then, we turned towards the front of the room, both of us clearly still at ease from the enjoyment of our pleasant acquaintance.

A few days later, as I was walking through the neighborhood, I happened to see my new friend out front in his garden, raking some pine cones together that had blown down in the wind.

"Hello", I called out as I raised my arm in greeting, glad to see him again and looking forward to another warm interchange like the other night.

He stopped raking and stood there looking at me, immobile – as if suddenly intruded upon by an unwelcomed stranger. Then, he raised his hand at the wrist slightly, moving as little as possible while still officially performing the act of greeting another person. Then, he returned to his gardening.

The only sound to be heard was the scraping of the metal teeth of the rake across the lawn.

"The hydrangea looks nice and healthy", I complimented him, referencing our social success from the other day.

He just turned his head slightly in my direction, smiled politely and went "Hmm" without looking, and continued raking.

I stood there and watched him for a while, until he had accumulated a little pile of pine cones at his feet in front of the hydrangea.

Then, seeing that the conversation had run dry, I turned and moved on.

I walked past one charming little house after another.

'What is wrong with these people?', I thought to myself.

Between Democracy and Nazism

Democracy

Democracy has been a foundation of German society for nearly a century already, and the country has become a leader on the world stage in the application of this particular social form.

Considering the length of the history of the German people, though, the institution of democracy is a relatively recent import to the German culture.

Prior to the current governmental and legal structure, there had been century upon century of cultural habits as well as generation upon generation of child rearing that occurred, of course, innately resulting in a cultural fabric which has its own deeply entrenched habits and tendencies, as is always the case in every group of people.

When people change, it usually occurs in increments, little by little over time, and the new ideas and approaches are gradually added as the old norms and beliefs are slowly relinquished, to whatever extent that occurs. Germany, though, was democratized literally over night, from one moment to the next, and that is a stark contrast to the way human development naturally occurs.

Even in this day of internationalization and a globalized globe, there is a clear difference in what it means to be part of the culture of South America, of Asia, of Scandinavia and of Europe. And within Europe, although the various Europeans share certain characteristics in common, there is a big difference between each group of European peoples –

between the Germans and the French, for example (just ask one of them, or follow the news from Brussels about the European Union).

Therefore, the process of the German culture adopting democracy is like the effect of water on a stone: the stone gets wet immediately, but it only changes its fundamental shape slowly, ever so slowly, and over the course of many, many human lifetimes.

A part of what a human personality is results from the movies a person has seen, his birth order in his family, the modern trends of his generation, etc. Among the countless influences are likewise characteristics that date back centuries. There are noticeable differences even today between people who come from cultures which had once been under the charge of ancient Rome and those which had not, and this difference is a part of every single, individual human being today, as we sit with our friends and have a beer, as we sit with our friends and smoke shisha from a water pipe, and so on.

The last 75 years of democracy in Germany has been added to the thousands of years of group behavior and group thinking that have been handed down from one generation to the next, somewhat changed each time but never deviating fully from the immediately prior pattern. Just think of yourself and your own parents; there are inherently similarities, no matter how different you might be, and differences no matter how great the similarity. This has, of course, been happening one generation after another, which is why there is still a difference between the cultures of Spain, Finland, China, etc.

Germany had been a loose network of individual tribes long after some other cultures had already organized into their own respective, more cohesive groups. There was not originally the sense that "we are all in this together", "let's talk about that and see how we each feel about it", and this basic component of the democratic process had been very much delayed in its development among the members of the German culture, regardless of whatever the reason might have been.

Germans have long tended towards the small group structure with an individual group leader. How close is the sense of mutual identification between one little rural German town and the rural town that is three bus stops away from it, or between the northern states of Germany and those of the south? Which is more different from Hamburg: the German state of Saarland or the entirely different country of Austria? It's a rhetorical question, yes, but that discussion could go on all night.

For those of you who live in Germany or deal with it as a whole on a regular basis, consider these words placed directly next to each other: Mecklenburg-Western Pomerania, Baden-Wuerttemberg, Berlin.

Did your brain explode?

You can even do it just with the older states (so as to avoid the excuse that the difference is only the result of the Second World War, and that it's really due largely to the influence of other countries upon Germany): Schleswig Holstein, North Rhine-Westphalia, Bavaria.

The different parts of Germany, though united, still have their own particular characteristics.

Germany is one country, but its individual groups have never, ever identified themselves, psychologically, fundamentally, as being part of a larger whole, beyond what is practical and necessary – and that applies even before the division of the country into east and west after the war.

In the first half of the 1800's, there was the "Zollverein", a "customs union", a collaboration between the hundreds of separate German territories and states. The purpose, though, was essentially to increase trade among the individual groups. There was no sense of, "You know, you like Schnitzel, I like Schnitzel, why don't we all just get along?".

No – it was for money, a convenience. In other words, they dealt with each other because they *had* to, not because they *wanted* to – not from a sense of shared personalities, but shares circumstances.

It's like the difference between the relationship between residents in an apartment building in a city, and the relationship between family members. The neighbors in the apartment building live next to each other, they deal with other, they might even become good friends with each other, *almost* like a family – but they still consider themselves to be psychologically separate: there is me and there is you, regardless of how close we become. In contrast, among a family, the members identify themselves as being parts of a group, regardless of whether they want to or not.

Germany and the German people are more like the residents of an apartment in a city, or rather, like the individual residents of many individual apartments in many different cities. They do not perceive of themselves as fundamentally, psychologically, one.

The basic concept that we are members of the same family, with deep similarities that we appreciate and value in each other, performing that illusion that humans perform among family members that *although we are separate, we still conceive of ourselves as one, as parts of a united whole* – that is not noticeable among the Germans, whether on the federal level, in the communal level, or on the individual, interpersonal level.

The Germans generally do not approach life as if they are all on the same team, negotiating among each other the direction in which the team is to go.

Every German is an island.

And they deal with each other as such.

The Germans work together and form associations of the different islands, exchange products between the different islands, consume confectionary goods and coffee with the different islands sitting at the same table – but the psychological demarcation of the boundaries of one island and another, where one ends and the other begins, remains.

In Germany, there is no sense of the individual parts, of the individual people, fitting together into one, cohesive whole.

In so many of the automotive engines and industrial machines that Germany is famous for producing, there are often countless metal teeth on various metal cogs of all shapes and sizes, and they all integrate into a single, functioning system.

If only the Germans could manage for the individual people in their culture (including the native-born Germans themselves) to interrelate with each other the way the individual teeth on the metal cogs of their machinery do, now *that* would be something – but that would involve people skills, and it's not the same thing.

In other words, in Germany, the people skills and not as strong as are the people's engineering skills. And the difference seems to be that people skills are not a matter of precision. They require flexibility, adaptation to the spontaneous and unpredictable, a perception of how one's own actions impact the other person and a response to this impact – and that just doesn't fit in here.

Now, add to this the ingredient "democracy".

It has worked (thank god!), but it has worked in a particular German way and not in any way that is especially democratic.

That particular German way is that democracy involves a constitution – so, a set of laws, a set of *rules* ("Did you say *rules*?", says the German. "I'm listening!"), and the Germans *love* to follow rules. It gives them a sense of order ("Ordnung - muß - sein!"/"There - must - be - order!"), and when they have a sense of order, they feel secure. And when they feel secure, that insane cuckoo bird that flies around haphazardly in their heads from time to time settles down and is lulled to sleep (though only for as long as the sense of security lasts).

So, democracy works in Germany *not* because the individuals recognize that they are united, or that they have an earnest interest in the concerns of the other members of the group, in listening to those concerns and discussing them with one another to reach a mutual consensus – perhaps a bit different from what each individual originally wanted, but something that works sufficiently for each party so that they can go back to the daily business of being close with one another again, like before, now that any differences of opinion have been resolved.

No, that is not the democracy of Germany.

The democracy of Germany is "You want to do it your way and I want to do it my way. Na, jaaaaa... let's see what the rules demand us to do". Then they look at the rule book (the laws, the constitution), look suddenly up at each other, and say, "OK, that's it, then. The rules say so, so it's settled."

And that works well enough, it's functional, but nowhere in that process is there a mutual give and take, a mutual exchange and recognizing of interests and concerns, and a cooperative resolution to the best of both parties as far as possible.

In German democracy, there is no collaboration, no togetherness – there is merely a bowing down to the great master that is "*THE RULES*", but there is no sharing.

Yes, the television channels are filled with panels of politicians and so on talking and discussing, but their approach is generally as follows:

Speaker A: "*This* is *my* idea."

Speaker B (crossing his arms over his chest): "Well, *this* is *MY* idea!"

Speaker A (now crossing *his* arms across *his* chest): "Well, your idea is not at *all* like *my* idea!" (his voice escalating noticeably).

And they sit there and pout, arms crossed, speaking unilaterally at one another, and nobody really listens, and nothing really evolves.

That's not democracy.

There is no place in the world where democracy is doing particularly well these days, including the USA. Nevertheless, there is something in the fundamental psyche of German individuals and the German culture whereby, while democracy is currently working, it is not the German's natural state, and the Germans don't really get it – they don't really see that democracy is more than just everyone following the same rules, bowing down to the same regimentation – democracy is a fundamental interest in one another, and a manner of dealing with each other interpersonally that results from that fundamental viewpoint.

Instead, the Germans continue to function according to that psychological social structure that they have been following for as long as they have been making hearty sausage – the "Führerprinzip", the concept that whatever the guy one step higher on the ladder says, that is what I must do.

Today, the constitution is the German "Führer" – but what happens when some individual or group comes along and tears up the constitution? Will the German people come together and say, "Now, let's all talk about this thing here, together", or will they just follow whatever new "Führer" is set in place of the current, constitutional one?

It is in the Germans' nature to follow the leader, and once that leader is no longer a constitution but something far worse, it is in their nature (with exceptions, of course, but on a culture-wide scale) to follow that leader – whoever or whatever kind of leader comes out as the strongest.

That is what scares the hell out of me regarding German democracy.

And there are a lot of cockroaches out there trying to nibble away at constitutions these days, and there are a lot of shaky, unstable conditions in the world – in the economy, in the environment, in the family units, and so on.

This world today is so ripe for dictatorship, and the Germans are so fundamentally vulnerable to its intoxicating, illusionary allures – and I just don't want that to happen. Germany has been doing so well for so long now. If only the Germans could understand that democracy is more than just about following rules, but rather about actually giving a damn about what the other guy wants.

That is what would prevent the next German meltdown.

And I don't see that change happening.

A simple example from day to day life displays this clearly.

While the autobahns in Germans are famously and luxuriously spacious, the small streets in German cities and towns tend to be too small for anything more than two narrow lanes of traffic. When a car happens to be parked in the street (which, in many cases, is fully allowed), the car behind it has to wait if there is a car coming from the opposite direction in the other lane. Only after the other car passes is the car behind the parked vehicle permitted to continue driving on.

That's fine, but notice how the two drivers, the two people, generally handle this situation. While they are driving along in complete isolation from one another in different directions, a circumstance from the external world (the parked vehicle) causes them to suddenly have to deal with one another, so as to avoid an accident and so the two drivers can then continue to carry on with their own individual lives.

What happens is that, apart from exceptions (there are always exceptions), the car behind the parked vehicle usually waits obediently for the other car to pass before driving around the parked car and moving on.

But try this: if you are in the car in the free lane which is not blocked by the parked vehicle, *wave and smile* to the waiting driver as you pass, thanking him for having performed this small civilized sacrifice.

The result has amazed me every time I have done it – there is a look of actual aggression, of anger, as though the waiting driver wants to make clear "I am not standing here for *you*, whoever you are. I am stopping because of the *rules*. It is the *rules* that say I must stop here, so I stop here. I am certainly not doing it out of any personal consideration for *you*!"

The little thank you wave and smile in such situations clearly aggravates the Germans in most cases. It's fascinating! It seems that they feel that actually sacrificing their own interests for that of the other person would somehow be belittling for them, not quite Nietzschean enough for them, and they rile at the mere suggestion that they might have sunk to such a low level of weakness.

They also don't seem to feel comfortable with this sense of mutual intimacy that is suddenly imposed against their will upon them through the thank-you wave and smile, because, in the end, they are *not* in this thing together with you.

There is absolutely no sense that we are both fellow humans who, out of mutual consideration and valuation, have just successfully negotiated an otherwise potentially confrontational situation, instead resolving it with collaboration and in peace.

That is not democracy. That is not all being on the same team, considering the interests and wellbeing of the others as of equal value to those of ourselves.

That is mere blind obedience to the leader, the rules, and if the leader that is the rules were to tell the waiting car to smash into the other car (to prevent it from producing so much carbon monoxide, perhaps), or to detain the other driver and have him sent to a work camp, then that is most likely what would happen – obediently, according to the Führerprinzip.

Incidentally, when the driver is waiting behind the parked vehicle, you will almost always see his car nudging impatiently and progressively forwards, millimeter by millimeter, instead of just fully stopping, as if the stopping for the sake of the other is actually against his own will.

That is not an acceptance of the concept of sharing. It is self-subjugation to force, the force of the rules.

And that is really not the point of democracy.

Nazism

In general, Germans tend to have a lot of positive characteristics, for which they are well known internationally (such as reliability, honesty, directness, perseverance, focused thinking, and so on).

Along with these virtues, they also tend to lack certain interpersonal subtleties which are at least more common in many other cultures. Specifically, Germans usually display the tendencies of:

- A) being inconsiderate and/or unaware of the effects of their actions upon others and
- B) losing control of their negative emotions when they feel insecure.

Living in Germany, along with the pleasantness and politeness that is often exhibited, it is simply not possible to avoid running into some people who respond to a different opinion with a shocking degree of aggression and combative defiance, or who perform acts of daily existence that display a stunning disregard of any and all human beings in their vicinity (including of other Germans).

Yes, all groups of people have such individuals among them, and we are all that way from time to time, but the proportion and degree of such behaviors in Germany, in spite of the many other positive characteristics, is one of many unique and defining characteristics of their culture.

Germans are known for working hard and doing their share, but they are also known for sometimes not even noticing that they have insulted other people (intentionally or otherwise) while doing their duty, just as they are known for being somewhat unduly stern in their behavior from time to time. There are Germans who do *not* work hard, and there are Germans who are normally *very* polite, but there is a cultural inclination that displays a unique cultural pattern.

This is simply a part of who Germans are. There are positive and negative tendencies in all cultures, and in Germany, the positive tendencies are particular ones and the negative tendencies are also particular ones, and (as applies in every culture) the combination and balance is uniquely their culture's own.

In the lives of most Germans, they will complete their duties, they will celebrate their social events, they will raise their families, and in the mean time, they will make their contribution to society, and although they will often manage to violate an array of social considerations towards others here and there along the way (whether they notice that they have done so or not), they normally do not intend any harm and have no intention of intruding in the wellbeing of others. In fact, they generally approve of others having the chance to live well. They still might erupt when their sense of security and order is jeopardized, but that can (depending upon the person) be temporary and situation-dependent.

This cultural propensity towards not seeing things from the other's perspective, together with the tendency to lose a grip on their self-control, *can*, however, under certain circumstances and depending upon the background of the individual, be exercised in the direction of being hateful and destructive towards others.

In other words, there are some Germans who, although sometimes stumbling crudely when it comes to social graces and a little volatile when it comes to moments of tension, are otherwise fine members of the human race (aggravating in their way, perhaps, but respectable and generally kind). In contrast, there are some Germans who not only stumble when it comes to social graces and are a little explosive, but who perform gross violations of human consideration and, in extreme cases, of human rights.

There is a difference in these two types of German personalities, as well in the results of their actions and behaviors, but it is interesting that the source of the lack of social consideration and emotional self-control is more or less the same.

What this means is that there are those characteristics within the German personality which (again, along with other positive characteristics) tend towards a temperamental disregard of other people, to one degree or another. This tendency can either lead to a) a mere irritation and social bluntness in an otherwise pleasant (or, if not, tolerable) fellow human being, or (in an entirely different individual) b) a hateful destroyer of the peace and wellbeing of others.

The source is the same, but the result is different.

In other words:

```
                   | > Normal aggravating
                   |   German (but nothing worse)
Interpersonal      |
disregard    >     |
and volatility     |
                   |
                   | > Nazism
```

The characteristics of lacking interpersonal sophistication and emotional self-control only lead to severely destructive behavior in a minority of the more extreme Germans. However, the fact that the majority of (if not all) Germans share these characteristics with their more extreme countrymen is what creates such a tender sensitivity when a typical German runs across the topic of Nazism.

Such Germans are not Nazis and have no intention, thought or desire to do anything that is in any way related to Nazism.

In spite of that, they do tend to lack natural skill at taking the needs and interests of other people into consideration (at least to the same degree that this skill is normally present in many other cultures), and they tend to become a bit overheated at times. In these individuals of the German culture, these tendencies are merely simple personality flaws (and we all have our own particular flaws, culturally as well as individually). However, this same tendency to lack natural skill at taking the needs and interests of other people into consideration and to sometimes get a bit out of control is also a seed from which, in other individuals, the mentality of Nazism (or some other destructive ideology) *can potentially* grow, and without which such an ideology would not be possible.

And that is what makes so many Germans seem to need to go the extra distance to prove, not only to others, but also to themselves (and *particularly* to themselves), that they are not Nazis. They do *not* possess the type of personality that Nazis possess, but they share some characteristics *from which* the characteristics of Nazis can *result* (even though there has been no danger of such a negative development occurring in themselves).

Therefore, when a typical German goes shopping for a shirt and is slightly aggravated that he cannot understand the accent of a foreign worker who is helping him in the store, he might feel a tremendous sense of guilt, worrying that this frustration with a foreigner might mean that he is really a Nazi deep down – even though he might actually find it interesting to have people from other cultures living amongst him, as long he can do his shopping and go about his day without any frustrating impediments.

In other words, if you're the kind of person who just grabs a paper that somebody is handing you without saying "Thank you" or yells at the passenger in your car because *you* missed the highway exit, you might just be a regular German.

Nazism takes a lot more hate than that.

Another type of German is someone who might want to be open minded, who believes in the principles of democracy and equality in theory and who aims at treating people cordially, but (through his upbringing, etc.) simply cannot keep his innate dislike of foreigners from boiling over from time to time, even though he does not like this part of his own character. Such a person lives in a constant struggle between wanting to be more open-minded and self-controlled than he actually is, versus giving in to that ever present urge of being irrationally judgmental.

For such a person, the disproportional potential to become inconsiderate and aggressive is always there and can be activated at any time, if the social conditions are right (or wrong) enough to trigger it.

Then, of course, there are actual Nazis, those people who are more than just a bit lacking in social grace and steady rationality, and who actually have a need to hate and destroy in order to counterbalance their own unfortunate lack of self-esteem.

The particular type of German who is mean and disturbed enough to potentially become a Nazi but whose environmental circumstances are not quite problematic enough for him to take that step of actively becoming interested in Nazi-like ideology is a "proto-Nazi" – all the internal ingredients are apparently there (the narrow mindedness, the boiling aggression), and it's just that no lighted match has been dropped yet to set the pile of dry hay on fire. It's as though they are a "carrier" for the susceptibility to hateful ideology, like people who carry a gene for cancer: maybe it will become active, and maybe not.

If you spend enough time in Germany, you will come across a disturbing amount of locals who seem to fit this description. It's not all of them, and it's not most of them – but it's still far too many.

Apart from the minority of Germans who are openly members of movements that have a dangerous similarity to the dysfunctional ideology of Nazism, most Germans want very much to not be mistaken as part of that group. More profoundly, they do not want to identify *themselves to themselves* as being believers in any ideology of hate and destruction.

What becomes difficult for so many Germans as they try to distance themselves from the recent dark past of their culture is that, while such individuals do not uphold the principles of Nazism in any way whatsoever, they do have as part of their nature some interpersonal shortcomings which, for *some people* and *under certain circumstances*, can be a seed from which the mentality of Nazism *could* grow. Even though this mentality of Nazism is not something that would grow in *them*, just the similarity of also being a bit less refined in the handling of other people can be enough to make the kinder, more functional of the Germans feel nervous – in some cases to the point of feeling ashamed and self-conscious, as if to say "We talk briskly and are impatient, and the Nazis talk briskly and are impatient, so maybe we're Nazis".

No, such Germans are not Nazis, and they do not have any intention to be so.

If two Germans have a shortcoming when it comes to considering the effect of their behavior upon other people, and they both have a tendency to become aggressive if a failure in some performance leads to their feeling insecure, then one of them might handle this reaction like the civilized (though imperfect) member of a modern society that he is, and another might see that seed in himself grow into a weed of destruction and hate.

Being German certainly does not mean someone is a Nazi, although there are some particular characteristics in the culture which, in some individuals and under certain dysfunctional circumstances, can provide the raw material for those particular members of the group to want to adhere to Nazism (or some other hateful ideology).

One such characteristic is the tendency to think according to the "Führerprinzip" – the concept that the leader must be followed, blindly and at all costs. Another is the tendency to need to blame someone else as a scapegoat to relieve oneself from feelings of insecurity during situations of stress, and yet another is the pronounced need for a sense of order.

Such characteristics are tendencies in the German personality. They often appear in daily German life in varying degrees and proportions, but they do not, in and of themselves, identify an individual as a Nazi.

However, if a particular individual German is insecure enough, hungry enough, hopeless enough, these characteristics can make that person more susceptible to hateful ideology than would be the case for someone of another culture under similar negative circumstances.

The German personality (in all of its forms, I would say) also displays a unique relationship between the "id" and the "superego" – between what one wants to do and what one has to do according to external requirements.

Ideally, these two parts of a personality are in balance and relate smoothly together: I want a cookie, but it will ruin my appetite, so I will postpone it for dessert – no problem.

In contrast, it is possible for these two drives to be present next to each other but less integrated with each other, and in conflict with each other, and this type of relationship between the two is frequently observable in daily German life.

Instead of this smooth balance, it often seems that a German is responding to a "little dictator" in their heads who pushes them and drives them to do certain things that they seem as though they would not particularly want to do, if they had a choice (working *extra* hard, scrubbing the floor *extra* thoroughly, etc.). Even if they tell you that this is exactly what they want to be doing, Germans do not seem to be peaceful and happy in these moments, and they do not seem as if they are currently following their desires (their "id").

Rather, they seem tighter, edgier, and more disgruntled than usually, and as if they are listening to the voice of some scolding adult in their brain, some "little dictator", who is forcing them along against their own contrary wishes.

Therefore, you will often see a German doing something like rubbing and rubbing at her window pane with an aggressive frenzy, as if she hates that window, all the spots, perhaps all windows everywhere, as well as the act of cleaning the window itself, as though she is forced to do so, as opposed to someone whistling happily as she performs her chores.

Another example is something unique that often happens when you place an order of some kind, such as at a bakery.

If you are in a bakery in Germany and tell the friendly, smiling clerk "I'd like a loaf of rye bread, please", the clerk might suddenly stop smiling pleasantly, her eyes might suddenly focus with surprising sharpness (as if concentrating on something deep within her own skull) and she might audibly repeat the order "A loaf of rye bread!" to herself – sharply and in a somewhat elevated tone, almost militaristic, with all of the finer subtleties of politeness and interpersonal consideration purified away from the original request, like when melting steel – and it is not as if she is repeating it to you, as a kind of a question (with raised intonation at the end), such as in an act of asking for confirmation; it is rather as if one part of her is giving a command to another part, as if a "little dictator" in her brain is commanding that part of her that wants to just lay on the side of a lightly trickling stream in the sunshine and look at the golden daffodils, and the little girl by the stream is told, "NO!", is suddenly hauled upright, placed in a suitable and proper posture and instructed as to exactly which procedure she is to follow.

Then, you get the rye bread – or rather, the rye bread is wrapped and polished and placed on the counter between you and her (since her role as a server of other humans ends where her fingertips finish; there is often no handing over of the package, and clerks in Germany – no matter how friendly otherwise – tend to prefer that you place the money in the little plastic tray that is placed on the counter for just that purpose, even long before the pandemic was even dreamed of; you will sometimes get a rejecting and disappointed look if you offer to place it in their hands directly).

The procedure of fulfilling the order is performed as if the friendly bakery clerk who had greeted you at the beginning of the interchange had momentarily left her own body, which had been temporarily taken over by her leader, that voice in her head that tells her what to do, what is right and what is wrong, the "little dictator" that is not living in peace and harmony with the light-hearted girl who just wants to follow her impulses.

Why else would a bakery clerk need to repeat such a request at that point in the order (without the raising intonation that is natural to a question)? *You* know you want a loaf of rye bread, *she* obviously already heard that you want a loaf of rye bread, and she could just as well continue smiling and say, "OK, I'll get that for you. One moment, please".

And that might happen sometimes, but when this stiff repetition of the order occurs, it is a sign of the "little dictator" in the German personality forcing them along.

This psychological structure of having one's impulses clearly demarcated from one's sense of responsibility (instead of a normal, smoother integration of the two), this "little dictator", is another typical German characteristic which, under severely dysfunctional childhood and environmental circumstances, can lead a person who would otherwise just become a peculiarly tight German to being interested in Nazism.

Without those extreme conditions, though, it's just another weird little thing about the Germans.

This difference between the "little dictator" in them and that other part of their personality which makes them just enjoy the peace of the beautiful stream in the sun is exemplified in that famous first part of Beethoven's Fifth Symphony.

First, there are those ominous, domineering chords with their imperious eruption – "TA-TA-TA-tuuuuuuum... BA---BA---BA---buuuuuum", and you drop your half-a-roll-with-raw-meat smeared on it (yes, the Germans sometimes eat raw meat... and it's delicious) and you spill your coffee in awe of all that is foreboding and unknown...

... then a little later, in contrast, the more gentle violins begin to sing, like a young girl who is just coming of age while she watches a bird take flight as the clouds begin parting...

...and then, those powerful chords return, chords that remind you of every vague character and event from every nightmare that you have ever had since your earliest moments of childhood onwards.

That's Germany, and that part of that piece of music is the most perfect portrayal of the German soul in action, with all of its conflict and contrast between light and dark, good and evil, that I have ever known.

Whatever their political viewpoints might be, the Germans exhibit this conflict between peace and war, ease and tension in day to day life, and each of them handles this part of their German character differently – with minor oversights, fluctuating, or with hysterical outbursts, some tending more towards one pole and some towards the other.

Being so prone to aggression and defensiveness when they feel insecure and having a sharp imbalance between their impulses and their sense of responsibility is uniquely and weirdly German – but that does not mean that each individual German is a Nazi.

However, you never know where on this range any given German will be at any given moment – and some of them might not know, themselves.

It depends on the German you get.

Therefore, you can never let your guard down fully with the Germans… you really just never know what you're going to be dealing with.

This applies individually, on a personal level, but it also means that this productive leader of unification and togetherness that is standing at the heart of the European Union at this point in history can always, ALWAYS… flip.

It's not that all of them would want to, and there were many noble souls among them who tried to stop the mess last time in the 1930s. However, there can be enough members of the culture who will already be far enough to the dysfunctional extreme as well as enough who will have the potential to arrive there when the conditions are uncertain enough for them – then, it can happen.

The trigger can be a collapsing economy, a diluting sense of their own cultural identity, whatever makes enough of them loose that sense that "Alles ist in Ordnung" ("everything is OK"). Then, the cyber-tanks will have to roll, before the borderline-personality of the overall German culture makes another mess of things, like before.

Some Germans (a lot of them, in fact) have been pushed to the far end of the range between tranquility and agitation such that they are just constantly miserable, and they make everyone aware of it.

Among the other functional Germans, these broken psyches appear as if they are those heavy Germanic chords from Beethoven's Fifth simply being repeated, over and over and over again, unceasingly, without the counterbalancing sweetness of the lighthearted violins, until they drive that German himself as well as anyone involved with him raving mad.

These particular individuals are like a statue of the German poet Heinrich Heine which is located at the center of the University of Düsseldorf: it is a statue of a gaunt, black figure, standing in isolation and thinking in the rain under the oppressive, gray sky. There are many Germans who, after a few seconds of their company, can easily remind a person of this dark, gloomy statue.

Yes, everybody in every culture has their limits, and everyone can be pushed over the edge under certain conditions, but some of the Germans (again, only *some* of them) are constantly living directly on this edge.

There is a kind of sea clam which lives on the floor of the Arctic Ocean. Since it is so cold there, they can only survive if they live right along the edge of a deep crack in the ground, through which warm air rises in a current through an underground thermal source; however, if the clams stray too far from the thermal vent (however it is that clams can manage to perform the act of straying), they instantly freeze to death from the cold.

This is how some Germans are. Everyone needs to be warm enough, and we all get a little too hot under the collar from time to time, but some of the Germans are RIGHT ON THE EDGE, constantly, even when they are happily gardening or chatting over cards, and the slightest thing sometimes seems capable of pushing them over.

So here's the warning: don't get lulled into a false sense of peacefulness when you hear that sweet violin that rings out from a German soul as they greet you and chat about the beautiful trees, for at any moment – depending upon the subtle balance within that particular individual, if their viewpoint is challenged or if they feel their firm hold on their sense of order slipping (and, therefore, security is perceived by them to be shaken) – you might hear those resounding chords again… "TA-TA-TA-tuuuuuuum…"

In fact, Heinrich Heine, the subject of that lonely, dark statue, once warned us all to beware of "the German Thunder". He said that way back in the 19th century, long before either of the World Wars, and before the horrors of the Holocaust were even possible to imagine. Even before that time, when the Germans were known as romantic poets and crystal clear thinkers, the Thunder was noticeable, as an ever present undercurrent.

The Germans are very much like their weather – in some cases, and in some moments, you can bask in the warm sun, you can enjoy the fresh, cool breeze – but remember to heed the ancient warning, and beware of "the German Thunder"!

The Playground Incident

The mail box out front squeals open. Instead of the usual "Clump" sound of envelopes falling into it, there is a general rustling about and the sound of footsteps receding quickly.

'It's late for a mail delivery', I think to myself. At the sink, I clean the paint off my hands as well as possible (we've been renovating a few rooms, now that we've finally settled into the new house) and I go outside to check the mail.

Among the advertisements and the professional looking envelop from the electricity company, which must have been delivered earlier, there is a loose half-sheet of paper curled up, as if it is shy among the other pieces of mail.

There is a faded coat-of-arms as a watermark across the background of the entire sheet, along with bold font that states "Dear Rucklingsdorfers" across the top.

'So, that's the Rucklingsdorf coat-of-arms', I think to myself. It looks impressive, at first blush, but when I look a little closer at it, I see that it is only a shield with a few sprouts of some vegetable crops, surrounding a horse's head in three-quarter profile.

'We'll, that's appropriate', I think.

Under the rather large greeting, there is a tremendous amount of text, in astoundingly small font, like legal text, as though the person who wrote it doesn't want anyone to really know what is stated there.

It has clearly been prepared by someone at home on their personal computer (most certainly Kerstin

Stempelkauer, who is generally the driving force behind such revolutionary movements like this in the town). There is a lot of ink build-up on one side of the border of the paper, as if the printer jet had been clogged.

In the text, I can make out the German words for "together", "our town", "take part", "our children", and a few others.

Squinting, I manage to decipher that the leaflet is a call to all of the "Dear Rucklingsdorfers" to participate on the coming Saturday (today is already Thursday) in the creation of a playground on the lawn of "The Golden Mule" (the big restaurant and hotel that is also sometimes used as a kind of a town hall and for any other community events). "For the sake of our children", it says.

There's also a telephone number in small font buried in the middle of the text, and "interested participants" are asked to call to "provide notification of their plan to attend the event".

It has been a pretty hectic period for me, what with all the renovations at home, on top of the regular work week.

'I'm pretty busy', I say to myself. Then I read the text again, and when I get to "For the sake of our children", my resistance has been worn down.

'Well, I can't very well ignore them when they ask me to help them like this. And for the children', I think. 'You *have* to help the children.'

Even though my girlfriend and I don't have any children of our own, I imagine the other little boys and girls from the village, standing in the gutter, staring at a vacant patch of grass, perhaps overgrown with weeds, with the tall boy amongst them holding a ball, and then a car rushing buy and just swerving to miss them.

'OK, that's it', I decide. 'I'll be there'.

'They need me', I think. 'The children as well as the other people in town. After all, we'll all neighbors... and they were so nice about it in sending this letter to me, inviting me, including me, wanting me to be part of them...

"Dear Rucklingsdorfers", I read again at the top.

'And I'm one of them. What a wonderful town this is'.

———————

Later that day, I call the phone number that's printed on the leaflet to tell them that I'll be glad to help them out.

The phone rings, and rings a few more times, and when the fourth ring is suddenly interrupted... there is a long pause.

Peculiarly long.

And then there is a quiet, factual recital of the name "Stempelkauer" by a female voice. The lack of any modulation in the voice is noticeable and surprising, considering the number of syllables in the long name. It sounds as if she has picked up the phone, then looked suspiciously to the left, surveyed the scene, then flicked her eyes suddenly to the right, and then stated "Stempelkauer", as if about to relay a coded message from the underground to the front lines.

After a moment of adjustment, I say, "Hello, Ms. Stempelkauer," and I state my name.

After I wait for some sort of expression of welcome or reception, which I am used to from phone calling in other countries, I hear… silence. There is no, "Oh, hi, I'm so glad you called", or "Well, what a pleasant surprise. How are you doing over there?"

No, just silence, followed by a tentative and rather uncertain "Hello", but it has been painfully delayed by this time.

"I wanted to let you know that I'll be glad to help out Saturday with the playground", I say proudly, with a certain glee and optimism in my voice.

There is another pause.

'Maybe her phone is broken', I think, although I know at this point that this is not the problem.

"Oh", she says, before pausing again, as though she does not know exactly what to do with *this* particular kind of information, which she evidently had not at all expected.

"That's nice of you", she says, as if forcing the words to come out.

I wonder, 'Is someone there holding you hostage, Ms. Stempelkauer? Are you bound to a chair by rope, with your captor holding the phone to your ear and a gun to your head? Shall I call for help?!'

We say goodbye, and after I hang up, I wonder if perhaps it is a little too much at one time for these local people if a person from another country (a *foreigner*, an *unknown*) enters their world like this and helps them in a community event.

I look at the leaflet that I've been holding while I call.

'But they made all that effort to deliver this paper to my door directly… well, to my mailbox, anyway', I think.

I read over parts of the leaflet again.

'They *asked* me to help. They *begged* me'.

Then I remind myself that I'm living in a different culture.

'Maybe I'm just be misreading the situation', I think. 'They're country people. Maybe they're just a little shy, that's all.'

"Dear Rucklingsdorfers", I read again.

'Besides, it's for the children. I can't *not* help children. What kind of person would I be to not help children have a place to play?'

…and so I decide to participate.

———————

When I get up early on Saturday, the muscles in my back are still sore from all of the renovations at home, but I put the work clothes that I've been using to paint back on anyway, take a shovel from the garden and head down the street to the Golden Mule.

The sun has already been up for a while. It's bright out, but pleasantly cool, and the birds seem to be very satisfied about the way the day is unfolding.

I am aware that I am smiling as I walk along, and as I come to the Golden Mule, there is nobody to be seen. I pull on the door, and it is locked. There's no sign on the door other than "Open" (which had not been flipped to "Closed" at the end of the night last last) and no evidence of any congregation of people or activity of any kind.

'They said Saturday, didn't they? Did I miss it?', I ask myself, sure that I must have overlooked something. 'It can't be over already.'

Then I remember that this is farm country, and some of these people rise at 5:00 in the morning six days a week, permitting themselves to lounge in bed dissolutely until 6:00 once a week only because it's Sunday.

'Well, I have a lot to do, anyway'. I put the shovel on my shoulder and turn home, heading the other way around the block, past a small group of houses which look more or less identical to each other.

As I go, I start thinking about what to do with those floorboards in the bedroom.

Down a little ways, I notice a bunch of people moving around like ants in some well-integrated process. They seem to be working comfortably with each other, and there is a sense of peaceful productivity about the whole thing. It is clearly some kind of event, and as I approach, I see that they have shovels and other tools, and there has already been some digging.

'It's them', I realize, and I smile openly, looking forward to spending a lively afternoon working together with my neighbors to make a valuable contribution to the village – *our* village.

As I arrive, the people facing in my direction stop in the middle of a conversation they are clearly enjoying and look in my direction, and their pleasant facial expressions instantly disappear.

The man they have been talking to is wearing denim overalls. He has his back to me, and as they stop and look, he turns his head and watches me approaching, in my work clothes, smiling to them.

"Hi", I say, full of anticipation. "Are you guys working on the new playground?", still not sure why they would be so far away from The Golden Mule, where the work is supposed to take place.

The man in the overalls just keeps staring at me, over his shoulder, with his back still turned to me. He looks as if I have just insulted his grandmother.

In the void of human interchange, I kick-start the conversation by adding, "I got your leaflet, and I'm ready to help".

There has been no movement on the other side – no smiling, no blinking, and their fingers are frozen in place around their tools.

Then, the guy in the overalls says to me, "Those rocks over there have to be put in that trailer."

He says it like an accusation.

When he makes the statement, he points with his finger towards a pile of rocks, but nothing else about him changes, and he is still staring at me, as if to see what I do next.

I look at the pile near the trailer. Nobody else is anywhere near it, and it is clear that nobody has started shoveling the rocks yet.

He apparently expects me to run over and to work, alone, at the most unpleasant job that's available and which everyone else has so far avoided, while they stand and continue chatting.

There has also not been any sign of welcoming or appreciation from them of any sort.

I just stand there, and look back at him. He seems surprised that his command has not been immediately followed, but I don't care.

I see Ms. Stempelkauer not far away, and I walk over and greet her.

"Oh, you came", she says, upon seeing me – not pleasantly, exactly, rather more as an observation.

"Yes", I reply. "Is this where the playground is going to be put in?"

"Yes, right here, up to that incline there."

"I thought it was going to be put in at The Golden Mule."

"Well, this land here is part of The Golden Mule property."

And then she explains that the land for The Golden Mule used to extend straight from the building all the way to this plot, a long time ago.

As the story goes, Wolfbert Hauchgeruch, who came from "an old family" (as Kerstin Stempelkauer puts it), had inherited the building and all of the land in The Golden Mule estate. When he retired, he said he wanted to sell out and go live near his daughter, who had married a man from Baden-Württemberg and lived in the South of the country. Well, the Town Council (that is, six guys from Rucklingsdorf) told him that the town might be interested in buying The Golden Mule, as long as the price was reasonable.

There were a lot of arguments back and forth about the numbers, and a little ill will developed. Then, to the surprise of the members of the Town Council, Wolfbert suddenly agreed to sell beneath his price.

The man who was the mayor of Rucklingsdorf at that time ('They have a mayor here?', I think to myself) went with Wolfbert to the lawyer, and everything was all settled.

That's what everybody thought, anyway, until the work trucks started appearing.

It turned out that although Wolfbert Hauchgeruch had indeed sold the building of The Golden Mule to the town, he had been negotiating with a developer from the city to buy the open land the whole time, behind their backs.

Wolfbert wanted to sell all the land from here to The Mule to the developer, but the developer wasn't interested in this plot, because of that incline over there (without looking, Kerstin Stempelkauer gestures with her thumb towards a sharp, stony mound jutting out of the ground behind her and to the left).

Then she takes a slow, deep breath, as if in a kind of mourning, and explains that Wolfbert had managed to sell the land in between this plot and The Golden Mule to the developer ("*that* developer" is how she says it).

"I guess the mayor back then didn't read over the papers as closely as he should have", she says. "Wolfbert apparently got a pretty good price, because he bought a big place there down south."

I imagine palm trees and flamingos, and then I remember that Kerstin Stempelkauer is referring to the south of Germany.

"Well, the houses went up, and they sold like hotcakes", she concludes, staring hard at the houses in the new development as she says so.

"But this plot here still belongs to us and The Golden Mule", she adds, changing to a tone of defensive optimism and victory.

She seems to be glad that I listened to her while she told her story.

The other guys have meanwhile gotten back to work, and I join a couple of them digging out a big boulder in the middle of the field.

"I hope we don't find somebody digging back up at us", I say to the guy next to me, and he chuckles spontaneously, although without looking up at me, and then he just returns to his work quietly.

'Well, at least I know he can understand me', I say to myself in consolation.

After we're done, a little bit later on, a truck rolls up and a few guys go to it and start taking out bags of sand from the back. I join them, and we are all working like a well-oiled machine, walking down one side of the field carrying the bags, and then returning along a path a few feet away, so as to stay out of the way of the other line of workers who are just loading up.

As I'm walking back to the truck, I start up conversation with the guy walking behind me, but he responds as minimally as possible, and he doesn't look up once from the ground to make eye contact with me.

It's not that he says anything negative, exactly. He's just not participating with me in the dialogue, and it's as though the minimal response is more extreme and less personal than if he were to be confrontational. After all, aggression involves acknowledging the presence of one's adversary. This cold ignoring of one's existence is even worse.

'For people making a playground, they're not playing very well', I say to myself.

After the sandbags have been emptied out of the truck, a couple of the guys go over and talk with the man in the denim overalls about what has to get done next.

As I'm standing there near the edge of the property, a young woman holding hands with a small child walks up from the road, more or less right to where I am.

"Hello", I say, looking right at her and smiling. We are two feet away from each other.

"Hello", she says, without making eye contact and as if the greeting is a responsibility to be done with.

Then, she starts to look behind me, on all sides of where I am standing, as though tracing the outline of the space I am in with her eyes. Her head moves around from one side of me to the next, like someone trying to see around another person who is sitting in front of them at a sports event – except that we are directly facing each other.

She is apparently trying to find someone in the group of workers and has absolutely no interest in speaking with me, although we have never met.

She does this with the child still holding her hand next to her.

"For the sake of our children", I remember reading in the leaflet the other day.

'This is one of the mothers whose children I am here to help by installing a playground', I think to myself, 'and she doesn't even care to acknowledge that I exist!'

Then I see Kerstin Stempelkauer nearby, and we start talking again.

As we're chatting, we both notice that all the other people who are there to work this morning (they are all men except for Kerstin Stempelkauer) are gathered in a semicircle, talking and laughing easily together, a few steps away from where she and I are standing.

She raises her voice a little bit and says to them, "I don't know if you have all officially met our new neighbor here."

"Hello", I say warmly, and I smile and walk over to them as I tell them my name.

Then, I stand there in front of them – and they all just look back at me, silently.

No names are offered, not a single word of greeting. There is not the slightest sign of a smile, and they stare at me as if they suspect me of stealing something from them.

One of the guys picks up the conversation where it left off, and they all start talking with each other again, warmly and easily, but not a single one of these statements is offered to me. Nobody asks me anything, and not once does anybody make eye contact with me or smile kindly to me while something is said.

It's as if they are passing a ball back and forth between each other, and nobody bothers themselves to ever pass it to the new guy.

It's too late and awkward now for me to walk away from them, so I just stand there, leaning on my shovel with the tip of the handle in my palms.

I watch the conversation, completely and utterly disregarded in this group of human being I have come to help today at their request.

I consider jumping into the dialogue myself by responding to something or another that one of the other men says.

For some reason, though, in spite of my having listened to countless hours of audio books in German over the years, I realize that I cannot understand a thing the other men are saying. When I notice this, I make the effort to catch individual words, sentence fragments, but every word from every one of the speakers is indecipherable to me.

I stand there in front of them, more thoroughly alone than I have ever been in my life. I start to slump in embarrassment, and I become painfully aware that it will not be possible for me to hide completely behind the handle of the shovel, which suddenly seems extremely thin to me.

Kerstin Stempelkauer appears nearby, and she and I return to talking together. It is obvious that she realizes what has just happened, and that I have been blatantly excluded from the group.

We carry on our discussion for a few exchanges, and after a while, I see two men in the distance behind her, walking to the back of a house nearby. They are still talking cordially with each other, smiling, looking in each other's eyes, and responding with interest to each other. I see one open the garden gate for the other to walk through, before he enters as well and shuts the gate quietly behind himself.

He did not look in this direction before he disappeared. He did not wave.

I look around, and notice that the men are all gone, apparently behind the gate now, enjoying a little socializing after a busy morning.

Kerstin Stempelkauer sees me looking at the gate.

"We're going to have a little coffee", she informs me. "I don't imagine you want to come." It is stated as further information, and not at all like an invitation.

The answer she is clearly expecting from me is "no".

I would like to just go home and write the entire event off as a social failure on their part – but I have been asked to join them (in spite of Kerstin Stempelkauer's idea of social graces).

If I turn down the offer, then *I* will be the one drawing the line between us, *I* will be in the position of being rude by rejecting offered hospitality, even though I know that the offer is bogus – and that is just not something a person does (not where I'm from, anyway).

"OK", I say, and the skinny face across from me is visibly disappointed, even worried about the fact that I will apparently be joining them in the garden.

As I walk through the gate, I see that all the men from before are seated around a big picnic table under an awning. It's a very cozy setting, but they all look up at me and say absolutely nothing, making it clear that they did not expect me to come along with them this far.

A few of the guys talk back and forth, looking at each other in the eyes with easy attention as they do so.

Then, one of them turns to me and speaks to me for the first time, straight-faced, saying, 'That's where my wife usually sits.'

… and they all bust out laughing, all staring at me now with their mouths open and their heads bobbing up and down. Not a single person is looking away now, and the laughter has that harsh, aggressive tone that men's laughter can have when they're in a group. One of them is actually pointing at me while he laughs.

'Suddenly, they're interested in recognizing me', I think, 'when they've found a way to try to degrade me.'

The laughter doesn't die down right away, even though what the guy said wasn't very funny. It's as if they've been looking for a reason and are glad that they have found one, no matter how good an excuse it is.

"Well, she obviously isn't here right now", I say coolly, looking at some of them in the eye turn by turn.

Then, the laughter dies down immediately, like a stone being dropped. It is obviously clear to them that they are not dealing with an easy target, but rather a moving target, and they are not sure in which direction I might go next.

They return to talking with each other, but try as I might, I am simply not able to follow the conversation.

I think of the grade I received on that German language test I took so many years ago, a test that these local people might not even be able to pass. It established that I would be able to use German proficiently in professional and academic situations.

Kerstin Stempelkauer is looking at me, and she seems to feel bad for me. She whispers something to the guy sitting next to her, and he looks down at the floor and frowns. She keeps looking at him, and then he says to me, "So, why did you move here to Rucklingsdorf, anyway?".

Despite the stunning crudeness of the question, I tell him and the group cordially where I'm from and that my girlfriend and I have just moved into our house down the road.

While I am talking, the entire group is silent, silent as death, and every single one of the others are listening in full and undivided attention to what I say, with all eyes suddenly upon me.

After I finish, there is a rather long pause, and the man who asked the question turns away from me and says to the guy across from him, "Well that doesn't answer the question", and they both laugh together, with a few from elsewhere in the group joining in.

Then he turns away, not having said anything further to me, and the group returns to their dialogue.

I look across the table at Kerstin Stempelkauer, and there is a look of embarrassment in her face.

While the chatter goes on without my being able to follow it, I wonder about the language situation.

'Wait a minute', I realize, 'I understood what that rude jerk said to me just fine. And he obviously had no problem understanding me, based on what he said.'

Then I run through my efforts to talk with the others while we were working.

'And that man with the brown flannel shirt there to the left laughed naturally when I said what I did about someone else digging his way back up to us', I remember.

Then it hits me.

'Are these people speaking dialect?'

Like elsewhere in Germany, a lot of the long-time residents of Rucklingsdorf are able to speak a local dialect, usually (but not always) along with actual High German.

In English speaking countries, a very broken version of English is often spoken in poor areas where the people tend not to be very well educated. It's still English, just with lots of errors and mispronunciations.

German dialects are different. They are not just poorly spoken versions of German. They each actually consist of their own different words. They have different vocabulary, different grammar, and are absolutely not the same language as actual High German, like Germans speak in public. Educated Germans, or even Germans who speak their own local dialects, often have trouble understanding the dialect spoken in a different region.

'They *must* have heard that I am from another country, in a little village like this. Kerstin Stempelkauer would have told them after I called her, if nothing else. And they can certainly tell that my German isn't perfect, that I have an accent.'

'Can these people actually be sitting here and talking with each other in their local dialect, purposefully leaving me out of the conversation?'

The possibility stuns me.

'After I have sacrificed my time, with everything else that I have to do? After I have helped them, at their request, to install a playground in the town? So that their children can have a place to play?'

I can't believe that anybody would be so rude and inconsiderate to another human being, particularly with no motivation – and after that person has sacrificed his time and effort to help them, after they asked for help.

This is a low point of human civilization that I had never experienced before – until today, here in Rucklingsdorf, Germany.

'I already knew that people could lie to each other, steal from each other, even murder each other – but this today doesn't even have any selfish benefit in it... other than mere exclusion...'

... and I stumble upon it.

Exclusion.

Belonging. The security of belonging.

The sense of security that comes from excluding others.

I think of the white racists in the American south and the black people they burned and hung from trees. Of the racism in the factories and day-to-day life in the north there.

I think of the Holocaust and the people who were tortured and murdered.

I think of the people of this town, who asked their neighbors to help them build a playground in their village, so that their own children could have a place to play, and who did everything they possibly could to make sure that an outsider who mistakenly came to help them was excluded, and knew it, and that it hurt.

I think of a photo I saw once of a Jewish woman cowering in the street in the 1930s. She had been stripped naked, shoved down to the ground, and was surrounded by her German neighbors, who were standing there, encircling her, laughing.

Not so much has changed here in the charming little village of Rucklingsdorf, Germany – except that now they have a new playground.

Germans on the Job

Like butterflies studied more closely under a microscope, the Germans in their various iterations as "worker" display a multitude of diverse characteristics.

Let's take a look at the engineers.

Ah, the German engineers.

Where would modern civilization be without them? And where would the German economy be without them? While not exactly the *life blood* of Germany, they are more the hard, rigid bones that compose its skeletal system, enabling the country to hold itself upright.

After talking with the average German engineer ("Actually, we all scored far above average on our university exams, and therefore it is not exactly precise to say…") – after talking with them, one thing becomes clear: it is hard to tell the difference between the typical German engineer and the machines that he designs.

There are exceptions, of course. Occasionally, there is a sociable engineer who is no less capable with conversation and relating to other people than he is with numbers and formulae. For the most part, though, they are very similar to the character of Spock from Star Trek.

I have often wondered what German engineers (as well as most Germans) first thought when they saw that character of Spock. I would expect a reaction like, "Now *there* is an excellent model of how a person should be. Streamlined, efficient, not bogged down with all of those sticky, syrupy… what do they call them? Oh, yes, of course… emotions. It's too bad that he has to deal with those rather hysterical people running about him and getting into all sorts of trouble episode after episode because of their, their... *feel*ings."

It might be surprising to such a Germanic engineer that people from other countries see Spock as a being who is handicapped, a tragic figure, one who survives and produces but who never really lives; who can calculate the expulsion rate of the jet turbo engines so as to ensure that they travel in their spaceship as efficiently as possible but who can never really appreciate the moonlight reflecting off of the tips of the stars as they do so.

One thing is certain – you will never accidentally mistake a German engineer for a young girl picking flowers in a sunny meadow ("Why should the flowers be picked? They should stay where they are so that the bees can cross-pollinate them, and then there will be more food for people, so they can do more work and build more machinery").

There are fuzzy little kittens with big, soulful eyes, and there are German engineers. They are not the same thing.

Then, there is the German office worker.

While not as painfully and disturbingly rigid as the German engineers, they are also not anywhere near as productive ("The representative German engineer is productive at a rate per capita of...").

A German office on Monday morning will generally be populated with pairs or small groups of three standing around and regurgitating the more prominent moments of the latest soccer or European football game, as well as a mutual explanation of who did what where over the weekend and how great it was (regardless of how great it might actually have been).

It's not a surreptitious kind of conversation, either, stolen in moments at the copy machine or at the water cooler, as though they are worried about being caught while not being productive at the workplace.

There is a surprising sense of leisure among German office workers so soon after they have returned from their weekends and resumed their workweek, and there is a sense that they really shouldn't have to be there at the office at all again, as though the entire thing is just a big inconvenience, a burden mistakenly placed upon them by those people who expect them, *them*, to actually perform something as mundane as *working*. There is something uniquely socialist about their attitude on Monday morning, as though they expect that their government should find a way to divide everything up more effectively so that they can pursue their natural born right to devote their time, their valuable personal time, to the subtle art of watching more football.

This Monday morning coffee chatter can go on for a surprisingly long while, after which a supervisor might pass by and say, "Lukas, have you finished that report yet?" (after the supervisor has finished *his* respective coffee chatter about the football game and the weekend events, of course).

"Oh, Scheiße!", the worker will then erupt, with panic in his eyes, to then rush to his desk, rummaging wildly among his papers and banging frenetically at his computer keyboard, trying to complete the report that he could have finished on Friday, if he had not spent the hours of 3:00 to 4:30 on Friday afternoon talking about how great the next football game was going to be and what he was going to do where and with whom over the coming weekend. He then places himself under tremendous pressure to fulfill his duties promptly and properly, to the point of exhaustion, and he is already burnt out by the time the first lunch hour of the week arrives (entirely avoidably, of course, if he had merely managed his time more evenly).

If you have a company and you want to launch a new product on the market to crush your German competition, do it between 9:00 and 10:30 a.m. on a Monday. They won't even see it coming.

Now, if you should happen to find yourself in the woefully unfortunate position of needing to contact a German office worker to get some form or service from them during a week when there happens to be a holiday approaching, then you might as well put on your comfortable pants and take out that 800-page novel you've been wanted to get to but never found the time for.

The German bridge day is used as an excuse for a surprising degree of deviation from that responsibility and productivity that the Germans are otherwise famous for.

Let's say that you have been exchanging emails with an office worker, a certain Frau Schmidt, and you need to receive a signed form back from her by a certain deadline so that you don't become evicted and have to live in the street fighting with the pigeons over bread crumbs to survive.

Of course, if the holiday falls on a Friday or a Monday, the extended weekend is made use of, and nobody is there in the office but the one desperate and wholly uninformed intern at the bottom of the food chain who, in spite of Herculean efforts, simply cannot accommodate your request, perhaps because she does not have the little key to the cabinet in which Frau Schmidt keeps the rubber stamp that is needed to complete your form. Even if that is the sole act that is necessary for Frau Schmidt to perform, your document will sit there, sweating and shaking, until Frau Schmidt returns from her spa weekend and unshackles it, stamps it, and sends it along in the mail (after 10:30 on the first morning back, of course, following coffee and a discussion of the past wonders she experienced over the extended weekend).

Now, if the bridge day happens to be on a Thursday, clearly Friday will be used as an opportunity to apply one of the worker's available vacation days, and the one vacation day will be multiplied, like loaves and fishes, into two.

If the bridge day falls on a Wednesday, though, something magical happens, which seems to defy all rules of logic and mathematics.

Since the free day is in the middle of the week, a person could take of Thursday and Friday if they have enough vacation days remaining (or, they might suddenly develop a spontaneous elbow rash, which they're afraid might spread to their lungs if they don't take care of it right away).

Then, of course, there are those two other days remaining at the beginning of the week, that Monday and Tuesday.

"They're *just* two little days. How much can be accomplished in two little days like that? Especially with the holiday on Wednesday. Some people, somewhere, are surely going to be taking the first two days of the week free while I take the last two days of the week free, so nothing will really be able to get done, anyway. It would be *silly* to come into the office on Monday and Tuesday, since I will not be coming on Thursday and Friday after the holiday on Wednesday (my elbow rash, you know. I wouldn't want it to cause an epidemic). I would just be sitting around, and then they would be paying me to just sit around, and *that's just not right.* Why, it's not *fair*. I *have* to take the whole week off, since there's a holiday on Wednesday. If I don't, what kind of person would I be?"

And if you send in your form on the previous Friday for Frau Schmidt to stamp and sign, you will have to wait an abundant nine-day weekend (plus the first hour and a half of the next Monday) for her to return, open that little cabinet of hers, take out the rubber stamp and ensure that you do not become homeless. Notice the amount and degree of stress that you, the customer, can be forced to endure while Frau Schmidt enjoys her vacation, all due to one free day on Wednesday.

And as if just to rub it in, before Frau Schmidt goes on her extended holiday of pleasures, she might or might not take it upon herself to click that single, tiny little button that switches on her absence email while she is away. As a result, you might or might not just be sitting for nine torturous days – waiting, wondering, hoping, buuuurning – and trying to convince yourself "Maybe *today* is the day. I'll check my email just *one* more time this hour to see if she has responded to my... rrrrrrrrrghh!", and your salvation might still be more than a week away yet, for all you know, you mere customer.

Now, the same thing with holidays basically happens in the summer, just on a larger scale. If you ever wanted to sell your house and move to another country for a few weeks, explore volcanoes in Fiji or get a license to fly small planes, the summer is the time to do it.

I don't know how many people endure life-altering tragedies because offices grind to a halt for two and a half months in the middle of the year in Germany and are not there to handle correspondence.

Along with that, there are a couple of holidays scattered throughout nearly each month, like pepper and salt here and there, depending upon the region, some of them even impeding the national economy and scientific progress because of something involving ghosts.

The end of the year brings Christmas and New Year's, of course, and after the annual budget has been expended, not a lot really happens in January and February, to speak of.

And then, there are the school holidays in the autumn (immediately after school has just started, ironically, as if the Germans are training their children early for the self-indulgent scheduling of their future work lives, and to ensure that they do not accidentally develop that crude and unhealthy habit of showing up regularly). Each separate state in Germany has a different schedule for the school holidays, too, so overall, September and October are hit and miss, at best, when it comes to reaching all of your customers or suppliers, acquiring that artificial kidney, and so on.

As a result, we are left with one, single month of productivity in Germany: November.

Except for the Rhineland, that is, where November is the month when they start to celebrate Carnival.

Oh, just forget it. There is not one single month in Germany when everybody gets together and decides, "You know, why don't we all go to work together at the same time, and *stay* there. How would that be, do you think?"

And yet somehow, Germany is often at the forefront of the international economy. Just imagine the intense degree of focus and productivity that those Germans exercise on those collective eight hours of those three days per year when they actually appear at work and perform.

Incredible.

This balance of high tension and lackadaisical ease in the German work schedule is just another expression of that part of the German soul that is at war with itself; the little child in them who wants to just smile and play as the cool wind blows, and the firm dictator in their heads that shouts, "No! You will work and produce, NOW!"

And so Düsseldorf has its millionaires, and the houses in Munich are purchased for prices amounting to what some people earn in a lifetime.

That must be one hell of a three days.

That's the situation with German office workers. If you ever have the pleasure of witnessing a German tradesman in action, you will truly come to understand the meaning of the word "miracle".

There seems to be a sense of responsibility and high standard in their work that goes back to the time of Charlemagne and which has not yet been polluted by cell phone downloads and Kim Kardashian videos.

If you hire a German to build something out of wood or to install a piece of porcelain in your bathroom, you will be rewarded with stunningly effective, pristine quality of the highest degree.

Again, there are always exceptions, but generally speaking, German tradesmen are Germans at their best.

After a fence is taken down from your garden, for example, you will see the separate parts of the old fence piled evenly at the curb, with the edges of what is now garbage perfectly aligned with each other, with not a single edge protruding from the overall block, ready to be collected by a truck in due time. On the table in the garden, there will be a series of piles, as if an animal had crouched and deposited them there, one after another: one pile for the angular pieces of hardware that held the wood together, and then others for the screws, categorized according to thread width and degree of wear: one pile for the long screws that can be used again, another for the smaller screws that can be used again, and a forth pile for all the screws which are too rusty, each pile being centrally located upon its own individual little square piece of paper (where they get the pieces of paper from, I do not know) so that the piles do not soil your nice, clean table top.

If you have your cement terrace retiled, you will see similar piles: one for the old tiles which are unbroken and could easily be reused, one for the larger fragments of old tiles, and another pile for the smaller fragments which are not large enough to be categorized into the previous pile. And they will all be spaced equidistantly from one another, most often on a patch of dirt so that they do not inhibit the photosynthesis of the grass blades in your lawn.

You will see these signs of highly focused productivity erected before you, but as you hold the tray of coffee cups, eager to be a good host to the people who have worked so hard for the sake of your pretty little garden, you will stand there, alone, with the coffee cups and the tray in your hands, because the German tradesmen of stunning precision and high-quality performance will have left, immediately upon completing their duty, without having said a word to you, having informed you that the project has been completed or that they would be going, like dutiful robots who have not been programmed for human interchange outside of their crew (and a bill for the agreed price will arrive later in the mail).

Oh, and *never* thank a German. Whether an office worker, a tradesman, or any variation on the general model, the response will usually be a stern pair of steady eyes and the comment, "Of course! It's my *job!*", as if you have insulted them, as if, by thanking them, you have raised the dim possibility that they might have considered *not* performing their duty, and that you are surprised that they have actually displayed the respectable character to do so to the contrary, a surprising turn of events for which you are now thanking them.

So, *never* thank a German. It's not very polite of you.

The Doorman

There is a big social event at The Golden Mule tonight. While I get myself ready, I remind myself not to dress too fancy, since it seems to make the people here a bit uncomfortable.

There's a big crowd, and as I walk up the two cement steps out front, there is a woman directly behind me, and I hold the door for her, smiling politely to her as I do so.

To my surprise, she just walks through the door and ignores me, as though it is completely normal that I should stand there and hold the door while she enters.

As I turn to begin entering as well, a man follows close behind her and walks into the building, while I continue holding the door. He doesn't acknowledge that I am there, either.

'Her husband, perhaps", I think to myself.

And as I rotate slightly once again to enter, I find that there is a steady stream of Germans, marching in through the door one after the other, while I stand there and hold it.

Not one of them looks at me, not one of them says thank you, and none of them show the kindness of taking the door from me in turn and holding it politely to wait for me to enter before them.

After they have entered, I stand there holding the door, alone.

Then, I close the door softly and turn around.

'It's a good night for reading', I think to myself, and I walk home.

Guests from Abroad

Again, there was the sound of a squeaking mailbox followed by a rustling about on the front porch and the sound of footsteps receding quickly.

I went out right away but there was already nobody in sight.

'How does she get away so quickly?', I wondered, admiring her skills.

This time, Kerstin Stempelkauer had deposited a bright red sheet of paper, almost glowing, like a warning alarm. It informed the "Dear Rücklingdorfers" of a change that would soon be upon them.

The Town Council (it stated) had been informed by the State Social Services Department that a family of asylum seekers would be housed in "our town" starting on the first of June. They were going to be living at 31 Schnausastrasse.

"That's the Maier's place", my girlfriend said. "They haven't been able to rent it out for a while."

It would be a family with eight children, from East Bekistan, according to the leaflet.

"They can't even handle the fact that *we're* here", I said. "How are they going to deal with *this*?!"

Throughout the town over the next few days, a lot of phone calls were made, followed by a tremendous amount of coffee and cake being consumed, during which time this new shock to the system of Rucklingsdorf society was digested.

After a period of disturbing quiet, like before a storm cloud breaks open, the frenzy began of ensuring that these visitors to our town, these poor, unfortunate souls ("Did they say *eight* children?") would have absolutely no excuse to say that they had not been taken care of effectively and properly in the town of Rucklingsdorf during their stay in Germany.

Clothing was collected, dolls were donated, clothing for the dolls was donated (and, in one case, sewn by hand), a direct line of communication with the State Social Services Department was established, and a carpool schedule was organized to ensure that the children could be transported safely back and forth to school.

It was quite a whirlwind to see, this rousing up of a population in the accomplishment of a common goal, and a few hundred souls from among the village spent countless hours each week to ensure that these two parents and their eight children ("Did they say *eight* children?") were made to feel at home while they were here, by any means necessary.

The day the truck from the charity organization came and delivered the domestic essentials of pots, pans and so forth, there was already a noticeably thicker stream of people who had decided that it was a nice day to take a walk (in spite of the drizzle), perhaps past that nice little growth of birch trees, "You know, the one around the corner from the Maier's place".

As the locals passed the rented house, there was a lot of looking down at the street, and then suddenly peering as deeply as possible into the windows, before just as quickly looking back at the asphalt.

After a few weeks, the father sat outside, drinking his tea, alone, with his legs crossed. He was sitting in a green-upholstered chair that he had dragged out from the dining room.

When the first people passed him, his eyes suddenly sharpened and he had a look of fear. He griped his tea cup and saucer and his legs uncrossed, almost as if he was getting prepared to flee... but then there was a friendly "Moin" and a wave from the couple, and the man waved back and said "Hello" in English. As they turned the corner, his face melted into a look of warm relief.

After a few days, I saw him in his chair with his tea as I was walking back from the post office, and after a wave and a hello, he said "Komm" and gestured for me to join him with an inviting smile on his face.

We then greeted each other up close and shook hands, and I felt welcome immediately. The man clearly appreciated that someone had stopped for a visit.

There was the basic exchanging of names and the explaining of where I lived in town. Everything was performed with a lot of gesturing, like two emotional sign language interpreters in a bubble next to a newscast.

He held up his cup and asked "Tea?", clearly offering to get me some, although it looked as though he was asking if I wanted a sip from his cup.

I accepted, and as he went to get my tea, there were a lot of arm movements as he raised his forefinger and patted the air in front of him, saying some words in his own language which apparent meant "Wait here. Don't go".

He came back balancing the tea carefully on a little wooden tray with a bright floral blue and red pattern, and he offered the tea to me as if it was the key to his front door.

The cup was very small, more like an espresso cup, and as he placed the tray on the ground, he suddenly noticed that there was only one chair on the patio. He looked around from place to place as if trying to desperately find an escape hole in a prison cell and, finding no other option, he offered me his chair, with a gesture of a waiter in a very high-scale restaurant.

I politely declined and pointed the cup and saucer to my feet, which I stamped lightly up and down to show him that I was glad to stand, while I said so in German.

He persisted, though, patting the chair and saying "Du, zitzen" with an open smile.

His hospitality was like a warm wind, and it was clear that he would find it an offence if I were to decline, so I thanked him and sat down in the chair.

He looked around again a few times, and then just seemed to resign himself to the situation and stood next to me. We sipped out tea together with him standing there at my side, and we chatted around the language barrier.

As people passed, they waved and said hello, and then they stared closely with a confused look in their faces, as if trying to decipher what this situation could mean to them.

I imagined what might be running through their minds.

'Why is the American sitting in that chair with the refugee standing at his side? Is that his body guard?'

'Did the American hire him to stand there?'

'Do they know each other from before? They *are* both from somewhere else. Maybe they already met before they got here.'

My host didn't seem to mind at all, and he smiled back to the passers by, proud for others in his new home to see that he had his first guest.

Over the next few weeks, as he drank his tea alone on his new patio, people began to stop and chat with him (mostly with gestures and a few basic words in German), and he offered them a chair he had found in the garage and which he had pulled out for just this purpose.

The locals never wanted to sit in the chair at first, rejecting the offer with an anxious waving of hands, as if to wipe the offer away.

Their host was persistent, though, as if he assumed that this was part of a kind of ritual to the hospitality here and that the people actually intended to sit after making the polite show that they did not want to stay (when in reality, they actually did *not* want to stay).

It would be one thing if they were to both stand in the street together and chat (that would be O.K.), but this was different.

It always got to the point at which leaving would be even more awkward for the local passer-by than actually accepting the warm hospitality, and so they sat, but it was as though they did so against their will, and not comfortably – with a stiff torso and leaning forward, sitting on the edge of the seat a bit.

Over the next week or so, it started to become expected by people who walked by the house that they would be invited to sit in the chair and have some tea from the little cups.

It's not that they started to get comfortable so soon, exactly, but they became familiar with the procedure, and they began to accept it, in their way, little by little, as something that went along with having an asylum seeker in the neighborhood.

The man's name was Hassafaromed (actually, Hassafaromed Ben-al-Halambraye).

Due to various cultural, linguistic (and perhaps intellectual) difficulties in handling the pronunciation, it became settled among the locals who visited him that he would just be called "Hassa" for short.

One person even decided once to shorten the name even further to "Hass", but since that happens to also be the German word for "hate", it was quickly realized that this just wouldn't do.

When Lars Jansen called him "Hassa" for the first time, the asylum seeker's eyes sprung open and his eyebrows plunged in the middle, as though he was prepared to defend the honor of himself and his family from a heinous insult.

What Lars did not know was that "Hassa" just happens to be a word of great and terrible significance in the language of East Bekistan.

The asylum seeker was not able to explain the matter to him, of course, and he seemed to realize just as quickly that nothing was probably meant by it, anyway, since none of the locals knew his language.

So when people passed by and raise their arms up in greeting and yelled "Hassa" at him, he just smiled and waved back warmly, and the people of Rucklingsdorf had no idea what they were shouting at this man as they passed him in front of his new home.

After a few more weeks, one of the locals sitting in the chair summoned the bravery to ask Hassa if he had any coffee, instead of tea, and since then, Hassa began to have coffee together with his local guests when they came to visit.

One of these guests to the patio, Stefan Krautjäger, asked Hassa if he was making any progress in learning German. Hassa could not understand a single word of this question, though, so he just nodded his head up and down solemnly, smiling, and saying "Ja, ja."

In response, Stefan Krautjäger started in on a long story about the subtlety of the German language, assuming that, since the man was learning German, he would probably appreciate such things.

It was a summary of the comedy routine "Der Maus Ihr Gatte" by Heinz Erhardt, in which the fine detail of the case declension of the grammatic article "die" changes to "der" due to the exact position that the word has in the sentence, among other things.

At the end of the explanation, which was presented along with a brief lesson of German syntax, the man from

East Bekistan who had been in Germany less than three weeks after having snuck with his wife and eight children, hungry, across a border in a war zone under heavy machinegun fire, just looked at Stefan Krautjäger, smiling and nodding but with an added look of confusion that the local resident did not perceive.

As a result, Stefan Krautjäger smiled proudly, quite satisfied at the telling of his story, as well as at the sheer amazingness of the German language, which he was sure his conversation partner had now clearly appreciated to its full extent.

As time went by, it was not uncommon for a visitor to appear on the patio once in a while.

Each night, before going to sleep, Hassafaromed pulled the two chairs back under the overhang, so that they would not get wet, and he pulled them back out the next day once the first visitor happened to come along.

Word of the refugee inviting people to sit and talk over coffee on his patio started to spread, of course, and it came to pass one day that Stefan Krautjäger came back, hoping to see the man outside and be offered a cup of hot coffee, like the last time, only to see that the seat had already been taken by another visitor.

Stefan Krautjäger stood and chatted for a while, and when Hassa offered to bring out another chair from the dining room, Stefan Krautjäger explained that he had to go, anyway, to which the other guest responded by standing himself and saying something similar, and the two left Hassafaromed there on the patio alone next to the empty chair.

Noticing his popularity increasing, and realizing the furnishing arrangements that this would necessitate, Hassa started to experiment with all sorts of seating possibilities.

He first dragged out a big stump from the back yard (the homeowner had cut the stump on an angle, and so whoever sat on it was always leaning upwards, to the back and noticeably to the left).

He then added an expensive-looking oak chair that he had gotten for 10 euros from the charity foundation, as well as a chair that he had hammered together himself from a few pieces of wood that he had found here and there on the property.

Three legs of this chair consisted of parts of 2-by-4's he had found in the garage, and the remaining leg was just part of a thick branch from a tree – you could see the place on the tree where he had sawed it off, raging like a stump out from the back yard among the other full branches.

The lower trunk of this tree was actually on the neighboring plot, but its branches extend onto the property that Hassafaromed and his family were living at, so there had really not been any problem in his cutting the branch off like he did.

Nevertheless, during one of his visits, Stefan Krautjäger took the opportunity to explain to the asylum seeker the finer details of land ownership and property rights in the Republic of Germany, just to prevent any misunderstandings in the future.

The four chairs and the tree stump were often full, with the conversation among the locals sometimes becoming rather lively.

During these times when they met each other on the asylum seeker's patio, they didn't usually talk so much to him, but rather just to each other, tending to rather leave him to the side to nod and smile, as he listened to them chatting with each other and drinking his coffee.

Hassa's warmth and friendliness was infectious, like a pleasant bacterium which a traveler's body is not used to and which then spreads, and the guests started to gesture a bit more and adopt the higher pitch of their host's voice from time to time.

Over the weeks, the sitting area started to spill out onto Hassa's driveway, and since the asylum seeker did not have a car, he stopped pulling the chairs in under the roof every night, leaving them instead where they were, together with the tree stump.

The chairs began to show signs of weather damage over time, and when nobody was sitting there, passers-by looked at the empty chairs and the uneven stump, all of them discarded and in disarray in the driveway, a sight which is quite peculiar in a little German town like this.

The people started to talk about the location and the event, of course, and among its frequenters, it came to be known as "Hassa's café". Later, this just got shortened to "the café", and someone might say, "Ja, I was talking with Holfart the other day at the café, and he said he heard that…"

Hassa's wife, Zaraha, usually stayed indoors, but she was as overwhelmingly hospitable as her husband whenever anybody came in to visit her.

The first in the village to experience this hospitality was one of the other mothers from the carpool when she dropped some of the children off after school.

At first, after Zaraha came to the door and welcomed her in, the other mother declined and said that it was OK for her to just stand on the front porch, as the Rucklingsdorfers tend to do.

This resulted in the asylum seeker tilting her head to the side and scowling a bit in confusion, with her warm, cow-like eyes just looking back at the other woman, as if to say, "Why? Why?"

The further protests from the woman in the carpool were met with a haphazard wave from Zaraha, as if she were trying to get rid of a fly, and she repeated, "Komm, Komm", walking into the house and gesturing behind her for her guest to follow.

After the other woman was just left standing there alone at the front door for a while, she found no other choice than to just enter, treading cautiously into this new world, a world of foreign speakers and people not just standing outside on the porch when visiting someone else, but actually entering their home, regardless of what this casual discarding of habits might lead to.

After they entered the home of the Ben-al-Halambraye's, Zaraha would always lead her guests to the dining room, where they were shown with an open hand and a smiling face to a place at the table, and before they finished explaining the reason why they had found it necessary to bother her and what they had come there to accomplish, a cup of tea on a saucer was placed before them, as if descended from heaven.

Zaraha sometimes joined her husband outside for tea or coffee, but she spent the majority of her days indoors, tending to family matters.

Hassa himself, while warm and hospitable, was also a rather pious sort of person. He came across like a jolly priest, who could at times acquire an air of quiet gravity, according to the situation. He enjoyed eating, but he still remained very slim, and he never touched alcohol. When Paul Paulson offered him a cigarette one day, Hassa raised his hand like a barrier, as if giving a benediction, and said "Nein, danke" with a polite smile and his eyes closed.

Nevertheless, it was a fact little known to the frequenters of Hassa's café that their host had meanwhile developed the tendency to visit his neighbor, Tobias, in the man's garage at night, after the children had all gone to sleep. There, Tobias would open a drawer to an old tool cabinet in the corner and pull out a little hand-operated machine which Tobias and Hassa used to roll their own cigarettes.

Nobody else in the neighborhood talked to Tobias much, so the event remained a secret, and Tobias was glad to have Hassa's company.

In one of the first of these visits, Tobias offered his guest a beer as he pulled one out from the little refrigerator for himself. Hassa declined politely, but as Tobias popped the top off of the beer bottle, Hassa sniffed at the air a little. He watched with rapt attention as Tobias poured the golden nectar into a glass for himself, and after Tobias drank it and went "Aahhhh", Hassa raised his eyebrows imploringly and swallowed.

Nevertheless, he limited his evenings with Tobias to the luxury of smoking their homemade cigarettes.

The children of the Ben-al-Halambraye family adapted quite well to their new surroundings. They managed to talk with a surprising degree of fluency in a matter of months, and thoroughly charmed the mothers of the carpool. The children also became a main component of the playgroups in the town, and were much sought-after participants in the games and adventures among the local children.

This was not due to any shortage of toys for the children to play with at home. From the moment when the news of the arrival of the new family of asylum seekers had started to spread, the people of Rucklingsdorf had been falling over themselves to provide the family with every possible means of satisfaction and entertainment, as a result of which the children had come to acquire an overflowing treasury of playthings.

It quickly reached the point that the children had far more toys than they could ever play with, but since none of the family wanted to offend anybody, they simply accepted the generosity, and placed the extra toys in a large closet that was otherwise empty. Within a matter of weeks, the closet was nearly full, from floor to ceiling and side to side, with a multitude of brightly colored game boxes, pieces of sports equipment, and so on, which the children simply do not have the time to touch, or in some cases even open.

How many German children in Rucklingsdorf have closets that are full to bursting with toys like that?

Of course, since the children did not need any more toys at that point, there was the question of why the people of Rucklingsdorf continued to give the toys to the children, anyway. There was clearly no need, since the children always had something to play with (which everyone could see), and so it seemed that the people of the town were giving more for the sake of themselves to be giving, than actually to satisfy a need of any kind.

And the people gave, and gave some more. Zaraha was regularly bequested with so many cakes and deserts that she just fed them back to the other locals as they came to visit, on a kind of pastry loop.

It was almost as if the people of Rucklingsdorf *needed* to give things to the family, for themselves, somehow. After all, the charity organization already provided the asylum seekers with everything they needed to survive and live comfortably, and Hassa always had a few hundred euros in his wallet at any given time, since he received money from the State Social Services Department to handle other expenses.

Without a doubt, the people of Rucklingsdorf *got* something out of giving things to this family. Perhaps it was some sense of purging, some sense of atonement for generations past. Whatever it was, the presence of this family of asylum seekers provided a valuable service to the members of this little German farm community.

Something that I noticed rather early on in this experience was that, although the locals had been so eager to help this family and to make sure that they understood that they were welcome, the people who had been born and raised here had always been noticeably distant from me as an independent American in the village, a foreigner who has his own work, his own source of income, who could speak the language, and who expected to relate with them on an equal level in the community.

They were friendly in the street, without any doubt. They stopped and greeted me and talked about how good the flowers were growing, and that sort of thing. There was a noticeable void, though, in their development of any personal relationship beyond that level.

Any yet, they were stumbling over themselves to talk to this family, to give to this family, to carry them back and forth, to make sure that they were not in need while in their neighborhood.

And that seemed to be it.

I was not in need. I was a foreigner who they were not in a position to treat like someone who needed their assistance – I was not an underling.

While generosity can be very real and heartfelt, there *can* be a bit of a power position involved, in that relationship of the donator and the needy.

This is very common among the donations by wealthy or middle class white people in the United States who want to help black people: 'Those poor blacks, who can't do it by themselves', they say. There is no shortage of such people who donate to organizations that support poor black communities, but who are in fact actually racists.

Under such circumstances, it's a kind of power play.

It's not the helping of a friend, of a fellow human: it's more like taking care of a pet, a kitten they have found, who is allowed to stay in the house but is not welcome at the dinner table.

'We have, and you do not have, and we have decided to help you... oh, you don't need any help, and would like to become a full member of the fishing club, perhaps to run for a position on the Town Council? Well, now, that's another story.'

What would happen to most of these local donators after Hassa learned German and got a job and was able to support himself and his family, without the government asylum program? After he applied for a mortgage and bought a house in Rucklingsdorf? If one of his grown daughters wanted to marry their son? Would all these people who were so excited to be extending a hand full of extras still be there, as equals?

Some, yes, but most – I would guess not.

As I was bicycle riding with Hassafaromed and his wife one afternoon, for example, we passed the house of an old man who was well-integrated in the life of this little village. Zaraha was a little wobbly on the bicycle (they didn't have one in her village back in East Bekistan), and this mother of eight was laughing like a little girl, free and comfortable, as she flew along down the curvy streets. Hassafaromed was laughing with her, as he kept an eye on her, making sure she didn't fall, and as this beautiful sight went past, this old man scowled at it. Here were people who not long ago had been in danger of being tortured by warlords, and now they were floating (wobbly or otherwise) along the peaceful streets of their new home, in the company of a new friend, and the scowling old man found it a good time to shout out from his lawn, in place of a warm greeting, "Do you need any plates or silverware?", with the scowl never leaving his face.

It's almost as though it disturbed him that they were free, just like regular people, and not at all confined into that box, that compartment of the "needy foreigner" for just one happy moment.

Of course, this is different from those people in the town who actually cared, who actually saw human beings in front of them and wanted to make sure that they felt at home, and who befriend the newcomers.

There *were* warm-hearted souls such as this in this community, and they exercised a kindness to these people that could bring a tear to one's eye. Those were the local people who the children saw as their own extended family members, as a kind of grandmother or grandfather, aunt or uncle.

Then there was the young married couple that let the Ben-al-Halambrayes use the couple's wireless Internet connection, so that the asylum seekers could talk with their own family members who were still back home in East Bekistan, enduring the war and everything else there. The couple often joined Zaraha and Hassafaromed for tea inside, and sometimes at the café in the driveway, and it was just real friendship.

Such people were few, though, among the flood of the needy givers and the nearby-but-separate chatters, and the difference was noticeable.

Whatever the reason for each individual's interest and generosity, not *all* the local people were so content with the presence of the Ben-al-Halambraye family intruding in their quiet, predictable world as they had.

After a few months had passed, another flier appeared in the mailboxes of the town.

There was no "Dear Rucklingsdorfers" this time, and whoever it was who had sent it was going to be holding a meeting of a new group they were forming. "The Heart of Rucklingsdorf" it what they were calling it, and they wanted to invite to a meeting next Wednesday night all those members of the town who had noticed that the "feeling" of the town had changed and who wanted to do something about it.

The purpose of the event was noticeably vague, and I made sure to go to that meeting, to see what they were up to.

It was led by a man wearing blue denim overalls (I had already run across him when I volunteered to help with the new playground some time ago). Standing up in front of the others, he said that there had been a lot of changes in the town, and that "it just doesn't feel the way it used to".

He talked about the way things used to be in Rucklingsdorf, how everybody knew each other, all the way back to their school years, even, and how it used to be like one tight-knit community. He said that back then, everybody knew that they could trust each other, and that if somebody needed help, like when we had that snowstorm a few years ago and a couple of people got snowed in, they knew who to call, they knew who they could *talk* with.

He said that things were different now, and that he thought there were probably some other people in the town who had noticed that, too.

There was some low rumbling in the audience, nothing clear or identifiable, but it was there. I noticed that none of the people around the table were among those from the carpool who drove the Ben-al-Halambraye children back and forth to school, and I had never seen any of them at the café in Hassa's driveway.

I didn't like the direction this seemed to be heading in, and so I stood up and told the group that I would like to say something.

"Go ahead", the man in the denim overalls grumbled, but it was not like he meant it.

I said that when my girlfriend and I first moved to Rucklingsdorf, we were glad to find a place where the people were so friendly. I mention that everyone talked to us when they saw us out front. I said that it was nice to live in a neighborhood in which people cared about each other, where they wanted to help each other, where they wanted to work together with each other and not against other people (I was exaggerating their social graces somewhat, but the situation seemed to call for it).

I looked at the man in the denim overalls at the head of the table when I said this, and he frowned at me and then looked away.

I mentioned how the world had become so angry and aggressive, with people hating each other so much, and that what was nice about this town was that it was a place where people still greeted each other, they still spent the time of day to chat with each other, they still cared about people, about other *human beings* – and I stressed those last words as I said them.

I saw that the crowd had become calmer, and some of them looked as if they had been caught doing something and were embarrassed… "and that's something that I hope never changes here in Rucklingsdorf", I said.

There was a long silence.

'This thing could go either way', I thought to myself, and then…

…and then the knocking began, with nearly all the people around the big wooden table banging their knuckles on the top of it, to express their agreement, some of them as if against their will but doing it anyway.

I sat down, and then the man who had started the meeting began to talk about their parents' generation, and their grandparents' generation, and how they had had a strong town – but he saw that he had lost them for now.

The meeting dragged on a little longer and then just broke up, and everyone went home.

The man in the denim overalls looked angry and disappointed, and he threw a pretty heavy look at me as I left the room.

After a few months of things going on pretty much as they had been, it got around that Hassa and his family would be leaving in a few weeks.

The government said a space had opened up in a residential unit in a small city further south where there was a language school, and where Hassa could get work a few hours a week doing some kind of manual labor.

We all said our goodbyes to the family, and pretty soon the charity organization came to handle the move.

In a few days, Hassa, Zaraha and their children were gone, starting their lives over again, and we all remained behind without them.

The town has become quieter since they left. The café is gone from Hassa's driveway, and there is not all that stress with the carpool and the donations.

Now, without the old chairs and the tree stump in the driveway, that part of the town looks more orderly, more like it used to.

There is a sense among the community that things are back to normal, a sense of relief, in a way – it went well; the family felt welcome, and now everyone can go back to their regular lives.

But there is an absence: an absence of lightness and openness, of people inviting you into their homes for tea and nuts and some unidentified sweet candy – all this is gone, and now it is just Rucklingsdorf again.

The Dark Side

Germans can be pleasantly light and airy when you socialize with them.

Depending on the particular model of German you happen to be dealing with at any given time, as well as how well they know you (*not* how well *you* know *them*), you can often expect a friendly greeting of "Hallo", as if it's being sung to you by a playful child – actually, it's more like "HA--loooo!"

If your greeter is particularly cushy and inviting, you might even be the receiver of the more intimate "Hallöchen" (in the art of song, "Ha--LLÖÖÖÖÖÖÖ-cheeeen), which literally means a "little hello". Isn't that cute? A tiny, little hello, *just* for you.

And then when the chat ends, there is always, without exception, those same, standard two notes, always on perfect pitch, of "Tschüss!" ("TSCHÜÜ--üüüüss"). It rings with a first high note, which is gleefully drawn out a little (actually, for precisely two beats), followed by the remainder of the word, exactly two notes lower and for precisely four more beat, for a total of a Germanic six.

The notes are even always precisely the same on a music scale: a cheery "A" descending down one step to a "G". There is the natural sense that the entire composition trends towards resolving to the next lower note of "F" (like when church music descends three notes to come to a final conclusion) but it never does. The last note just hangs there (according to the prescribed rhythm), suspended in time and space, as if it is a cordial reminder that the chat was so pleasant that it is not really finished and could continue again next time (no matter what argument might have occurred between the greeting and the ending).

It is truly amazing that every single German says goodbye with precisely the same word, using exactly the same notes and pitch, and according to the regimentally agreed rhythm of a certain number of beats. How have the Germans managed to standardize something as spontaneous and personal as "goodbye"? Perhaps the relevant criteria are downloaded automatically from the appropriate governmental agency, once the Germans get home at night and plug a cord from the wall outlet into their belly buttons to get recharged.

Whatever the case may be, there is no friendlier greeting or closing to a chat than the one you will receive from Germans. It could easily be developed into a symphony.

This tone of optimism and leisure just makes it all that more shocking when, while innocently minding one's own business and expecting nothing other than a smooth continuation of an otherwise normal and productive interchange, a person happens to inadvertently navigate themselves into what turns out to be the German's "dark side" – a sticky, glutinous amalgamation of half-ideas, wayward vengeance and irrational accusations.

The first time it happens, it can leave a foreign conversant speechless and gaping, wondering what primitive, pagan spell had accidentally been cast to result in your nice, friendly German being transmogrified into this raving horror-movie character that is raging and growling before you like a cornered animal, and all because you dared to suggest, "Why don't we just talk this thing over?".

There are not always any signs that the transformation will occur, though it is usually limited to situations in which there are no other witnesses (just like always happens in movies when the main character turns into a werewolf).

These are moments when your friendly, responsible, rational German has crossed over to the dark side of the moon, and there is really no telling when they will be coming back.

You can't pull them out of it, either – you can try magnetism, alchemy, a few phrases you might have read in a book about young wizards in boarding schools in England.

The only thing to do is to let it run its course, or, preferably, to exit the vicinity, taking any small children and sensitive glass objects with you, and, if necessary, to contain the German in a sealed-off area.

For in these moments, what you have just inadvertently stumbled upon is the ancient and unsolved mystery of "Deutsche Wahnsinn" (the "German craziness" or the "German insanity").

It's like a dark, musty room in a haunted mansion, that room which nobody ever enters and, if they do, nobody ever escapes from unchanged.

Or, you might prefer to think of it as a brown, clammy moat around an old, medieval castle, with alligators and crocodiles chomping and snapping at the air just below your feet, as you walk across the shaky wooden bridge that is suspended between you and your conversation partner.

The trigger for entry into this twilight zone of irrationality and negative emotion is usually the fact that the German has, for whatever reason, come to feel insecure about himself. Something has made the formerly civilized German to be unsure, and (following the ancient Germanic pattern) this "self-doubt" leads to his feeling that there is a lack of order in his environment. Since "order" for a German is like water for a fish, the lack of order flows instantly to "insecurity", which in turn just rushes headlong over the cliff into "irrationality" and "aggression".

It is not an attractive process, and at such moments, you will find yourself wondering 'Is the bread and beer here really *that* good to put up with this?'. And that is a question that every soul on this earth has to answer for himself.

Strangely enough, "Deutsche Wahnsinn" can appear when it is least expected.

There are some Germans who are just fine (wonderful and refreshing, in fact) until their sense of self-esteem is challenged, and then they apparently feel (rationally or otherwise) as though the fact that the hedge they are trimming turned out a little uneven suddenly places before their memory the scolding, dissatisfied face of some giant parental figure from their past (who, in turn, apparently had also been hovering somewhere along this continuum of light and darkness in their own day) – and if you happen to get in the way accidentally, that sweet, easy-going, placid German responds as though they have every intention to do whatever is within their power to thoroughly and completely annihilate you, and, moreover, to enjoy it as they grin and watch you suffering as a result.

The worst and most extreme case of this on a larger scale has been people being placed on those trains to Auschwitz, and a question that I always have during these extremely severe Germanic outbursts is just how far the particular angry version of a German across from me would go if he were in a position to feel insecure and unsafe enough, depending upon the situation.

And the Holocaust was far too horrific a tragedy to have been mentioned here as a light comment; the Germans, when they enter this state of switching to their dark side, when they feel or perceive themselves to be countered or cornered, really seem, standing right there before you, as though they have an earnest desire to annihilate what they perceive to be (again, rationally or otherwise) the source of their own self-hate – and, in my experience, it does not seem as though they would stop and maintain this desire within the boundaries of anything civilized or humane, if given the chance.

Like any demonic monster, this "German Insanity" can take many forms, but it can go something like this:

(An office, 7:15 p.m., after everyone else has already gone home for the evening)

Employee: "Hi, Max."
Supervisor (smiling): "Ah, Philipp! You're working hard tonight, I see!"

Employee: "Yes. I had to stay late again, to work on the customer portfolios."

(The supervisor just continues to type at his desk, as if not noticing the introduction of the topic).

Employee: "Max, these sales regions are a little mixed up. The customers are all over the place in different parts of the country, and the other salespeople and I are crisscrossing each other all the time, going from one customer to another."

Supervisor: "That's ridiculous. The sales regions are fine the way they are" *(not looking up from his typing at his computer, as if there is no reason to pursue the matter any further).*

Employee: "Actually, I've got two of my customers way out west, right next to Franziska's main client."

Supervisor: "Well, Franziska's customer is a major purchaser of our products!"

Employee (pausing briefly, confused at the irrelevance of the supervisor's response): "I don't really see what that has to do with it."

Supervisor: "You just said you don't want Franziska to take care of that customer she has out west."

Employee (his eyes narrowing and turning his head slightly to the side, as if trying to see something more clearly): "No, I didn't. I said that the salespeople are all crisscrossing each other's territories."

Supervisor: "All the territories are distinctly separated from each other"*(still typing, but faster, and with louder clicks coming from the keyboard).*

Employee (trying to prove the obvious through reason and evidence): "I have two customers within 10 kilometers of

Franziska's customer, three in the same county as Michaela's, and another directly across the street from Alexander's regular stop."

Supervisor (scowling now at his computer screen): "I don't see why you have a problem with your colleagues having so many customers".

Employee (visibly frustrated): "I *don't* have a problem with my colleagues having so many customers. I have a problem with the division of the sales regions."

Supervisor (suddenly leaping up from his chair, and throwing his hands in the air as the chair rolls back noisily behind him): "I don't have time to bother with this tonight!" *(and he storms out of the room into the hallway, as though he has an important reason to go there)*.

Employee (leaning suddenly back at the hips upon the unexpected movement of his supervisor and the chair): "Well it's important, and all the other salespeople have been talking about it, too!" *(he calls into the hallway)*.

Supervisor: "These are the sales regions we've had for a year and a half, and they've been working just fine!!" *(he shouts back from the hall)*.

Employee (following his supervisor into the hall): "Alexander is having problems at home because he can never get back until after eight at night!" *(Then, trying to collect himself and be reasonable)* "Why don't we just divide the map up into equal parts and split the customers among ourselves evenly?"

Supervisor (strutting quickly back into the original room, as if trying to escape his pursuer, who is following behind him): "Divide the map again? That's ridiculous! Everybody would have to relearn all the routes from the beginning! *(shuffling around papers and objects on his desk unnecessarily, and then shouting)* This entire conversation is a complete waste of time!"

Employee: "No, it would save time, and then the other salespeople could all go home at a more reasonable hour."

Supervisor (turning to stare suddenly at the employee now): "You always have problems with everybody here, don't you?! You never want any of your coworkers to be more successful than you! Why do you hate them all so much?!"

Employee: "We all went to the stadium together last Saturday!" *(completely surprised by what he has just heard)*.

Supervisor: "Oh, Mister Popular! I guess you're the only one anybody likes around here! Sorry!!"

Employee: "What?"

Supervisor (in a sharp, scolding tone): "I wish you would just stop always telling everybody else what to do! As if you're the only one who knows anything around here! What do you think I am, an idiot?!" *(shouting now and staring hatefully at the employee)*.

Employee: "What? No, of course not!"

Supervisor (clearly yelling now): "I'm the only one is this whole damned place who has any idea what he's doing!! This company would probably be out of business now if it weren't for me!! And I *still* have to deal with idiots like *you* every day!!"

Employee: "Max, calm down! I'm just trying to suggest that we reorganize the sales regions a little smoother, that's all."

Supervisor (standing face to face with the employee, bending at the waist and screaming into his eyes): "It's TOO BAD you all have to deal with an INCOMPETENT MANAGER like ME!! Why don't you just complain to the head office?! Maybe you can get me FIRED!!" *(He turns back to his desk)* "I don't deserve to have a job, anyway! I'm too STUPID!!" *(suddenly turning back to the employee as he says that last word).*

Employee (as if he is at a complete loss as to how to handle the situation and not understanding how it came to this): "Max, nobody thinks that! We're all happy with you here, it's just the sales regions, that's all."

Supervisor (as if he hasn't heard anything, or even been able to hear anything since he last spoke): "Maybe I should just QUIT!" *(slashing his hand across the air in front of himself)* "Maybe I should just throw all of this JUNK in the garbage RIGHT NOW!!" *(and he starts to rattle his computer screen with one hand).*

Employee: "Max, take it easy! We're just talking about the different regions!"

Supervisor (as if nobody is any longer in the room with him): "Then I can go and live in the street! *(He picks up a letter opener from his desk and clenches it in his fist).* And my wife and children can just STARVE! *(He suddenly whirls around to the employee, holding the letter opener at hip level in a tight, whitening grip).*

Employee: "Max!"

(The supervisor just stands there, frozen with rage, glowering into the eyeballs of the employee).

Employee: "Max! It's me! I helped you with those sales figures last month!"

(The letter opener shifts as the supervisor's fist slackens, and he turns, hunched, back to his desk. He lets his body fall dejectedly into his swivel chair, which almost slides out from under him. The employee lunges cautiously to catch the chair and stop it from moving back further).

(The employee just stands there, speechless and confused, looking at what his supervisor has become, as the supervisor stares unfocused in front of himself, his eyes heavy, like a fish on a line that has finally given up and just can't any more).

It can get pretty horrible, and the scene above, while a general description, is no exaggeration.

"Deutsche Wahnsinn" can be exhibited by an individual, by a group, or even by the entire population (as we have already seen many decades ago).

The unsuspecting party who is confronted with it can tend to try to use reason to return the situation to a rational conversation. However, considering that this phenomenal behavior is apparently based upon the performer of "Deutsche Wahnsinn" being irrationally aggressive in order to hide from others and himself his own sense of self-hatred, which results from some insufficiency he perceives in himself, there is no reasoning with such a person in such a state.

The only solution seems to be to address the original topic again at a later, calmer time, or to go around the individual and solve the respective matter otherwise (since a renewed approach sometimes just results in a re-stimulation of the soft-spot in the irrational party).

Here is a list of various stages that you might recognize (not necessarily in this order) if you are ever confronted with this very dark side of the German psyche. They are also portrayed in the scenario above::

<u>Avoidance</u>
- Denunciation of the opposing view as ridiculous and, therefore, of no value.
- Use of irrelevant topics and tangents.

<u>Manipulation</u>
- Altering the other person's statements.

<u>Denial</u>
- The stunningly transparent rejection of facts and reality.

<u>Altering Reality</u>
- Focusing upon what he imagines or wants the topic to be, not upon the actual topic.

<u>Escape</u>
- Giving up and walking away

<u>Devaluing the Discussion</u>
- Trying to prove his side of the argument as exclusively correct, instead of trying to reach a mutually agreeable compromise.
- Devaluing the other person's logical statements.

- Rejecting the proposed alternative as an inconvenient, unnecessary waste of time and energy.

Opposition
- False (particularly destructive) characterizations of the opposing party: the "Feindbild".
- Speaking like an adversary.
- Being defensive.
- Aiming towards argument and war, not peace and cooperation.

Megalomania
- Self-aggrandizement and devaluing of the other person who (wittingly or not) motivates this sense of offense (cause by insecurity and self-hatred) in the German.

Self-hatred
- Making statements of extreme self-hatred and even self-loathing and shame (unwittingly divulging that they have been covering up a severe sense of feeling insufficient by means of having been [in contrast] arrogant and aggressive).

Attack
- The end-of-the-world ("Weltuntergang") approach of slashing and burning everything so as to achieve total and complete annihilation with regard to the situation, instead of being proactive and constructive (the "Hitler-in-the-bunker" mentality).

Exhaustion
- Seeming as though they have nothing left in them and, although refusing to agree or give in, they are now a ghost of their former selves: empty face, heavy eyes, unfocused gaze.

If you look at videos and texts of what the German Nazi leaders in the 1930s and 1940s said and how they behaved, you will notice this process of "Deutsche Wahnsinn" being blatantly exhibited.

If you are a person who deals with Germans on a regular basis, you might suddenly find yourself one day face to face with this altered version of a formerly functional and otherwise responsible and logical acquaintance.

If that happens, you might leap suddenly over your desk to your bookshelf, rummage hysterically about the items there in search of this book again and, gratefully finding it, you might wave and flip your hands and fingers frenetically through the pages looking for this list again, in a fit of needy and frightened desperation.

If this book is an operating manual about dealing with Germans, then the list above is a survival guide about the German gone mad, the German who has entered a state that a team of psychiatrists and archeologists armed with the most modern technology and big, heavy shovels will scarcely manage to fathom: the German (or the Germans) at his or their worst – in the throes of "Deutsche Wahnsinn".

The Little Dog

As my girlfriend and I are out taking a stroll through the neighborhood, a little white puppy darts out suddenly from the house we are passing and runs up to us, barking and looking eagerly up at us as he jumps up and down in place, as if to say, "*There* you are, *finally*!", although we have never seen each other before.

We bend down to greet the little dog, and he responds with his eager little jumps, as if he's performing a circus act for us, when all of a sudden a young woman in jogging pants and a pale-blue T-shirt rushes out of the house and scolds the puppy.

"Nein, Wolfram! NEIN!", she says, as if she is shocked at the impetuous and improper behavior of the dog.

It's the first time we have seen anybody who lives there.

"That's OK", I say in German, as my girlfriend and I both smile back and forth at the young woman and the dog. "He's just a little excited today."

I already love the little dog enough for a whole lifetime.

The young woman doesn't respond, and instead just continues to reprimand the dog until he's corralled back into the red brick house, and the young woman follows him and closes the door behind her, without having said a single word to us and without once having looked at us to make eye contact.

We walk the few houses down the street to where we live (she's one of our nearest neighbors), and we go inside.

While I hang up my jacket, I think about the young woman, and how she didn't even acknowledge that we spoke to her, that we were even there – and I miss that little dog all the more.

Conclusion

Where is Rucklingsdorf?

There is no Rucklingsdorf, exactly – it is a German town which is both in the middle and on the edge, everywhere and nowhere; the place and its people are an amalgamation of various experiences I have had throughout Germany as a whole.

There is no one, particular man in denim overalls, no Kerstin Stempelkauer, and so on. These characters are all composites of so many people having done so many bizarre things over my years in Germany that they simply *had* to be portrayed in one place, together.

When holding a mirror up to the German culture, these characters and the little town of Rucklingsdorf are the overall, wavy image that has taken shape there to be seen.

The result is a satire of the German culture as a whole, to call attention to a few things that could be done a bit better (you're still not perfect yet, Germans, and you still have a ways to go, just like the rest of us).

As you can well imagine, this book is also a kind of revenge – a vendetta – not to any one person in particular, but for all of the cold, inconsiderate staring by people in public places, for all of the disparaging receptionists, the imperious highway drivers, for the xenophobia veiled in transparent politeness – and yet, the great contrast is that while writing this book, I have been sitting safely in my lovely German garden and enjoying the country's fantastic produce and high standard of living.

How can such a wonderful place be so damned aggravating and, in some cases, even personally repellant?

It's because of that unique schizophrenia of the German culture – that smashing together of gleaming high-performance and a stunning lack of personal finesse.

I like living in Germany – I just don't particularly like most of the Germans very much. I have met some who have been a breath of fresh air and a pleasure to know, and I think of them when I start to lose faith in these people – but I have met most of those pleasant individuals only in passing, and they have been a distinct minority, a minority which is far, far too small. For the most part, though, dealing with the Germans on a personal level has been like eating old cabbage – you immediately regret doing it and it leaves a bad taste in your mouth for a long, long time.

Stick a German accountant next to you while you're on a hiking trail through the woods, and there is a pronounced tendency that either he will inform you, in detail, about the average girth of the tree stems this time of year or he will make you feel that you are the most unwelcome intruder in *his* public forest. Sometimes you will receive a nice "Hallo!", but generally, that's like an occasional good scene in a very bad movie.

Even though they often socialize pleasantly with each other, sometimes it looks like even the Germans don't like other Germans very much. Their warmth and acceptance are usually strictly limited to close group members, and that is all. There are clear criteria to be fulfilled, and the rule book is seldom, if ever, flexible. If you are a German from a different little rural town with different trees and a different set of cows, then you will not find it easy to fit into *this* town, where we have our *own* trees, our *own* cows, and they are not at all the same as yours!

Besides that, other than drunken moments watching soccer, Germans generally do not have any sense of belonging to a nation. A person likes his buddies, of course, and perhaps some of his relatives, but a German's general opinion of other Germans (not himself, of course, but those other people) is that they are too uptight and too obsessed with rules (and he will tell you that with his hands held firmly at ten and two on the wheel as he drives). The fact that Germans don't like other Germans is proven by the decreasing population in the country. "Produce more Germans? Now, I don't know if that's such a good idea, honey. Can't we just work around that?"

They also generally don't identify themselves as being Europeans. Ask the random German, and he will say something like, "Yes, *those Europeans* are really making it harder for the rest of us." They seem to think that they are all independent little nation states, floating in isolation from all others around them, and only dealing with each other for business purposes, but not really being related in any communal sense.

How can a person like a country but not particularly care for the people in it? It's because there are certain characteristics of the Germans that lead them to create a very nice environment, when it comes to structure and nature preservation – the food is of excellent quality and relatively free of preservatives (depending upon your selection) and the nature is usually breathtaking and undestroyed.

One thing that summarizes this contrast between German excellence and deep Germanic disturbance is the Germans' Schwarzbrot (which means "black bread") – it is delicious, and it's hearty enough for a family of twelve to survive from a single loaf for months – but how can the Germans be so pessimistic that even some of their bread is black?!

Coming to Germany has been one of the best decisions of my life – but this place should definitely come with a warning label! While enjoying the high standard of living and the unviolated privacy that the country offers, though, I have also experienced here countless moments of stunning rudeness, personal disregard and, simply, very uncivilized behavior from those people who would otherwise be my fellow men, and it is honestly not seldom that, having had a spontaneous interchange with a German, I am immediately reminded that these are the people who brought us the Holocaust.

When I wrote this book, I wanted to *not* write a big book of hate – because there is far too much of that in the world as it is.

At the same time, I wanted to portray what I have experienced here as an outsider entering the circle of the Germans – and it can be a very cold, squared-off circle, indeed.

After everything that I have experienced in my many years among the German culture, what you have seen in this book is, I would say, a fair portrayal. The Germans are sometimes shown in their glory, interpersonal and otherwise – but changes clearly need to be made.

How?

Parents, don't teach your children to just stare silently at other humans as they pass by.

Don't talk with your children at the dinner table about foreigners as though they are "those people", but rather "fellow people with a different viewpoint and life experience behind them, and from whom we can often learn a lot ourselves, as they learn from us".

In your own way, adopt the many positive characteristics that you see in other cultures (on TV, when on vacation, etc.) without losing the many great virtues of your own.

And do it for real, deep down – not just on the surface with no actual difference underneath: if you are sitting in a pink living room with scented candles while you rub crystals to improve your aura, but your backbone is as stiff as an iron bar while you do it – that's not it.

Learn to relax, but without losing your sense of responsibility. A little order is a good thing – a *little*!

Teach your children so that what they *want* and what they *have* to do are not at war with each other, separate and compartmentalized, but rather mutually achievable through a smooth give-and-take – while at the same time not letting them play hide-and-seek in the supermarket.

You don't have to be exactly like the Italians, exactly like the French – just realize that you can be a softer version of yourselves – more aware of how what you do impacts the thoughts and feelings of other people around you.

Because after all, in spite of how it might look – we are all in this thing together.

About the Author

Jonathan Claay is an incredibly good looking guy who has everything going for him. Women love him, and guys love to be around him.

He has lived and worked in numerous countries, lived a generally wild life, and learned a number of foreign languages to varying degrees.

He is currently creating a new computer app: when a person just touches a button on it, they will become instantly happy, forever.

About the Book

What is it like to come from somewhere else and live among the Germans?

How do the Germans behave, how do they think, and what makes them... well, let's just say, "the way they are"?

Rucklingsdorf - An American Surrounded by Germans is a collection of short stories (and a few essays) that give you an insight into German day-to-day life, from someone who is simultaneously on the inside and on the outside.

If you were to crack open a German like an egg and pour the contents into a pan, the result you would see would be this book.

Buy it, read it, and love it!

(Also available in German, as an eBook or paperback, under the following title: *Rucklingsdorf - Ein Amerikaner von Deutschen umzingelt*).

MIX
Papier aus verantwortungsvollen Quellen
Paper from responsible sources
FSC® C105338